About the author

Catherine Byrne has always wanted to be a writer, and began at the age of eight by drawing comic strips with added dialogue and later as a teenager graduated to poetry. Her professional life however, took a very different path. She first studied Glass engraving with Caithness Glass where she worked for fourteen years. During that time she also worked as a foster parent. After the birth of her youngest child, she changed direction, studying and becoming a Chiropodist with her own private practice. At the same time she did all administration work for her husband's two businesses, and this continued until the death of her husband in 2005. However she still maintained her love of writing, and has had several short stories published in woman's magazines. Her main ambition is to write novels, and has now retired in order to write full time.

She was born on the Island of Stroma, and was brought up hearing stories from her grandparents about the island life of a different generation. An interest in geology, history and her strong ties to island life has influenced her choice of genre for her first novel.

Since first attending the AGM of the Scottish Association of Writers in 1999, she has won several prized, commendations and has been short listed both for short stories and chapters of her novel. In 2009, she won second prize in the general novel category for 'Follow The Dove.' She has attended an Arvon Foundation course and a Hi-Arts writing program, receiving positive feedback on her work from both.

Catherine Byrne lives in Wick, Caithness.

By the same author

Follow the Dove

The
Broken Horizon

Catherine M. Byrne

Matador
9 Priory Business Park
Wistow Road
Kibworth Beauchamp
Leicester LE8 0RX, UK
Tel: (+44) 116 279 2299
Fax: (+44) 116 279 2277
Email: books@troubador.co.uk
Web: www.troubador.co.uk/matador

ISBN 978 1780884 967

British Library Cataloguing in Publication Data.
A catalogue record for this book is available from the British Library.

Typeset in 10.5pt Book Antiqua by Troubador Publishing Ltd, Leicester, UK

Matador is an imprint of Troubador Publishing Ltd

Printed and bound in the UK by TJ International, Padstow, Cornwall

I wish to thank the following people for their help in getting this book ready for publication.

As always, the members of my writer's circle for support and encouragement.

Also those friends willing to pre-read, comment and give editorial and constructive criticism where necessary.

Margaret Wood, Jean MacLennan, Katrina Sutherland, Janis MacKay, Sheona Campbell, Hi-Arts W.I.P. mentoring service, and for supplying the cover photograph, Douglas Cowie.

http://www.cowiephoto.com

Prologue

On the 14th of April, 1920, Chrissie Reid received a letter from a dead man.

She met Sanny the Post at the gate of Scartongarth, the cottage where she had lived since the death of her in-laws. Wind loosened strands of hair from the bun she wore. It was impossible to get away from the wind on the island of Raumsey. It swept across the Orkneys, unhampered by mountains or the few straggling trees fighting for survival.

'Aye, Sanny. Have you anything for me the day?'

'I have that, Missus Reid.' He leaned his bicycle against the wall of upright flagstone and fumbled in his bag. 'Here we are.' He pushed his bonnet back, held an envelope close to his face, blinked a few times and squinted. 'I can't make out the postmark.' He moved it a little way from his eyes and squinted again. 'Not from your sister-in-law in Canada. Have ye got a secret admirer, Chrissie?'

'Secret admirer – hah, that would be the day!' Laughing, she snatched the letter from his hand.

'Dinna be so fast to say that. Ye're a fine-looking woman. Many a man would put his boots under yer bed. If I didna have my Nellie... who's it from then?' He winked and picked up his cycle but made no move to leave.

'Get away you old fool. It's...,' Chrissie's eyes skimmed the address, and she gasped as she recognised the writing. 'No one... nothing...' Shaking, she turned her back to Sanny and ripped the flap open.

'If that's the way of it, then,' said Sanny. He sniffed, turned and pushed his cycle slowly up the rutted track towards the main road of stone and clay that ran across the island.

Chrissie lurched to the front of the cottage, and her body folded onto the stone seat. Handwriting, barely remembered but still recognisable, slanted over the paper. As she read, her stomach tightened, and a prickly heat ran the length of her.

Dear Chrissie
You will be surprised to hear from me after all this time.
I've been thinking about you and Scartongarth a lot lately.
You and I were meant to be together for eternity. I'm coming home.
All my love,
Jack

Filling her lungs with the salt wind, she stared at the page in disbelief and reread it several times before pushing it into her apron pocket. Her gorge rose. She set one hand on the stone wall to support herself. Seagulls shrieked from the thatched roof; sunshine filtered through thin clouds and splashed across the landscape. The tide had reached its peak, and the waves washed up the shingle beach with an incoming roar and retreating rattle. Fourteen years ago that same tide had brought in an empty boat. It had been assumed her man had drowned. No one knew the truth – no one but herself.

She had been twenty-five at the time; a scared, confused lassie. What did she know of the world then? What did she know now?

'The letter can't be from Jack. Jack is dead.' She spoke aloud; words hollow sounding to her own ears. 'Who's doing this?' Her head tilted as if an answer would come from the elements, but all she heard were the thin cries of new lambs and the cawing of seabirds.

Part One

Fourteen Years Earlier

Chapter 1

The knock startled Chrissie. She grabbed her medical bag. Someone needed her skill as a healer, no doubt; friends did not call round any more. Her hand flew to her neck. Was a bruise there? She couldn't remember. She opened the door and raised her eyebrows at the young man who greeted her.

Charlie Rosie stood on the flagstone path smiling awkwardly. 'Is Jack here, Missus Reid? Is it true he's giving me a job on his boat?' His red hair lifted in the wind.

'He... he didn't say, but he needs a hand, right enough.'

'And I need the work.' His smile was tentative, almost scared.

The lad should be scared, going to sea with Jack, Chrissie thought. She avoided Charlie's direct gaze. Behind him, bushes that never grew beyond the garden wall dipped and swayed. She should warn the youth, tell him to run and forget about ever setting a foot aboard the *Christina* as long as Jack held the helm, but Jack's own parents, with whom Charlie lived, sorely needed the extra money. She was glad Jack was giving him the chance.

'Jack's away to the mainland.' She indicated the hazy blue outline of the northern coast of Scotland. 'He's helping with the post-boat.'

She looked into Charlie's clear, grey-green eyes and eager freckled face. His smile broadened, a hint of mischief sprang in his eyes. Charlie. The lad who used to cheek her when she was seventeen and he was eleven, the lad she had many a time chased from her yard with a broomstick, laughing so hard it hurt as he and his brother, Angus, performed their devilment. He had stretched in the last few years and was now taller than her five

3

feet four inches. She wished she could invite him in, but she wouldn't dare. Jack, her man, would see a lad, even several years her junior, as a threat. She pulled her corn-coloured braid across her neck.

'Are you all right, Missus Reid?' Charlie's voice sounded uncharacteristically serious. His forehead furrowed.

Her eyes flicked from him and over the countryside to where the low, stone-built houses of the crofters and fishermen with their assortment of outbuildings and thatched roofs spread haphazardly over both green fields and heather clad moors. Beyond that, the black ribbon of rip-tide split the expanse of the Pentland Firth. 'Jack won't be long; the boat's halfway across the sound.' Unable to remain still, she fingered the folds of her apron. She wished he would go, before Jack found out he was here.

'Um... do you need... any help?' his question was unexpected.

'Why should I need help?' She was suddenly wary. She understood how gossip spread around an island this size. No matter how much she'd tried to hide the truth, if one person had seen a bruise, that's all it would take. She felt a failure as a wife as it was and didn't want to add disloyalty to her list of faults.

'With work and that...' He bit his lip. 'I mean...'

'There's nothing you can do.' Her voice sounded much sharper than she intended. Charlie's face turned scarlet.

'I'll be away, then,' he said quickly. 'I'll meet Jack at the pier.'

Instantly contrite, she grabbed his arm. 'I'm sorry…I didn't mean to snap…'

Charlie cleared his throat and shuffled his feet. 'I just thought...'

'I know what you meant, but I'm all right. Just be careful what you say around Jack. Keep the peace, eh?'

'Aye, I'll do that.' He studied his fingernail. 'I'm off, then. Don't worry about me.'

I hope I don't have to, she thought as she watched his retreating back. Rain had fallen in the night, and his bare feet splashed through puddles on the rutted cart track that led to the metal road. A few of the hardiest lads left their winter boots in the cupboard until the ground became white with frost. Although the weather wasn't too bad yet, the wind nipped her face and fingers.

Charlie turned and waved. She lifted her arm in acknowledgement. How old would he be now – nineteen – twenty? She had not been much older the day she married Jack. Five years ago, yet it seemed like decades. Without thinking, she set her hand on her stomach. If she'd been able to give Jack a child things might have been different.

Back indoors, she adjusted the faded curtains until they hung in exact symmetrical folds. Breathing in the scent of burning peat and the geraniums sitting on the window sill, she looked around the living area of her three-roomed cottage. Everything was in order. The yellow and blue wax-cloth covering the table had been wiped clean. The water in the kettle hanging on a hook above the open peat fire would soon be hot enough for tea. She moved a hard-backed chair, and the legs squealed over the flagstone floor as she set it in its own space. All the china she possessed shone from the shelves of her pine dresser.

Specks of ash sprinkled the rag rug in front of the fireplace. She picked up the mat, went outside and hung it over the washing line. That done, she fetched the carpet beater and swung it over her head, imagined Jack's face and brought the stick down against the rug repeatedly until her muscles ached and sweat ran down her forehead.

With her breath laboured, she returned to the house and studied the floor for signs of dust. Thank God she had enough milk to buff the flagstone to a shine. She glanced at the clock. Jack wouldn't be long now. Her stomach clenched. A generous portion of smoked ham hung on a hook from the rafters above the fireplace, but she still had to peel the potatoes and turnip. There had been a time when Jack appreciated her cooking skills and complemented her after a good meal. But now she seldom saw glimpses of the man she once loved.

She should have listened to her sister-in-law, Isa, while she lived on the island. Isa had suspected what was going on and had encouraged her to leave, an unheard of act of rebellion by a local wife. It was a woman's lot to cope with whatever God put in her path. In any case, she could not run away. There was nowhere for her to go. Without the croft, boat and house, everything her grandmother had willed to her, she had nothing.

Isa was married to Jack's brother, Davie, but he had joined the herring fleet in Wick and not returned. Since she'd heard not another word from him, Isa believed she'd been abandoned and had gone to join her parents in Canada.

What Isa didn't know, however, was that it was not all Jack's fault. To her shame, Chrissie had not come to his bed a virgin. Davie had been her first love, long before Isa came over from Kirkwall. She understood how the knowledge wriggled like a maggot in Jack's brain. She'd hoped that in time he would forgive her, that in time he would open his heart and tell her what else caused the deep torture in his soul. Because, even as a young lad, there had always been an anger in Jack. Now, after five years, the hope that she could mend him was all but gone.

She turned and looked at her grandmother's chair and imagined her sitting there. With her parents both dead of consumption before her tenth birthday, Chrissie's grandmother had been the most important person in her world. As a child, she'd followed her granny over moors and fields, looking in ditches and under hedgerows for roots and leaves to make her medicines. They used to sing together, their voices rising in harmony. How Chrissie loved to sing. *The child has the voice of an angel,* her father used to say. She began to hum a well-remembered tune.

Jesus loves me this I know
For the bible tells me so
Yes, Jesus loves me,
The bible tells me so

Sometimes she and her grandmother went to the mainland to collect plants which did not grow locally. Chrissie loved those trips, picking the plants the old woman pointed out. With the nearest doctor on the mainland and most folk unable to pay his fees, Lizzie Adam's skills were essential to the islanders.

'One day, my lasgie, you'll be the spaewife and the howdie,' her granny had said. Chrissie had loved learning which herbs cured what and which to avoid. She helped to dry, grind; label and store each leaf, root and seed. In front of this fireplace, Chrissie had watched the wrinkled hands record every detail, the pen scratching over the surface of the paper, the brow furrowed in concentration, the tongue occasionally flitting over thin lips. God, how she missed her granny.

The clock whirred and struck four times. She walked to the window and once more fingered the curtains. Had she ever truly loved Jack? She thought she had at the time. Her grandmother had died and her relationship with Davie had ended. She had been lost and unhappy in an empty world, with a strong desire for love both physical and emotional. And Jack had been there. Strong, handsome and in love with her. Two emotionally damaged people drawn together by a mutual need. She had believed, back then, that she could mend him – that they could mend each other. The raw passion which had consumed them in the beginning had filled her world until his unreasonable jealousy sucked the love out of her. He had ruined the bold self-confidence which was once so much part of her. What had she become? She had even been too afraid to invite Charlie inside the house.

***

A girl of about six or seven came running up the path, her shouts startling Chrissie from her reverie. She opened the door, and the child, her cheeks wet and snot running over her top lip, barrelled into Chrissie's legs. 'My mam's bad. She's... she's going to die.'

Chrissie bent down and took the girl's face between her hands, wiping the tears away with her thumbs. 'It's all right, Daisy. Your mam is going to be fine – you'll see.'

Daisy's mother was about to give birth, and Chrissie did not foresee any problems. The woman had three children already, and

7

all her labours had been short and straightforward, but nevertheless terrifying for a six year old to witness. No one would explain the process of birth to a child. At least Chrissie hoped that was all that was wrong.

Daisy sniffed and wiped her nose on her sleeve. 'Promise?'

'Come on, darling. I'll get my bag and write a wee note for Jack, and then we'll go see what ails your mam.' She stroked the child's fair curls back from her face and took the small hand in her own. Glancing round the kitchen, she shivered at the thought of Jack returning to find the dinner unmade. Maybe if the birth was not imminent she would be able to rush back and set bread and ham on the table. But the one thing Jack could never take from her was her dedication to her patients.

The minute she entered Daisy's house the woman on the bed shouted, 'Thank God you've come. This bairn'll no wait another minute.' Her face was red, and her fair hair was plastered against her sweat drenched forehead.

'Take your wee brothers outside to play, and I'll make your mammy better. And you know,' Chrissie bent down and stroked Daisy's head, 'there might be a grand surprise for you in a wee while.'

The little girl stared at her with trusting eyes then did as she was bid.

***

'You're an angel. I had to send Daisy – the pains came on so sudden like. I didn't know what else to do with Bill at the sea.' The mother grasped Chrissie's hand and pressed her lips together as her body arched in another spasm.

Chrissie rolled up her sleeves and washed her hands in the basin which sat waiting for her. She examined the woman quickly. All was well. Less than ten minutes later, a baby girl slipped into Chrissie's hands. She cleaned out the child's mouth, cut the umbilical cord and wrapped the infant in a towel. 'She's real bonny.' She clutched the tiny bundle to her, just for a second, but even in that second an ache swept through her. Too quickly she placed the child into the mother's outstretched arms. 'If only all births were so easy,' she said, forcing lightness into her voice.

After a quick tidy up, she went to the door. Daisy sat on the wall biting her lip. Her brothers played in the earth, oblivious to what was going on. Chrissie called the children inside, and they gathered around their mother, faces lit with wonder. Chrissie stood for a heartbeat, watching the family gaze at the precious babe. Moments like these made all that was wrong in her life melt into nothingness.

'Take a hen for your services, Chrissie,' Daisy's mother said without lifting her head, 'it's all I have.'

Chrissie didn't want to, the family had little to spare, but Jack would be in a sour enough temper as it was, let alone if she returned with no payment.

***

Charlie walked the two miles to the harbour down the long straight road of broken stones and clay. To either side the fields lay bare, waiting for the crops to be sown, reminding him of how much work there was still to do this year. Grazing grounds, sloping towards the sea, were dotted with sheep on tethers. The wind tugged at his clothes and stiffened the skin of his face. He thought of Chrissie. She used to be such a laugh and a real beauty with her round, happy face and glowing skin. All the young lads teased the life out of her just to be near her, and he was no different. Then she married Jack Reid. Of all people!

Och aye, Jack was a handsome man and all; a lot of lassies hung around him at the time – and he was kindness itself to the fools who came from institutions on the mainland to work as servants on the crofts. Stuck up for them, Jack did, against those who would tease them for their slow speech and ignorant ways – but, by, he was wild tyke if anyone got on his wrong side. And Chrissie, she'd changed so much – seldom seen out and then with hardly a word to say for herself. She'd lost weight and her cheek bones were better defined. That, if anything, made her more attractive. But those eyes that used to sparkle like the sea beneath a summer sky had lost their lustre. There must be truth in the gossip. Was that not a bruise on her neck she'd been trying to hide?

He reached the top of the slope which led to the bay. Before him, the ocean thundered against the shore, and the post-boat rolled from side to side, rising in the peaks and dipping in the troughs. A larger yole should be used on a day when a north-westerly wind drives the sea, Charlie thought. Barely sixteen feet of boat and Sanny the Post was not the best of seamen.

At the same time as the boat sailed into the lee, Charlie arrived at the pier. He leaned against the parapet and waited and watched as the sails billowed and snapped in the wind, and the boat rose and fell on the slate grey water. He watched Jack throw out strings of corks which served as buffers, leap onto the pier and hold a hand towards Daft Larry, a soft lad who worked for the post office. Daft Larry tossed the mailbag ashore.

Charlie tensed when Jack opened the bag and rifled through it. Surely that wasn't allowed?

'I wish ye'd stop doing that,' shouted Sanny the Post. 'That's His Majesty's mail ye're tampering with.'

'I'm looking to see if there's anything for my own folk. I'm saving you a trip,' said Jack.

Sanny spat a stream of tobacco coloured liquid into the sea. 'You still shouldna' be doing 'at.' He slipped the rope from the boat's prow into the iron ring on the pier and secured the knot.

Jack threw the bag back to Larry and held up a letter. 'You can have the rest. This is for us. I'll let you read the address if you don't believe me.'

'Suit yerself,' said Sanny, 'But I'm no happy, and you, Larry, I'll have words with you later.'

Charlie pushed himself from the parapet and walked towards Jack. 'I... wanted to thank you for giving me a berth.'

Jack started, his fingers tightened around the envelope. He

rammed it into his pocket. 'What? Aye, well, come tomorrow, if you think you're man enough.' His eyes slipped passed Charlie's and up to a sky pregnant with unshed rain.

'Right you are.' Charlie forced his voice to remain pleasant. It would be hard, working alongside this man. With a 'humph,' Jack turned and strode up the road. Charlie watched him leave and blew out some air. If only he was older. If only he did not desperately need this job. If only Chrissie would take him seriously.

Something else was niggling at him. Jack had acted guiltily. The way he'd jumped when he realised Charlie had seen him, the way his fingers had closed around the letter. And he shouldn't have interfered with the mail. 'It's not right,' he said to no one. As he returned to the pier to help Sanny and Daft Larry tie up the boat, he suddenly realised he had not asked Jack what time he was sailing tomorrow.

He looked up, but Jack had disappeared over the brae. Charlie hurried along the rough road until he reached the crossroads then took a short cut along a meandering sheep track over the fields. A little way ahead of him, Jack, almost home, glanced at the house and dodged into the barn. Strange that, Charlie thought.

A few minutes later, his jacket slung over his shoulder, Jack reappeared, a satisfied grin on his face. He flinched when he saw Charlie. 'Why in the name of hell are you following me?' he snapped.

'I forgot to ask you what time tomorrow.'

A flush crept from Jack's neck and across his cheekbones. 'Three o'clock – in the morning. Now bugger off before I change my mind.' He spun away and headed to the house.

Jack was guilty of something, as sure as eggs were eggs. Charlie believed he could lay a bet it had to do with the letter he had taken from the post-bag.

Chapter 2

Chrissie hurried up the road with the hen under her arm. Jack would be home now. She let the hen go, moistened her lips and opened the door carefully.

'Where have you been?' Jack sat in her granny's chair, his hands clasped before him. His eyes settled on the medical bag. 'Who needed you this time?'

'Elma Manson had another bairn. She gave me a hen. I'll just get the dinner made.' She set her bag in the corner and went to the back porch to retrieve the enamel basin where she had left the potatoes.

'What was it, then?' asked Jack, his voice almost normal.

'A wee girl.'

'Funny how some women can pop them out like peas, while I come home from work to an empty house. Get me a cup of tea at least.'

'Yes. Yes.' A heat rose up from her neck and travelled across her face. His constant snide remarks directed at her inability to conceive twisted her heart. After making the tea, she walked to the passageway where the lidded milk pail sat on top of a wooden cupboard. 'No mail for us the day?' she asked lightly.

He didn't answer.

She filled the jug and set it beside his cup on the table. 'Is ham all right, or would you rather some herring? It won't take long.'

He said nothing. As he drank, she sensed his eyes on her. Hesitantly, she met his gaze. Not to do so would be a fault.

'Why did you ask about the mail?' he said.

She shrugged her shoulders not knowing what she had said to upset him. 'I thought maybe there would be something, that's all.'

His eyes remained on her, and a tremor ran down her backbone. 'There's been nothing for a while.' Chrissie tried to swallow but her mouth was dry.

Jack stared into his cup, black hair falling over his eyes, then finished his tea with one gulp and rose, knocking the chair over. 'I've to mend that dyke by the sheep pen. Shout on me when the dinner's ready. He marched out slamming the door behind him.

Half an hour later, when he returned, he ate his food without speaking.

For the next week Jack seemed in fairly good spirits, but as always, Chrissie strove not to do anything that might upset him. She never knew what might set him off.

'I'm going to St Margaret's Hope,' he said on Friday morning. 'There's a crofter died, and his stuff is being auctioned.'

Chrissie wondered where he found money for an auction. She wondered whether she should ask him what he wanted to buy, wondered whether that could be construed as poking into his business. On the other hand if she said nothing, he would accuse her of not being interested. She searched her mind for some suitable answer.

'The weather looks promising,' she said. Surely he would find no fault in that.

'There's a thick fog rolling in. How stupid can you be?' he snapped.

She flinched. 'Are... are you still going?'

He turned dark, angry eyes on her. 'Have you no faith in me at all? You know I'm a good seaman. Why do you constantly put me down?'

'I'm sorry. I didn't think. Will I make you some bread and dripping to take with you, then?'

'That's the least you can do.'

Without speaking, she prepared the sandwiches and wrapped them in a dishcloth.

It was a long sail from Raumsey to St Margaret's Hope, but

the weather was mild for the time of year. After he had left, she heaved a sigh of relief. At least for a while she could be normal. She washed the porridge pan and plates before starting the chores she had set herself today.

A few hours later the wind had stilled completely, and the mist lay thick across the land, shrouding the islands of Orkney to the north and turning the farm animals into eerie, shadowy shapes. But Jack would be all right. He had a compass and, as he said, he'd sailed through worse. A large part of her wished he was not such an able seaman, and a tremor of unease ran through her at the wish.

After the cow was milked, the hens fed and the eggs gathered, Chrissie went to flit the sheep. She trailed across the fields, her shawl tied at the waist with a length of twine and work boots on her feet. The hem of her skirt, wet from the hummocky grass, chafed miserably at her ankles. She pulled each long, steel backie from the ground and led the tethered sheep to richer pastures. Nineteen sheep. She owned twenty. Damn this fog. Difficult to see a yard in front of her let alone where an errant ewe might have strayed. Only the occasional bleat, the distant bark of a dog and the mournful drones of foghorns from this and other islands, each with their different tone, told her she was not alone in the damp, unnerving stillness. She followed the edge of the ditch.

A ewe materialised before her and tried to bolt away, but the tether had become entangled in an abandoned cartwheel. With her skirts hitched up, Chrissie jumped across the trench to where the wheel lay. Her boot slipped on the wet ground, and she went down heavily. Shocked by the pain, she heard no more than a whisper in the grass before she heard the voice.

'You should have pulled your skirts up a wee bit further.'

She looked up into Charlie Rosie's grinning face. A silvery sheen of moisture outlined his head and dampened his shirt. My goodness, he was forward!

'Where did *you* come from?' She struggled to stand and

winced as pain shot through her ankle.

Charlie's smile vanished, and he reached towards her. 'You're hurt.'

'I'll manage.' She stepped away, but another stab of pain forced her to admit that she did need help. 'Are you following me?'

'Hardly. Mind you, if I wasn't so busy…' He laughed when he said it.

'You've got the cheek of the devil. What are you doing here?' In spite of her words, her heartbeat quickened at the sight of him.

'I came to find out what time Jack wants me tomorrow, like.'

'The same time as yesterday and the day before that. Did he not tell you he was away the day?'

He shook his head. 'Just that he didn't need me. Anyway, it was your bonny face I wanted to see.' He winked.

Her heart flipped. What a cheek! Yet, could it be possible that this young man found her attractive? It was unthinkable, and yet... Ach, he was just being his usual impudent self. 'Behave, I'm a married woman.' She tried to sound stern. 'Could you let the ewe go?'

He unravelled the tether, led the animal a short distance away and pushed the steel backie into the ground. 'That should hold her.' He returned and offered Chrissie his hand.

Afraid to put her whole weight on her ankle in case she caused further damage, she clasped his arm. She sensed the heat from his body and was surprised at the solidity of muscle in one so young. Each step he took was measured and careful. 'Tell me if I'm walking too fast,' he said.

She leant against him, enjoying his concern and thanking God that Jack was far away. It had been so long since a man had shown her any kindness. Once they reached the cottage, she let go and leant against the door for support. 'Thank you kindly.'

'I'm not going,' said Charlie. 'Not until I'm sure you're all right, like.'

She looked into the clear, grey-green eyes and came to a

decision. 'Come away in, then.'

He helped her inside, grabbed hold of her hands and lowered her into a chair. A sparkle flooded his eyes. 'I'm glad Jack's not here.'

Her cheeks flamed. She gave an embarrassed laugh, and her eyes slid away. 'I'll have less of your nerve.' But her voice had no firmness.

He knelt down. 'Here, give me your foot.' He removed the boot and carefully felt around her ankle. Something in his touch sent a barely remembered quiver to the pit of her stomach. Her skin prickled.

'Good news in the letter then?' asked Charlie. 'It's not broken – only twisted.'

'What letter?' His fingers burned into her flesh.

'The letter Jack took from the mailbag. Have you anything I can use as a bandage?'

'I didn't get a letter.'

'Mind you, I thought it funny he didn't go to the house. That ankle will swell to twice the size if I don't wrap it up.'

'Bandages are in my bag in the corner. What letter?' A stab of alarm had grabbed her attention. Jack did seem to have more money lately, bringing home new clothes and often foodstuff from the mainland. She had wondered where it came from, but knew better than to ask. 'What letter?'

'The letter Jack took into the barn.' Charlie found the bandage and returned to her side.

'How do you know – did you follow him?'

'Yes. I needed to talk to him. You mean you didn't get the letter?' He began to bandage her ankle.

'Course I didn't. But... but even Jack wouldn't interfere with the mail.'

Still holding her foot, Charlie lifted his head and their eyes locked. 'I know what I saw. And Jack's up to something.'

A flush raced up Chrissie's face. 'Stop this, Charlie.' What was he trying to do to her? 'Just stop it.' But in her heart she was afraid he was right. Jack must have a reason to hide a letter from her. She would never dare to touch anything addressed to him.

'I'll stop if you listen to me.'

'Enough.' Ignoring the pain, she stood up and walked across the room, testing her weight. 'It... is a fair bit better. You're good, you know. At bandaging.'

'You'll maybe give me a job next time you're called to an accident.' He gave a slight laugh.

'I might at that.' A dog barked outside, and Chrissie jumped. She knew Jack had gone for the day, but she was nervous out of habit.

'You sit down. I'll get you a cup of tea.' Charlie jumped to his feet.

Returning to her seat, she forced herself to remain still. Her vision blurred, and she blinked away tears. In the last few minutes, she realised what she missed more than anything – tenderness – a bit of caring – nothing to do with the physical side of love. Jack wouldn't have worried about her ankle swelling up. He would have called her a clumsy bitch.

Charlie took the mugs from the dresser and set them on the wax-cloth covering the table. The kettle, hanging on a hook above the open peat fire, was already singing.

'You can make tea? A young lad like you?' she said.

'Young? You're not much older than me.' Charlie gave a laugh. 'Hey, I remember when you used to threaten to tan the arse of us lads. You scared the living daylights out of me and Angus.' The lightness was back in his voice.

'No wonder.' Relieved at the turn of the conversation, she looked up at him. 'Remember the time you put a peat on top of the chimney and smoked me and my granny out of the house. It's a good job there's not a constable on the island.' They both laughed. Suddenly Chrissie's lip trembled, and she became aware of tears on cheeks, tickling like ants. How long had it been since she laughed? With the bottom of her apron bunched in her hands, she pressed the material against her eyes. 'Don't mind me.' She gave an awkward laugh.

Charlie said nothing, but poured the tea and handed her a cup. As they drank she sensed him watching her. Hesitantly, she met his gaze and his eyes flew away.

He knelt beside her and took the cup from her hands. He was near enough for her to sense the warmth of him; near enough for her to be aware of the faint scent of sweat, of salt air and something she couldn't put a name to – nothing like a boy at all.

'You'd better go now.' She turned her head so that she would not have to breathe in any more of him.

'I'll go. After we've looked in the barn. I want to know what Jack was hiding.'

'Why? Even if Jack's keeping something from me – I'm not touching his mail.'

'Fine. We won't touch it. But I'm going to look anyway.'

She wanted to tell him that it was none of his business. To leave well alone. Yet those precious minutes with him had reminded her of the person she once was – the person she thought had gone forever. And she was curious herself. She glanced at the clock. Jack would not be home for hours. Once they knew what he was hiding, she would make Charlie go away and stay away and stop making her feel things she was afraid to feel. These were stolen moments. Charlie must never come here again.

Outside the sun, warm against her skin, was fighting its way through the fog as she followed him. She noticed how his shirt strained across his shoulders, the way his hair curled above his kerchief. In the barn, she watched him search along the walls, behind the horse's tack and among a pile of hay.

'Are you satisfied?' she asked when he found nothing.

He turned his eyes towards the ladder leading to the hayloft. Chrissie swallowed. 'Nothing's up there,' she said hurriedly.

'I'm not so sure.'

'It's... well...' *What did it matter? Charlie was going to find out the truth as soon as he climbed the steps.* 'He sometimes sleeps in the loft, when he's late and doesn't want to bother me.' She didn't say, *after he can't stand facing what he's done to me.*

Surprise flitted across Charlie's face. 'Good place to look, then.' She climbed after him, her injured ankle slowing her down.

The attic space was largely empty with disused harnessing and a coil of old rope in one corner. A musty smell of mice thickened in her nostrils. Cobwebs hung like gauze across the skylight. She blinked, focused her eyes and limped across to the make-shift bed in the corner. Lifting the single blanket, she rummaged through the hay that served as bedding. 'Nothing here.'

'And here?' said Charlie. An upside-down fish box held a partially burnt candle and a mug. He removed the mug and candle and turned the box over. It was empty.

Chrissie stepped away. 'You're wrong Charlie.' The board beneath her foot creaked. One end raised a fraction. She moved back.

He bent down, prised the board up and reached into the cavity. His fingers fumbled around until, with a whoop, he pulled out a bundle of envelopes.

Chrissie snatched them from him and read the address. 'These are for Isa.' She recognised the neat handwriting. 'From Davie.' Davie had left to chase the herring over a year ago. 'We have to put them back.'

'Put them back – are you mad?' Before she could stop him, Charlie pulled one from her and tore it open. Something fell out and fluttered to the floor. He picked it up. 'A postal order – for two and six.' Jack's been stealing her money.'

Suddenly everything became clear to Chrissie. It was not about the money. 'Jack wanted rid of Isa,' she said. Isa had encouraged Chrissie to leave. But Davie appeared to have abandoned her, and with no money coming in, Isa had had no option but to join her parents in Canada.

'He won't get off with this.' Charlie's breathing quickened. 'You know what Isa went through. And all the time... Maybe I could still catch her . . .'

'Don't be daft. She's been gone near three days. The ship'll be well into the Atlantic by now. I'll write to her, tell her.' She had to get rid of Charlie. Put the letters back, pretend this never happened.

'I can't believe what you're saying. If you won't do anything, I will.'

'No, Charlie. Please. It's my business not yours.'

'I was fond of Isa and Davie. Jack stole the mail. He could be locked up for a long time.'

Her head whirled. Jack locked up. For a mad moment she considered what that would mean – a solution – and she could stay safely in her own house. But Jack could be plausible when he wanted; he would get out of it somehow. Then he would make her suffer. She had to make Charlie understand. 'I'm as angry as you, but let me deal with this.'

'And how will you do that?' Charlie turned irritated eyes to hers.

'Please. You don't know what Jack's capable of.' Her heart thundered. Why had she allowed Charlie to come up here?

'Isa was a good friend to both of us.' He spun from her and climbed down the ladder. Slowly, she followed him, limped out of the barn and into the damp day.

'Listen to me, Charlie. Jack's ill – in the head. Oh he gets mad, but he's usually sorry after it. It's not all his fault. There's things you don't know about me.'

Anger flashed in his eyes. With his hands on her shoulders, he bent down until his face was level with hers. 'Apart from what he's done to Isa, look what he's doing to you. You're terrified. You don't deserve to live like this.' His voice shook with barely controlled anger. She had heard red haired people had a temper to match, but she had never before seen signs of it in Charlie.

She swallowed with difficulty; her mouth dry. 'For goodness sake,' she shouted. 'Let me handle this.' Charlie was, after all, just a daft wee laddie, too impulsive to act wisely. 'Let me talk to the minister, he'll know what to do.'

Charlie shook his head. 'I don't understand you, Chrissie. Working with him's bad enough – he makes me feel this size.' He held his finger and thumb about an inch apart. 'I'm sick of him.' He turned from her. 'I'll catch Sanny the Post before he gets to the shop. He should be on his rounds by now. I'll have words with him. He surely can't know what Jack's been doing.'

A prickly heat took over her body. 'Wait, wait, give me time, please. And your job, you need it.' Her braid fell away from her shoulder.

'If you call being Jack's whipping boy a job. I've had enough.' With his jaw set, Charlie started towards the road.

'I'm coming with you.' The pain in her ankle was nothing to the fear in her heart. 'Charlie, please don't. Leave this to me. Jack'll kill you. He's got the strength of the devil.'

He flexed his muscles. 'I'm pretty strong myself. I could take him in a fair fight.'

She didn't doubt it. The lad was brought up with years of physical work, but hate did not drive him the way it did Jack. Fear twisted like a great worm in her gut.

'No, please don't get on his wrong side. There's nothing fair in Jack.'

'You stay here. Your ankle...' Charlie shouted over his shoulder.

'I can walk. Even if I have to crawl, you're going nowhere without me.' She hobbled after him and grabbed his arm. It was as rigid as steel.

'All right, all right. Look, there's Sanny, over by Black Maggie's place.'

Together they walked across the field in the direction in which they had seen the postman. He had disappeared.

They stopped on the brae-head and looked around. The fog had largely dispersed and lay in thick banks, fading the hills and the horizon. 'Sanny can't be too far,' said Chrissie.

A sudden shout startled them both.

'What in the name of hell are you doing with my wife?'

Chrissie spun around and screamed. Jack was standing on the beach by the upturned *Christina*, a black dripping paintbrush in his hand.

Jack. Here. 'But ... I thought...'

'... I was off to St Margaret's Hope. The fog was too thick after all. Just as well, by the looks of things.'

Panic stricken, Chrissie's eyes flew over the surrounding countryside, but no one was within earshot. Thoughts tumbled around in her head. What could she do now – what could she say? She had been clinging to Charlie's arm for support. How must that have looked? 'I ... I hurt my ankle. Charlie helped...'

From beneath a sweep of raven-black hair, Jack's eyes bored into her. He wiped his tar-blackened fingers on the leg of his dungarees and stepped towards the bottom of the slope.

'You thought I had gone,' he shouted up the incline, his voice heavy with suspicion.

Chrissie's eyes darted to Charlie and back to the man staring up at her. 'No. He helped me.' Her voice faded as each breath shook itself to her lungs.

Jack's eyes moved from one to the other. She could sense the anger gather around him like a black cloud. 'Go away,' she hissed to Charlie through her teeth. Charlie's fists clenched and clenched again. She had the impression of a tightly wound spring ready to be released. 'For God's sake. You're making it worse.'

Charlie remained solid and unmoving.

Jack nodded slowly. His voice took on the raw edge Chrissie knew too well. 'Thought I was away for the day, did you? Thought you slip down here for God knows what.'

'No...' Chrissie dropped her hand. 'Jack listen...'

Jack snorted. 'Is he the best you can do, Chrissie? My God, if he's touched you.'

'Shut up! I haven't laid a hand on her, and that's more than you can say.' said Charlie.

'You little shite. You live with my folks – wormed your way in – I give you a job, and now you want my wife. Get down here, Chrissie. Now.'

'Leave her alone. And I've been more of a son to your folks than you ever were.'

'Bloody hell, what is this? Come down here and face me like a man. Or are you scared?

'I'm not scared of you.' Charlie leapt forward and skidded down the slope towards Jack.

Desperately Chrissie looked around. Where was Sanny the Post? There might be people in the fields, hidden by mist and distance, too far for sound to carry. There was no help from any direction. She stumbled down to the beach, shouting as she went. 'Charlie, please. Go home.'

Jack's eyes flicked from one to the other. 'I'll kill the little bastard.' He drew back his fist.

'No, stop,' cried Chrissie. 'It's not what you're thinking. The letters. We found the letters.'

Jack stopped, his fist held high. He turned granite hard eyes on her. 'Letters?'

'Davie's letters to Isa,' said Charlie.

'How dare you rake through my stuff?'

Chrissie stared at this man with whom she had once believed she could build a future. The years she had spent with him had become a never-ending nightmare that had sucked her dry. She marvelled at how she could be so hot, yet so cold at the same time.

Jack's darkening eyes flashed towards Charlie. His colour heightened. A muscle contracted along his jaw. 'This is his doing.' He lowered his head and ran straight for Charlie. Ramming the boy in the chest, he lifted him off his feet. They tumbled backwards, a mass of flailing legs and arms. Jack was first on his knees. Roaring, he grabbed Charlie by the throat and pinned him against the ground.

The air swirled about Chrissie in a red haze. 'Stop it,' she shouted, 'You'll kill him.'

Charlie's face was turning a purplish shade, and he grappled with the hands that held his throat. Without any conscious thought, Chrissie grabbed a stone and aimed for Jack's head. She brought it down with all her strength. At the same moment, Charlie twisted, and Jack was thrown off balance; just enough so that the rock glanced off the side of his head, peeling skin and flesh with it. He gasped and fell to the ground, hands clutching his skull.

Chrissie screamed. Events had taken a life of their own, spinning out of control. Time slowed down, like a dream. She stared at the man she had married. Blood ran freely from between his fingers.

Charlie pulled himself upright, coughing and rubbing his neck.

Jack stared at her as if he had never seen her before. 'You... you tried... to kill me.' He struggled to rise, then sank back. Blood dripped onto the sand, black holes in the golden grains.

For a moment Chrissie hesitated, then the healer within her jerked into action. She lifted her skirt, tore away part of her petticoat, folded it quickly, knelt beside him and pressed the wad to the wound. 'No... no. I didn't mean to.' Her voice trembled, and she could say no more.

'Come away from him, Chrissie,' said Charlie. 'I'll go to the mainland and get the law.'

'Don't listen to him.' Jack reached out and grabbed her arm. Her flesh contracted with disgust.

'Everything I do is for you.' His fingers tightened. 'I thought things would be different with Isa and Davie gone.' He blinked and pressed his eyes closed for a minute. 'Now... this wee shite has to interfere. . .' He turned and spat at Charlie. Rage flowed from him in a wave. Chrissie could smell his madness.

The realisation of what he had brought her to terrified her as much as anything. She was the island howdie, the spaewife, delivering bairns and treating the sick; committed to saving lives. She had never believed herself capable of violence. Yet, a minute ago, she had really wanted to kill him. Violently.

'Let me go. I need to bandage your head.' Forcing a smile, she kept her voice soft, fear of reprisal dictating her actions.

When he loosened his grip, she wrapped the makeshift bandage around his wound. Blood seeped through the cloth. 'I... I can't cope any more, Jack.'

'It was all for you. But you don't appreciate anything. I've tried so hard. This is the worst, Chrissie – you and him... you tried to murder me.'

'I didn't. I was scared. The rock slipped... I'm so sorry.'

'I don't believe this,' said Charlie. 'After everything he's done. Leave him now.'

Jack narrowed his eyes. 'And who's to say when you fall down a cliff that you didn't slip while collecting sea-maws' eggs?'

A sudden hopelessness washed over Chrissie. She looked up at Charlie silently pleading for understanding. 'I can't,' she said. 'It's not all his fault.' She had to pacify Jack somehow. His wound was not too serious, but his reprisals would be. There was nowhere she could go where he would not find her. Even if there was, the threat to Charlie's life was real.

'I'll go to the law anyway,' said Charlie.

Jack slipped his arm around Chrissie. 'When I tell them Chrissie knew about the letters – will you see her put away too?'

Charlie cursed and threw the stick on the ground.

'Just go Charlie,' she said, 'God go with you.'

'And you, Chrissie. You need God more than I do.' He spun round, kicked at a stone stormed up the rise.

She looked at this man she had married, and a deadly calm filled her. There was only one way she would ever be free. She had prayed and still did, even now, it would never come to that.

'I had to do what I could to make Isa leave. She was turning you against me. And Davie – it was always him you wanted. Why can't you understand?' Jack pushed himself to his feet.

'I do understand.' Her voice was low. She watched as Charlie disappeared over the brow of the hill. He found her attractive and that made her feel special. Nothing must come of it of course, but she would need something to hold onto in the months to come.

'What went wrong, Chrissie?' Jack's voice was soft now, full of self-pity.

'You need help, Jack. If you'd see a doctor...' She had heard there were doctors of the mind. Maybe there was still a chance he could be helped, although she doubted it.

'No doctor. You're the only one who can save me.' He held out his hand. His face twisted, as if he was fighting the urge to cry. 'I love you, Chrissie. I don't mean to hurt you.'

'I know.' Ice water ran through her veins. She'd lost track of the times he'd said the same words.

As they made their way home, he held her against him. The pressure from his body made her feel sick. Even the softness of his voice made her cringe with terror at what might come. For his mood could change with the bat of an eyelid. His grip tightened until it was painful.

'I won't leave you.' How easily she could say the right words when they had no meaning.

Back in the house, Jack was quiet for a long time, and his silence unnerved her more than his anger would have done. He allowed her to change his dressing and kissed her hand when she finished. 'I don't know what I'd do without you,' he said, but his eyes were cold and glittering.

He watched her every move as she cooked. Her back was to him as she set the table but she could still feel his eyes as they bored into her. She went to the porch, but he followed her.

'Did he touch you?' The iron edge was back in his voice.

'What? Who?' Fear clamped her in its vice.

'You know damn well who.'

Her heart beat like a trapped fist. 'If you mean Charlie, no of course he didn't touch me.'

'If I find out he did, I'll kill him. I'll kill you both, understand?'

'He didn't. I swear. As God is my witness.'

He reached past her to the shelf and brought down the bible. 'Swear on this.' He carried it to the kitchen and thumped it on the table so that the crockery rattled.

Chrissie set her hand on the book. 'I swear. He helped me because I fell and hurt my ankle. Wouldn't you do that for someone?' She watched his face tighten. Had she said too much? She waited. 'I swear.' She dropped her voice to a whisper.

His eyes blazed through her for a while. 'Don't let me ever catch him near you again.'

'I won't.'

He took his seat at the table. He lifted his knife and pointed it at her. 'I don't want you going near Scartongarth again. Not as long as he's living under that roof.'

Chrissie gasped. She had helped Mary-Jane's bairns into the world and loved them like her own.

'If... if you want.' She lowered her head and stared at her plate. 'Will... will I say grace?'

The hand that held the knife relaxed slightly. 'Go ahead.'

She clasped her hands and repeated the words of thanks that she said every night, but in her heart she prayed for strength.

After his meal, he rose, finished his tea, took her face in his hands and kissed her lightly. 'I left the *Christina* loose. I'd better go make her safe.' He sounded normal again.

Night was beginning to ink out the day. Chrissie lit the lamp and the flame flickered to indicate the oil was nearly dry. She added paraffin and the flame steadied. That done, she paced to the window. Reflected in the glass was the shadowy room; the stove, the dresser, the box bed, the glow of lamplight, and among it all, she saw herself. At twenty-five, her bone structure was good. She might have been bonny. She had been once. That night she only saw a distraught face. Closing the shutters, she banished the image and went into the back porch, reached up to the shelf and pushed some of the containers of herbs to one side. Right at the back, covered in dust and cobwebs, was a jar of ground laburnum flowers. In small amounts, the crushed leaves of the laburnum were useful for gallbladder complaints and melancholy, but the flowers themselves were highly poisonous. Her grandmother had told her so when together they had brought the straggling young tree back from the mainland and planted it in the shelter of the barn. Yet Chrissie herself had plucked, dried and ground the poisonous petals only last year. Even then, she had known that one day she would be forced to use them. At that time, she had intended them for herself.

Every sound, every click, every creak of the timbers startled her. The slightest rustle in the thatch of the roof made her heart skip a beat – a mouse maybe, or a bird nesting in the eaves. The wind gusted around the house and rattled the loose window panes; the clock on the mantelpiece struck eight times; the fire settled; the kettle started to hum. In spite of the heat in the room, she shivered. Why had Jack not returned? Dear God, she hoped he had not gone after Charlie. There was nothing she could do, other than wait.

Chapter 3

From his armchair in the corner of Scartongarth, Dan Reid rubbed his twisted leg. It pained him badly since the accident that had almost crippled him. He glanced at the smoke-blackened wall above the stove and along the smoke-blackened ceiling. The whole room could do with a whitewash, but money was needed for other things; salt for preserving the meat and fish, oil for the lamps, fuel for the fires, twine for the nets, lead for the sinkers, new boots for the winter. Apart from which, in his eightieth year, he no longer had the strength. Three sons he had brought up. Jamsie had been lost at sea, and neither his body nor his boat, the *Silver Dawn*, had ever been recovered. Jack lived on the island but he was a dark, troubled soul, and they seldom saw him. Davie, his youngest, was God knew where.

'Ganda.' A small hand smacked his arm.

His heart filled as he reached over, picked up the three year old and set her on his good knee. She was slight for her age and as light as air. His granddaughter, Bel, and her brother, Jimmy, were the glow in his darkness. Bel snaked her arms around his neck, and they rubbed noses. Her laugh was like a tinkling brook.

'Mind your granddad's leg now,' said Tyna, Dan's wife, looking up from her knitting. Her needles had once chattered like teeth, but now her twisted fingers took their time with every stitch.

The door opened and, Mary-Jane, Jamsie's widow, came in with a basket of eggs. 'Not so many the day.' Her voice was soft, and she walked with a grace more fitting to a lady of a manor than to an island woman. Her pale hair was knotted behind her head in a severe bun. Almost three years after her man's death, she still wore black, the sleeves of her jumper growing wide and accentuating the thinness of her arms. Each year she seemed to diminish. The birth of her twin babies had almost killed her, and she had never regained her strength. It twisted Dan's heart to watch the bluish tinge of her lips grow ever more pronounced as the life was slowly sucked from this beloved daughter-in-law.

It had been a sorry time for the croft after they lost Jamsie, and Dan himself became unfit to turn the soil. Mary-Jane had suggested bringing her brothers to live with them and work the land, and the boys had proved to be a blessing. They were young lads and full of mischief, but strong and willing. Unlike their solemn sister, Angus and Charlie had filled the dark corners with their jokes and laughter. And now that Charlie had a berth with Jack, there was more fish for the table.

Ah, Jack. So full of darkness and angst. Although he would not admit it except to himself, Dan had been relieved when this son had left home. He worried about Chrissie, and if truth be told, he missed her visits much more than those of his middle child.

'The lads'll be in for their tea soon,' said Tyna setting her knitting on one of the two padded stools that sat at either side of the fireplace. She pushed her body up slowly. 'There's rabbit stew left over from dinner. Bake a bannock to go with it Mary, there's a love. Where's Jimmy?' At that moment, the boisterous, red-cheeked little boy barrelled into the kitchen and slid on the flagstone floor, his corn-coloured curls a tangle around his face. He looked so like Jamsie it hurt. 'The cockerel chasing me again! Want a stick.'

'No, Jimmy.' His mother caught his arm. 'You're annoying the hens. If you don't stop it you'll have to stay inside.'

'Leave the laddie be.' Tyna smiled indulgently at him. Jimmy was her obvious favourite, just as Bel was Dan's. The little girl looked at her brother, tightened her arms around Dan's neck and laid her head on his shoulder. 'My ganda,' she said, claiming ownership. Tyna smiled at them fondly, her sharp intelligent eyes and high cheekbones still showing traces of the bonny wife he had brought back to Scartongarth all those years ago, and his heart filled. At moments like these, he wanted to say something kind, to tell her the feelings he still held in his heart, but words were not his way. He cleared his throat and kissed Bel's cheek.

***

Later that night, Charlie took his place at the table, but he could not settle. He could not forget the warmth of Chrissie's body as she clung to his arm, the butterfly touch of her hair, the faint scent of soap from her skin and the deep sorrow in her eyes.

She was terrified of Jack. Who could blame her? Since he had gone to sea with the man, Charlie had seen first-hand the way his moods could change from rational to menacing with no provocation. Although driven like a slave and often ridiculed, Charlie had, until now, held his peace for the sake of a wage and a few extra fish on Scartongarth's table.

The room was overwarm with the heat from an iron range. The aroma of rabbit stew, fresh baked bannocks and burning peat thickened the air. As the year lengthened, the days grew shorter, and dark shadows were already filling the corners and hiding among the rafters.

Charlie pushed the food around his plate. One time he had even felt sorry for Jack. He had come upon him unexpectedly. Sitting on a rock, shoulders hunched, staring out to sea. A giant cormorant. As Charlie approached, Jack started, spinning round. His cheeks were wet, and there was more pain in his eyes than Charlie had ever seen. He dashed his sleeve across his eyes and stood upright. 'Did you see it – on the horizon?' he said.

Charlie scanned the faded line that blended sky and sea together and shook his head.

'Sometimes,' Jack said, 'I see the *Silver Dawn*. I see Jamsie coming back.' He pressed the heels of his hands against his eyes. 'Why could it not have been me instead of him?'

Charlie suppressed a shudder.

Then Jack had caught himself, shook his head as if to clear it and gruffly gave out orders. Charlie had never seen that side of him again.

'What's up with you, lad? Do you not like the food I've spent all day cooking for you, now? And me an old wife bent near double with the rheumatics,' said Tyna jokingly, bringing him back to the present. Tyna was not bent double with rheumatics. In her seventy-eighth year, only her knotted fingers bore testament of the arthritis that plagued her. 'He's not himself.' She looked at Mary-Jane, who nodded in agreement.

'Mind, you do look awful pale, Charlie,' his sister said, tucking a loose strand hair behind her ear.

'Aye, you've usually finished before I've started, and then you drool over mine.' Angus shovelled another forkful of meat into his mouth. Apart from Angus being slimmer, the twins were identical.

'Don't speak and eat at the same time,' Tyna said. Since the boys had moved in, she had treated them like sons.

'Stop your fretting. He's not a bairn.' Dan's grey, bushy brows met and parted. A man of few words, Dan Reid was obeyed when he did speak.

Mary-Jane leaned across the table and tried to set her fingers on Charlie's forehead. Irritated by her attention, he dodged the hand.

'You're maybe coming down with something. This isn't like you at all, Charlie.' In the gathering shadows, Mary-Jane's eyes appeared dark and large. Almost like hollows in her too white face. Charlie loved her desperately.

From the box bed in the far wall, one of her children stirred, cried out and went back to sleep.

'Ach, I am tired. Maybe I am coming down with a cold or something.' Needing to be alone to relive the events of this day, Charlie agreed with her.

'Well I hope you're well enough for Saturday night. Beeg Jeemie's home from the navy, and he's a dab hand on the accordion. He's brought a few bottles of fine whisky and all. We'll have a good night. And Alexina Laird's got a fair fancy for you.' Angus pushed his brother lightly on the shoulder.

'Well she can have *you*. She'll not be able to tell the difference especially with her glasses like bottle bottoms. I'm going up to my bed.'

'Then you'll not mind if I have this?' Angus reached for the plate of uneaten food.

'That you will not!' Tyna snatched up the dish. 'I'll heat it for Charlie later. Jack works the lad far too hard.' She rose and set the plate on the pine dresser.

The cat, washing herself on the rag rug before the fire, lifted her head and eyed the food with interest.

'Better put it through to the porch before the cat gets it.' Mary-Jane made to rise.

'Will you women sit down and you too, Charlie. No one will leave this table 'til the reading's done.' Dan slapped the flat of his hand against the table top. The globe of the brass lamp rattled in its cradle. He seldom put a foot over the kirk door, yet he was unfaltering in his reading of a verse from the bible after every evening meal. He pulled the lamp towards him, removed the globe and lit the wick. Once the flame had settled, Dan took the large heavy book from the shelf above the box-bed and leafed through it. Peering over the top of his glasses, he began to read.

Let the wicked forsake his way,
And the unrighteous man his thoughts
And let him return unto the Lord.

Charlie, the events of the day uppermost in his mind, closed his eyes and waited, not hearing a word.

That night, in the attic room he shared with Angus, Charlie lay awake, staring at the rafters and the thatch beyond. He had no desire for rest, but neither had he any stomach for the banter of his family. When Angus finally climbed the stairs, Charlie closed his eyes and breathed deeply, feigning sleep.

Before the clock struck one, the urge to check on Chrissie became impossible to deny. He looked at the now slumbering Angus, his twin, his confidant in every thought and deed. Not this time, not yet.

Boots strung over his shoulder by their laces, he crept downstairs and into the kitchen, surprised to find Tyna still up.

But he should have guessed, for, plagued by the pain in her bent fingers, she slept little. With her long flannel nightgown covering her slender frame, and with her stringy grey tresses hanging around her shoulders, she hunched over the iron stove stirring something in a pot.

An ache welled in Charlie's chest. In the time he had lived with this feisty, often awkward, woman he had learned to see behind the sharpness of her tongue to the good heart beneath. With two strides, he crossed the floor and placed a kiss on the back of the bent head.

She jumped, spun round and threatened him with the spurtle. 'You devil – frightening an old wife half to death.'

Charlie dodged out of her way. 'But what would you do without me?' he teased, at the same minute stifling a strong desire to hug her and protect her from further pain. Though she saw little of him since his marriage five years ago, Jack was still her son. Tyna always spoke well of Chrissie, and whether or not she had any suspicion of how violent Jack had become, Charlie had no idea. Tyna would not tolerate gossip.

'What are you doing out of bed at this hour – spying on an old wifie in her nightclothes?' she said.

'Aye, you're a fine looking woman and all. If I didn't know you'd choose old Dan snoring in the bed over a fine lad like myself, I'd ask for your hand, so I would.' He forced a laugh.

She screwed down her rheumy eyes and, reaching up, touched his cheek. 'What is wrong, lad? You're not in any trouble, now?'

'No. A ewe's been on her back too long the day. She was still a bit unsteady after I righted her. I forgot to check in case she tumbled over again.'

'Hah. Ewe on her back indeed. I can always tell when you're lying, Charlie Rosie. Is it a lassie?'

Charlie opened his mouth, but before he could stutter any kind of explanation, Tyna said, 'I hope you've not got some lass in trouble. Oh my, you've never?'

'What – no... no, no, I haven't.' He felt the heat rush to his cheeks. Tyna could be very forward when she'd a mind to.

'Well there's something far wrong. One thing I'm telling you is that you won't be leaving this house on an empty belly, ewe or not.'

He peered into the pot at the oats and water she had been stirring in preparation for the morning. 'A wee drop of brose, then.'

'And you'd best get things sorted. I'll not have comings and goings at all times of the night. This is a God fearing home.'

***

Fifteen minutes later, with the oatmeal he had forced down an unwilling gullet warming his insides, Charlie hiked across the field towards Chrissie's house. The full moon glinted on the haar: low rolling mist creeping in from the sea to cling to the land and circle about his ankles like smoke. The countryside before him lay in a panorama of weird shadows and plains. In the bay to the east, the seals sang their heart-breaking songs and a solitary sea bird yelped in warning. Every so often, a creature of the night scurried across his path. He set his hands on the top of the dyke, the cold of the stone cooling his palms. He moistened his lips. He had no idea what he intended to do once he got to the house. If all was silent, he would go home; he could do no more.

Chrissie's cottage stood before him less than a field's breadth away, light falling from the window onto the grass in small squares. The door appeared to be partly open. His brain took a few minutes to register what he was seeing. An open door – at this time of night? Something was wrong. He vaulted over the wall and ran up the field.

He found her outside between the byre and the house; her face white, her eyes almost shut and swollen; her lip split, a dark bruise stretching from cheek to chin.

'Jack came back, he... he...'

Charlie reached out his arms, catching her as she fell. 'Oh God, what's he done to you? I swear I'll kill him.' He picked her up; felt her heartbeat against his chest, fast and irregular; smelled sweat and blood. Her head fell back, and her thick curls tumbled over his arm. A patch of bloodied scalp showed where her hair had been torn away. Her tense body suddenly fell limp.

'He's gone.' Chrissie's mouth barely moved, and he wasn't sure if he had heard her correctly. 'Boat... he was going to tell folks you'd drowned.'

'It's all right, you're all right now. Don't try to talk.'

She turned her face to his neck, and her breath warmed his chilled skin. Holding her as gently as he could, he pushed what was left of the passage door open with his elbow and stopped as the horror of what had occurred in that room lay before him.

Chapter 4

Chrissie gradually became aware of pain. As consciousness bled into her, the pain increased. A hammer thundered inside her head; arrows stabbed her chest with every breath. The remnants of a dream stayed with her. Something terrifying. Something she knew was important. Yet it slipped from her mind as she fought to recall even the smallest fragment.

She forced her eyes open. Sunshine cast a shaft of dust-speckled light across the floor. In the grate, the fire crackled and spat on sea-bleached wood. Hanging on the iron hook above the flames, the kettle made a rushing sound.

The room was tidy, the curtains open, the pine dresser stacked with dishes, everything in place, yet something seemed wrong. She glanced at the clock. Half the morning had gone. Why was she still in bed? What had happened? Her eyes were drawn to the bronze statuette on the mantelpiece. Something about it stirred a memory that vanished just as quickly. Trying to recapture the brief flash increased the pain in her head.

Footsteps in the hall. A man's work boots hitting the flagstone. The knob turned, and the door creaked. Heat rose inside her like a stove in winter. Her skin prickled as sweat coated her skin. She clutched at the covers so tightly her fingers went numb. No, it couldn't be. Not Jack...

Then Charlie's face appeared. The corners of his mouth tugged upwards when he saw her awake.

As she released the breath she had not been aware she was holding, her body sagged into the mattress.

He came to her bedside, knelt down and tenderly stroked her forehead. 'Do you think you could take a wee bit brose?'

'What happened?' She grabbed his hand and pressed her nails into his flesh. 'What are you doing here?'

'Hush now. Don't worry.'

'But... what happened? I can't... remember.'

'You were outside in a state. You didn't even recognise me. Oh Chrissie, you scared me. Thank God you've wakened.'

Her eyes scanned the room, and fear rose within her as if Jack might materialise from the shadows. 'Why can't I remember?'

'Jack's gone, Chrissie. He...'

'Did you... did you fight again?'

'What's the last thing you remember?'

'Jack went out.' She put her hands to her head. 'What's happening to me?'

Charlie turned away. He stared at the floor. 'And then?'

'Nothing. Jack went out. I was waiting for him.' A thin whine escaped from her lips.

'He must have hit you lots of times. Good job I came back when I did.' His moist eyes avoided hers. His nostrils flared slightly with each breath, his Adam's apple bobbed as he swallowed. 'Do you really not remember any of it?'

She shook her head. A pain shot through. She raised her hand and winced as she touched the lump above the temple.

'The door had been kicked in, and you were outside. The room was a mess – chair upside down, the rug crumpled, the tin bath before the fire.'

A frisson of horror raced through her, a memory she couldn't quite catch. His words echoed in her head bringing with it pain. 'No,' she shouted. 'Don't say any more.' Every nerve, every sinew of her being was stretched to the limit; any moment she would go hurtling over the edge of sanity.

'Jack's gone. So is the *Christina*,' said Charlie.

'Don't say any more. I don't want to hear.' She held her head and squeezed her eyes shut.

'Let me get the doctor.'

'No doctor. No one must know.' A deep anxiety gnawed at her, like the knowledge of something black and evil skirting the periphery of her mind. It seemed impossible that only yesterday morning everything had been normal for her – just another day.

'I'll look in when I come back from the sea.' Charlie rose to his feet, turning his face from her. He wiped at his eyes as he made for the door.

As soon as she felt able, Chrissie dragged herself from the bed, and, holding on to the wall for support, made her way to the back porch. She picked up an empty jar from the shelf, turned it over and glanced at the label. 'Oh dear God,' she said. The jar, which had once contained powdered laburnum flowers, tumbled from her hand and smashed on the floor.

She crawled back into bed and lay there, her head swimming and throbbing. The door opened. Charlie came in and behind him were Mary-Jane, Dan and Tyna.

Chrissie felt her expression arrange itself to one of horror. 'How could you,' she whispered.

'It was time they knew what was going on,' said Charlie.

Mary-Jane gave a cry and ran to the bed. Tyna started to weep. Dan turned on his heel and went outside.

'Jack'll have gone,' said Tyna. 'He won't be able to face people after doing this to his wife. Please, Chrissie, don't tell anyone else. Let them think he got lost in the fog.'

Chrissie understood. Tyna couldn't face gossip. The shame would destroy her.

***

Charlie followed Dan into the yard. The old man shook his head, his cheeks wet. 'I always knew he had a temper. But this – I never thought he'd stoop to this.' He stared across the moor and over the flat grey of the Pentland Firth.

'He's been violent for a while,' said Charlie, his voice low.

'What could we do? She made her bed the day she married him. But to hurt her so badly...' Dan's voice broke, and he ran his hand over his weathered face. 'We'll see her all right. Between them, the women will nurse her. God knows, she's done enough for us. But if he ever comes back, old as I am, I swear...' He turned and gripped Charlie's arm. 'Not a word outside, not about this.'

'You don't need to ask.' Silence was the least he could give this broken family.

***

Later that same day, Robbie MacDermid and his brother Sandy decided not to go to school. They'd already had time off for the potato picking and, neither being particularly good scholars anyway, found the fine day too much of a temptation. Together they crept to the Laries Geo, an inlet where the high sloping cliffs hid them from prying eyes. If they returned home with a decent fry of fish, their parents would not take their truancy too badly. Their father already thought bookwork a waste of time.

The boys grasped their homemade rods and tins of worms, slid down the steep incline and scrambled across the shingle beach. Expertly dodging the slippy, green weed, they made their way over the slanting rocks to the furthest point.

'You know what I'm going to do with one of my fish?' said Sandy.

His brother glanced back at him.

'I'm going to put it inside Taylor's desk, way at the back.' He grinned.

'Good idea,' said Robbie. Neither of them liked the belt-wielding schoolteacher.

'He never opens it – he won't until the smell...' He pulled a face, screwed shut his eyes and held his nose.

'He'll have to give the whole class the day off 'til they find out where it's coming from,' said Sandy, mimicking the other boy's grimace.

Robbie opened his eyes, grabbed Sandy's arm and gave him a little shake. 'Look,' he said, pointing. Sandy followed the line of his brother's finger. An empty boat bobbed in the bay, each wave bringing her closer. 'I saw her first. She's mine,' said Robbie.

'We could share her.' A worried frown creased Sandy's forehead. 'But she must belong to somebody.'

'Maybe not.' Robbie, barefoot already, edged downwards until his feet touched the sea-bed, and he began to wade towards the yole. The sea grew and swelled around him as if considering spilling over the land. His body swayed with the force of the wave, and he fought to keep his balance. 'Give me your hand,' he yelled to Sandy.

Sandy took a step into the water. 'And you'll share the boat with me?'

'All right, all right. Help me.' Robbie's feet slipped on the rock below. The water swept in again, bringing the yole with it and smacking the keel against the boy's face, knocking his glasses from his eyes and throwing him backwards into the water.

Sandy grabbed the neck of his brother's shirt and clung on as the retreating wave fought to take both the boy and the boat with it. Robbie coughed and spluttered, one hand pressed to his damaged face.

'We're soaking. You've lost your glasses. You'll get it from Mam,' said Sandy. The next wave knocked both boys off their feet. They scrambled up the beach out of harm's way.

'I want to go home,' said Sandy.

'Stop being such a cry-baby. The tide's bringing her in. Wait here.' Robbie had started to shiver, his face where the yole had struck him was numb, but the prize of a boat of his own was too much of a temptation. Once more, he waded into the water and grabbed the prow. 'Help me,' he shouted as the tide fought to drag her out again. With the next wave, they hoisted her onto the shingle. Robbie squinted at the letters making up the name of the boat, but saw only a blur of shapes. As the next wave retreated, he hurriedly scrabbled under the water to find his glasses and when he did, they were smashed beyond repair. Both boys had missed so much schooling, reading would have been difficult for Robbie even with his glasses, and Sandy hadn't learned at all. Neither could they recognise the boat by its colour. Every boat on the island was the same, white with green deck and keel.

Sandy backed away. 'It must belong to somebody – we'll get into trouble.'

'Haven't heard of nobody losing a boat.' Robbie rubbed his face, the excitement of his find raising him above his pain.

'We'll have to tell Dad.' Sandy's lip shook.

'We'll not need to. We can keep her – we found her below high tide level. Dad says anything we find below high tide level is ours.'

'Folk might think we stole her.' Sandy sniffed, pressed his lips together and wiped his nose on his sleeve.

Robbie kicked the sand. 'We'll pull her into that cave. If nobody reports a lost boat, she's ours. If they do, we'll pull her out of the cave and pretend we just found her then.'

'But... someone might find out, and we'll get a leathering.'

'Just keep your mouth shut.' Robbie started to pull the boat along the sand. 'Help me will you – or we *will* get in trouble.'

In spite of the tears now leaving slug trails down his face, Sandy pressed his back against the stern and pushed on the sand with his feet. Progress was slow, but between them, the brothers managed to manoeuvre the boat into the cave. They spent another hour building rocks around the mouth of the cavity.

***

Charlie sat at the end of the pier with his fishing rod. It was difficult catching enough to feed a family with nothing but hand lines. The thing that bothered him most was Chrissie's state of mind. He wished he knew how to handle this. Did she really not remember – or did she just not want him to know? It was obvious she did not want to think or talk about it. Whichever it was, he would not harm her further by forcing her to relive that night. Maybe someday she would trust him enough, but for now he would have to go along with her wishes. He would not say another word until she herself chose to bring up the subject.

Even now, she had still wanted to protect Jack. Charlie had angered her by telling the folk at Scartongarth, but she was badly hurt and needed to be taken care of, and this was more than he could cope with on his own. No one but the family knew that Jack had not set sail for St Margaret's Hope that day, and they chose to believe that his conscience had driven him away. The other islanders would assume he was lost in the fog. Charlie would keep his secret close to his heart, next to the place where Chrissie lived.

Chapter 5

Chrissie awoke in the grainy light of early morning to the crowing of the cockerel. Fourteen days had passed since that night, and every night the dream had come. For the first time, the vision had remained long enough for her to grasp an image. She saw herself crouching in the byre and before her, something dark, ominous – what? She didn't want to think about it – not now.

Swinging her legs over the bed she reached for her shawl which she wrapped around her shoulders. She wiggled her feet into her roughly-woven, twine slippers and opened the small cupboard door beneath the box-bed. Once she removed the chamber pot, she squatted over it and relieved herself. In the gathering light, she carried the pot outside to where the wind was soft, bearing a hint of warmth from the south and ruffling the hummocks of grass. Squawking hens rushed at her, expecting food. In the firth, the water rippled, beads of spray lacing the surface.

She emptied the pot on the midden behind the byre where the animal dung was heaped: fertilizer for the land. Then she rinsed the chamber pot with a can of water kept for the purpose and washed her hands in the rain barrel.

Back inside, she stirred the oats steeping in the large pan, raked out the cinders, set and lit the fire and swung the iron hook holding the pan of porridge until it hung directly over the flames. Then she carried the ashes outside to the ash-heap on the far side of her garden wall.

From the rainwater barrel, she filled a basin, which she brought into the kitchen. After stripping off her long cotton nightdress, vest and drawers, she washed herself with a flannel and carbolic soap. By the time she had donned her underclothes, her teeth were chattering. She pulled on her petticoat, her blouse, cardigan and skirt. After dressing, she ate a few mouthfuls of porridge, put water in the pan, left it to soak, made herself a cup of tea and drank slowly. Although she had tried not to think about it, a memory of the dream still lingered. Suddenly, she knew what it was. An open grave in the byre. She set the cup to one side and rose.

Outside the byre she stopped, reluctant to enter. What was she afraid to remember? She forced her hand forward and pressed it against the door until it swung open. There was a frantic fluttering, and a large blackbird flew past her face, its wings brushing her skin. Screaming, she stumbled backwards. She ran back to the house, slammed the door and leaned against it. A vision of the door bulging inwards, of the bar splintering and breaking sped through her mind too quickly to grasp.

Something about the door. The hinges. They were black, shiny and new. Struggling to sort out the jumbled mess inside her head, she sat down.

Later, if anyone had asked her how long she sat before Charlie's step resounded on the flagstone path, she could not have told them. Recognising his gait, she stood up, her body tightening. Simultaneously, she found herself wanting his company, yet wanting to strike out at him.

'Did you replace the hinges on the door?' she asked, the minute he entered the house.

'Do you remember something?' He looked hopeful but wary.

'No, no, I don't. I noticed the hinges.'

Charlie rubbed his neck. 'I tried to tell you. The door had been kicked in. I fixed it while you were still asleep.'

'Where exactly did you find me outside – at the door?'

'No, you, well, you were nearer the byre. Chrissie, are you all right?'

'I'm fine.' Breathe deep. Breathe slow. Keep control, she told herself. 'And the *Christina's* definitely gone?'

'She's gone. Chrissie, maybe I should...'

'What's being said round the island?' she said, without meeting his eyes.

'They believe he'll come back.' Charlie took a seat at the table. 'Did you sleep last night?'

She shrugged her shoulders. 'On and off.' She lifted the teapot, poured two cups of tea and sat down.

'They know fine how island men disappear for months at a time.' His fingers tightened round his cup.

It was true. Young men often ended up on some other island with a broken sail or rudder. Many years ago, her uncle had been swept away in a storm and ended up in the Faeroes. He had not been able to sail home until the weather settled in the spring and then he had returned with a Faeroese bride. No matter what the fears, there was always that shred of hope.

'They'll think he's on Swona. Folks say they're so short of men on that island that the women steal the rudders of any boat that berths there.' Charlie laughed awkwardly.

A sudden vision of Jack's crazed eyes, his bared teeth as he came towards her filled her head. How could Charlie even try to joke? And Jack's poor parents. She wanted to scream, but she couldn't, not in front of Charlie. 'I think you'd better go.' She stared into her cup, the tea untouched.

'Chrissie...' Before he could say more, a sudden knock startled them both. Chrissie's hand strayed to her hair, and she pulled her braid across her cheek. She went to answer the door.

Alec MacDermid stood on the doorstep, a shamefaced lad on either side of him. 'The boys have something to tell you.' he said, and jolted young Robbie's shoulder. 'Go ahead, lad.'

Robbie stared at the ground and shuffled his feet. 'Sandy and me...' He looked up at his father who poked him again. 'We found Jack's boat in Laries Geo.' The lad's voice weakened; his lip wobbled.

Chrissie grabbed the doorframe. Another fleeting rush of memory – Jack vomiting and doubled up on the floor. 'No!'

'They got a tanning for not telling me sooner. I'm sorry Chrissie, but they found it the day Jack went missing.' If MacDermid was surprised by the now yellowing bruises on her face, he did not show it. 'When they heard about Jack, they were too frightened to tell. Robbie said he'd got in a fight at school –

broke his glasses – I should have known he was telling lies. Robbie's not the fighting type.'

Stepping backwards, Chrissie steadied herself against the wall.

'Is there anyone I can get for you?' asked MacDermid, his brow creasing.

'Scartongarth.' She coughed to unclog her throat, thick with fear. 'Go and tell them. The men'll know what to do. Th... thank... you.'

Her eyes met Charlie's when she returned indoors. She bit down on her lip to stop the tremble.

Charlie half rose, reaching towards her.

She backed away.

'Don't worry. You don't need to worry,' he said.

Another memory flashed into her mind. Of her screaming, falling to the floor. Then it vanished.

'Chrissie...' Charlie set his hand on her arm.

'I don't want to talk. Not about Jack, now or ever. I want you to go.' She pushed him away. 'Go and tell them the boat's been found.' Those flashes of memory were hurting her head, making her irrational.

Charlie looked uncertain, opened the door and stared at the firth. He stopped and turned to face her. He opened his mouth as if he had more to say.

'No! I want to hear no more. Just go – I can't stand this.' She pressed her hands to her head, willing herself not to scream. She needed to be alone.

He hesitated.

'Do you not understand?' she shouted.

He shook his head and looked at the floor. 'If you want to talk...'

'I do not want to talk. I do not want to think. Leave me alone, please.' She slammed the door at his back and leaned her forehead against it, unable now to stop the memories tumbling into her mind. Pressing her hands against the wood, she closed her eyes. Her knees buckled, and she sank to floor. 'God help me,' she whispered.

Suddenly the smallest details became clear, dropping like rain into the void of her recent past. Her armpits prickled, her blouse dampened and stuck to her skin. And she was back in that fateful evening, reliving every heart-stopping emotion of the nightmare she had fought to blank from her memory.

She had been sitting in her grandmother's chair. On the mantelpiece, the bronze statuette that her father, a Navy man, had brought back from some foreign country, glittered in the firelight. As a child, she had loved that statuette. A naked man wearing only a fig leaf and holding a horse by the reins. Not a heavy hooved, stocky horse like those on the island but a slim, muscular beast rearing up, his forelegs pawing the air. Trim legs they were, expertly crafted. She studied each muscle imagining them quiver. The nostrils of the steed flared, his eyes opened wide; yet the man had a serene expression on his face, caring nothing about the raging beast beside him.

Footsteps outside. Growing louder.

Jack.

She stared at the fire. The flames, licking up and over the driftwood burned blue with the salt of the sea. Her breath quickened. Her fingers plucked at the material of her skirt.

The bricks behind the fire were black with soot. The chimney would need cleaning soon. The easiest way was to 'put it up.' She would stuff it with paper and allow the flames to burn the brickwork clean. As a child, she had often seen flames shoot out of chimney pots. She would do it ....

The door knob turned.

. . . tomorrow.

Jack stormed into the room. 'Is he here?'

Her hands tightened on the arms of the chair. 'Who? No one's been here.'

'Is he hiding?' He began opening cupboard doors, pulling back the curtain covering the box bed. 'Are you here, Charlie?'

'There's no one here.' Chrissie stood up to face him, saw the wild glitter in his eyes and knew he was beyond listening.

'But he was here, wasn't he?' Jack walked towards her. His face was twisted, and he slouched so that his eyes were level with hers. His arms bent at the elbows; his hands hung loose.

She stepped backwards, out of his reach. 'I promise you, please.'

'Have you been searching through my things... have you found anything else? He kept coming. In desperation she grabbed the statuette from the mantelpiece and swung it towards his head.

Jack's hand shot out blocking her swing. She staggered and tripped on her skirt hem. She tumbled slamming her head against the flagstone floor. Her fingers still clutched the statuette.

'Threaten me would you? Bitch.' He kicked out; his boot caught her wrist and jarred the bone. The statuette fell from her grasp and skittered across the floor. He gripped her hair and yanked her to her feet. His fist struck her mouth. She tasted blood.

'I wouldn't... have touched the letters. It was Charlie. I tried to stop him... At this stage she would say anything, agree to anything, to make him stop.

He grabbed her chin between his thumb and forefinger. 'Do you know where I was?'

She tried to shake her head.

'I was in the byre digging a grave for Charlie.'

Her legs turned to rubber as she fought to stay upright.

'Look at me,' he said. She forced her eyes open. 'Say you love me.'

Her mouth was so dry she barely formed the words. 'I... love... you.'

'Louder.'

'Love... you.'

He laughed. The mad laugh she'd come to hate. 'Aye, I knew you would never stand up to me yourself. When we get rid of him, we'll be back the way we were.' He threw her aside and began pacing the floor punching the flat of one hand.

Whimpering, she crouched to her knees. She touched her head, and felt wet stickiness.

He continued pacing. 'Charlie put you up to this. We were happy until he came.' He suddenly spun round to face her. 'You do understand why he's got to die?'

She nodded silently.

'An accident at sea. That's what they'll think. You'll help me. Prove to me you love me.'

'Aye. I... will.' Speaking was agony.

'Get me a whisky, and get the tin bath out. I need to wash – but first.' He grabbed her crotch so hard she screamed. With his other hand, he pushed her towards the bed in the recess in the wall. His fingers closed around her bodice, ripping the thin material apart.

'No Jack, no, please.'

'But you like it like this.' He held her down as she twisted her head this way and that, closing her eyes tightly so she would not have to see his face. One bent arm pressed against her neck until she feared she would suffocate. She lay, stiff as a corpse as his free hand fumbled with her clothing. With his knee, he forced her legs apart. When he finally entered her, roughly, painfully, she swam in and out of consciousness. Once finished, he jumped up. 'Now,' he said, 'Whisky. The bath.'

Beyond hurting, she dragged herself from the bed and limped to the back closet, closing the door behind her. She studied the broken nail on her thumb, the rough dryness of her skin, the blue raised swelling on her wrist where Jack's boot had landed. Her grandmother's voice floated towards her through the years. 'There will be times when you will hold life and death in these.' A bright memory filled her head; of how the old woman had held the child's small, smooth hands in her aged and gnarled ones and said, 'Choose wisely'. A cold calm filled her – a deadly calm.

Closing her eyes against the pain, Chrissie lifted a half-empty bottle of whisky from the shelf. She stopped and stood still, willing the blackness not to overtake her; willing her thudding heart to settle to a more even rhythm. Beads of sweat ran down her face. She grabbed the jar containing the ground laburnum, twisted off the lid, emptied the powdered contents into the whisky and stirred the mixture. The liquid in the glass settled. The ground flowers appeared undetectable.

Holding the container against her body, she limped into the room.

'About time,' Jack said. His lips stretched into a parody of a smile.

She handed him the whisky, and he threw it back, swallowing the liquid in one gulp. He gagged and wiped his mouth on the back of his hand. 'Bloody hell woman – did you wash the mug? It tastes like pish.' He held the mug towards her. 'Wash it and get me another.'

'Yes…yes.'

'Well go on. What are you staring at me for?'

All conscious thought gone, she dragged herself into the closet, poured the remainder of the whisky into the tin and brought it to him. As he drank, she fell to her knees and heaped more peat on to the fire. Every movement was performed automatically, as if she had left her body, and it now moved and acted of its own accord. She left the water pot hanging on the iron hook above the flames. Yesterday's soup sat on the bricks lining the sides of the fireplace. Sweat stood out on her brow as she struggled to move the heavy pan closer to the heat.

'I'll do it.' His voice was suddenly soft. He stroked her face and gazed at her, something like surprise in his eyes. 'Did I do that? Chrissie I didn't mean to hurt you. You make me so mad… you… you…' He waved his hands. 'Why do you do it? *You* make me do this to you.'

He straightened up and took her hand so tenderly her stomach roiled. He helped her into the seat as gently as if she were made of glass. 'I didn't mean you any harm… it was him… Aye, he'll get what he deserves!'

'Charlie… would never… he didn't…' Fresh blood dribbled from her split lip each time she spoke. Why did she bother? Jack wasn't listening. He knelt before her and kissed the swollen wrist, his lips like warm slugs. His eyes turned upward and met hers. 'I'll let loose the boat and fling the empty whisky bottle in her.

She'll drift, ha! She'll drift way out to sea. It'll look like he drowned, and only us will ever know the dirty bastard will be five feet under the soil. Salt water's too good for him.

An hour later, after he had bathed and dined, the vomiting started. Chrissie said nothing. She had no feelings left. She brought him a basin and a damp towel for his head. When his stomach emptied and only saliva filled the basin, the convulsions started.

'What have you done?' The words wrenched from him. From then on he was unable to speak, but his eyes flashed with hatred and disbelief.

A strange, cold calmness had filled her. She imagined she had risen above herself and was watching the scene from afar. When his breath became rasping and difficult, she left the house and went to the byre. She lifted the lantern above her head until she located the grave Jack had prepared for Charlie. She fell to her knees and stared into the black corners. 'You prepared your own grave, Jack.' Her words had been barely more than a whisper. There the memory splintered and faded, leaving her drained and still unsure of what had happened next.

***

When she thought about it later, she could not be sure how much had been an actual memory and how many blank spaces her own imagination had filled in. She could never swear an oath in a court of law that everything had happened as it had played out in her mind.

The clock struck four times, and the afternoon sunshine slanted through the window. Her hand shook as she pushed herself upright. She paced the floor, opening and shutting her hands. One thing she knew, however difficult she found it, she had to go and look in the byre – she had to make sure.

The byre door creaked open, and the dank air filled her nostrils. The light filtered through the dusty interior. Instinctively she walked to the corner looking for flagstones which had been disturbed. Fresh crumbling earth around the edges and the absence of dust and straw told her all she needed to know. She prised the first flagstone upright, bent down, grabbed the edges and moved it from its place. Then she began to dig. The first spadeful revealed nothing. The second time the blade sank into the soft earth, it hit something solid and slithered sideways. As she lifted the blade away, the earth crumbled and fell back into the hole. But not before she glimpsed white bone and blackened threads of dried blood where the sharp edge of the spade had sheared away skin. Her gorge rose. She tossed down the spade and ran to the corner of the byre where she threw up into the straw.

'Oh God, Oh God,' she said into the emptiness, as the realisation of what had happened hit her. She had killed Jack. Had somehow found the strength to drag the body into the byre and bury him. By the time Charlie had arrived it was all over. Charlie, like the rest of the family, believed Jack had taken the *Christina* and in his distressed state had either fallen overboard or faked his own death. He could tell her no more, because he knew no more.

Wiping her mouth on her sleeve, she swallowed the bile. Once she got hold of herself, she returned the earth and the flagstone to where it had been and stared at the disguised grave. In that moment came a flash of determination. Whatever he had done to her, she would survive. Her soul might be condemned to hell, but there were sick people on this island who needed her. And there were two wee bairns with an ailing mother at Scartongarth. She made herself a vow. She would never tell the family that her memory had returned, and she would never again speak about that night.

She could not remember later how long she had sat in her grandmother's chair, quietly rocking to and fro that night. Only when she realised that the dying day had already painted the sky black, did she rise and light the lamp.

Something still plagued her. If Jack lay beneath the flagstones in the byre, how had the boat ended up in Laries Geo? It had to be Robbie and Sandy. They were right devils. They would say they found it to save their own skins. Either that, or Jack, in his desperate hurry for revenge, had forgotten to make the boat safe from the rising tide. Whichever it was, she was glad of it. How else would she have explained his disappearance?

In spite of her resolve, the thought of facing another night alone in this house became almost more than she could bear. The lamplight flickered over the walls and every shadow reached out menacing tendrils. She was aware of a pulse beating in her stomach.

Footsteps outside. Someone was coming. She tensed, as she still did at every sound. Then she recognised the gait. Thank God. Charlie. She needed him now. She needed someone – anyone.

'Tyna sent you some soup. She wants you to come down to the house.' He walked across the floor and set a bowl covered with a cloth on the table.

'I'm not ready yet.' She turned away, fingers intertwined, trying to stop the tremors.

'Chrissie, what's wrong?'

She spun round to face him.

'I don't know. I need... I...'

His hand reached towards her, hovered in the air then dropped to his side. 'Are... are you sorry he's gone?'

'No, I'm not sorry.' It was not a lie. She heard the granite edge in her own voice. 'But don't mention his name, please. I never want...' Her voice quavered. Their eyes met and held. Behind her the fire settled, the cat purred, the clock ticked. Outside a ewe bleated, a seabird yelped. She moved closer and inhaled the scent of him. She needed to be held at this moment more than ever before.

Charlie's concern-filled eyes travelled over her face. 'I'd do anything...' his voice stuttered and faded.

She became aware that tears were streaming down her face. Silent tears without sobs.

Suddenly his arms were around her, and she clung to him, burying her face in his chest.

He stroked her hair. 'It's all right now. It's over,' he whispered.

'Stay with me,' she said, terrified of being alone. She did not want to leave the safety of his arms.

He placed a hand under her chin and turned her face up to his. He kissed her forehead, her eyes and finally her mouth. His lips closed on hers, hesitantly, inexpertly.

'Hold me,' she said.

'Chrissie... I've never...' His voice faded away.

'I need ...' What did she need? She didn't know. She just knew she wanted life and hope and to be held. She placed a finger against his mouth. 'Hush.' She drew far enough away to see the colour rise in his cheeks, and she kissed him again. This time his kiss was firm, his lips parted, his tongue meeting hers. When they finally broke apart their faces were flushed. With unsteady hands, she opened her blouse.

He noisily filled his lungs with air as she lifted his hand and guided it to her breast.

His fingers trembled.

She grabbed his shirt and fumbled at the buttons.

With half-closed eyes, he heaved the garment over his head and flung it to one side. He struggled out of his trousers and stood naked before her. His firm young body glistened in the firelight, the pale hairs across his chest no more than a dusting.

She drank him in with her eyes. The smooth lines of his muscles reminded her of the statuette of the naked man on the mantelpiece.

'You're such a bonny lad.' The words sat on the air between them as she touched his face and moved closer, gasping as his hardness thrust against her belly.

Taking her hand in his, he led her to the bed.

Some time later, she woke up, confused. She sensed another body beside her and turned to look at the head on the pillow. Charlie's eyes were closed, a small dribble of saliva escaping from his slightly parted lips. It took a couple of seconds for memory to return. What had she done? What had she been thinking? He was a boy: a mere boy. She was a grown woman: a married woman. She had been crazy – out of her mind. Remembering what had happened to Jack and her own part in it had unhinged her.

'Charlie, wake up.'

Opening his eyes, he blinked and a smile slowly spread across his face. He turned and looked at the clock. 'I could stay the night.'

'No!' She grabbed at the covers, hiding her nakedness. 'This mustn't happen again. I was... I don't know... I just don't know.' She stared at him, wanting him to go, wanting him to stay, willing him to understand her confusion, knowing he never would.

'Don't say that. I'd swim the Pentland Firth if you asked me.'

'You can't swim.' She gave a feeble laugh.

'I'd still try.'

'Go. Forget this happened.'

'Forget... I don't want to forget.' He looked dismayed.

'Please go.' She wanted rid of him now. She wanted to hide from her own shame. She wanted time to sort out her mixed-up feelings.

'I'll come back tomorrow.' Charlie rose and gathered his clothes. He leaned forward to kiss her, and she dodged the embrace.

'This won't happen again,' she said.

'Chrissie, I know you worry about what folks say, but we could leave here, take the *Christina* and sail to somewhere no one knows us. North Ronaldsay should be far enough.'

Not now, I can't face this now, she silently pleaded. But she only said, 'And how would Scartongarth fare with no boat?'

He paced to the window. 'We'll leave the boat then. We'll go to the mainland, and I'll work at anything. They say there's jobs breaking metal for the roads. We can go to Wick or Keiss. Or I can join a herring boat, like. Or we'll go farther. Far enough so if Jack does come back, he'll never find us.' He crossed the room and clasped her hands.

'We can do it. We can really do it.'

'You think I want that?' No, she didn't want to leave the island, there was no need. But only she knew there was no chance of Jack ever returning.

'You must feel something...' he said.

'Charlie go, leave me alone. You know I could never leave Bel and Jimmy.' How could she, with Mary-Jane's health growing worse every year? 'And... and don't tell anyone what happened.'

The hurt in his eyes tore her in two; he would never understand. How could he, when she didn't understand herself? She sank back against the wooden wall of the box-bed and listened as the door closed behind him and his footsteps faded. 'Oh God, forgive me,' she whispered. What had she been thinking? Charlie was a young lad with a boyish infatuation for her. Something which would disappear as he grew older. If the islanders linked his name with hers, questions would be asked about Jack's disappearance, and speculation would run rife around the island. The *Christina* had been washed up the day he disappeared. Jack was a good seaman in spite of the fog. It didn't matter that no one liked him. The islanders would pounce on a piece of gossip and devour it like hounds on a rabbit. She must not see Charlie again. She climbed out of the bed and took the bible down from the shelf and set it on the table. Leaning her forehead against it, she clasped her hands and begged desperately for God to have mercy on her soul.

***

Sunday came, and Chrissie shrank from the sound of kirk bells. In all her years she had barely missed a service, yet now, she felt unworthy of crossing the Lord's door. Instead she knelt to pray, but her prayers had no longer the power to give her comfort. Even God had deserted her. She picked up her apron tails and covered her face, but found herself unable to cry.

Chapter 6

From then on, Chrissie went through each day rigidly sticking to her normal routine. A round of rising in the morning, doing what work needed doing and collapsing in bed each night, too tired to think.

Charlie called often but she was always sharp with him. Seeing him reminded her of the shame of having given herself to him. The last thing she should have done was turn to another man for comfort. She constantly told him she was managing, managing fine. But night after night the nightmares came sneaking through the shadows and danced in the tangles of her brain. Not wanting to face the memory of what happened in the byre, she sang, filling the dark shadows with the sound. Singing kept her sane.

With every visit to Scartongarth, the weary lines on the faces of Jack's parents tore at her anew especially when Tyna hugged her, an uncharacteristic action for the island people. When Chrissie saw Charlie and his friends with a bunch of young, giggling lassies hanging around the shop, or disappearing over the top of the brae, she was glad. Glad for him, she told herself. Or she would be, if only she could banish the feel of his lips, the touch of his hands, the heat of his body.

One Monday morning, Chrissie answered the door to find the Reverend Donald Charleston standing there, turning his hat in his hands. 'I came to see how you were getting on, Chrissie,' he said. He had begun to drop by often since Jack's disappearance. Normally, if she saw him coming, she pretended to be out. Her guilt was intensified by his goodness. Yet she liked the minister. He was young, and his ideas were fresh. She knew why he had come today. She had promised to return to the kirk, a promise she had not felt able to keep.

'Come away in, minister,' she said, remembering her manners. A tall man, he ducked as he entered the doorway.

'I'm sorry I've not been in the kirk.' She moved the kettle over the flames of the fire.

'Can I help with anything, Chrissie?' He took a seat at the table.

She bit her lip, wondering how much she could confide in him. Would a man of the cloth understand? Yet something different drove Reverend Charleston. Unlike others of his ilk, he never condemned or passed judgement. Looking into the kind brown eyes, she came to a decision. She had to talk to someone. 'I don't feel worthy. I've done a bad thing.'

'God has a great capacity for forgiveness.' His long fingers played with the brim of his hat.

Tears threatened, and Chrissie didn't feel she could speak. No, she could not bring herself to tell him about Jack. He would surely want her to go to the law. She forced words from between dry lips. 'Jack's hardly gone, and I've had unworthy thoughts about another man.' There. It was said. At least some of it. She slowly raised her head, not knowing what a reaction to expect. His eyes were solemn and full of compassion.

'Sometimes God's laws seem very unfair,' he said quietly. 'He makes the same rules for a happy marriage as for one torn apart by strife.'

In the silence that followed the ticking of the clock sounded very loud. Chrissie stared at the floor, noticed a wood louse crawling across the flagstone.

'I wasn't happy with Jack. I'm glad he's gone. Is that a sin, minister – to be glad someone's dead?' Her voice gained strength. She leant forward, desperately hoping for absolution.

'No, for you are a good person, Chrissie. I cannot with my heart say it is wrong.'

'But I promised in front of God to love, honour and obey. I promised for better or worse. I tried, minister, I really tried. But he would have killed me...' She caught herself, and the tears she could not spill bubbled up from her heart.

'Come back to the kirk, Chrissie. Read your bible and pray. God will give you strength to do the right thing.'

'Even if I've done a very wrong thing?' she asked.

'Whatever it is, if you are truly sorry and sin no more, God will forgive.'

'Jack stole Isa's letters – the ones Davie sent her.'

'Yes, I know.' The Reverend lowered his eyes to the floor.

'You know – how?' Chrissie was suddenly alert.

'I accompanied Isa to the train, remember. The day she left. We found out he had been sending letters then. We assumed it was Jack.' He cleared his throat. 'How is she – do you hear?'

Donald Charleston had been a good friend to Isa. There had even been talk at one time that their relationship had been more than friendship. Chrissie noticed the slight dip in his voice at the mention of Isa's name, and she knew he would understand – about Charlie at least.

'I have had word. Isa's arrived in Canada. She's happy.'

'Good, good.'

'But it is a sin, is it not, to covet another?'

Sadness seemed to sit on the minister's shoulders. His eyes filled with concern. 'However hard it is, adultery, even the thought of it, is a sin. Do you want me to pray with you before I go – for strength?'

'Please do, minister,' she said. They knelt together. She did not listen to the words; instead she beseeched the Lord with her heart to forgive her for the deadliest of all sins. Murder.

Feeling less alone, she watched the retreating figure of the minister with even greater resolve not to let Charlie into her life. What good did loving a man ever do her? Davie had broken her heart, and Jack had abused her mentally and physically. Loving men had destroyed her very soul.

The next evening, as she passed the house of Jamesina Sinclair, one of her neighbours, the woman called to her from the door. 'Come away in, Chrissie. It'll do you no good sitting in thon house all on your own.' Strains of music flowed from behind the woman.

Chrissie hesitated. Although she did not relish mixing with others at this time, the thought of another night of shadows and memories was even less attractive.

Inside, a peat fire blazed, and several islanders sat around, all smiling a welcome. Charlie and some of his friends sat on the floor cross legged. Beside him sat Alexina Laird, a lassie his own age with a headful of dark curls, a turned up nose and thick glasses, and her older sister Ruby who was in service on the mainland. Home for a visit, Chrissie thought. They nodded at each other. Chrissie avoided Charlie's eyes as best she could.

'Come away and sit here, lass,' said Jamesina's man, vacating his rocking chair and guiding Chrissie to the overwarm position by the fire. 'Charlie is going to give us one of his stories.'

Charlie laughed awkwardly and rubbed his head so that his hair stood on end. It might have been the glow from the fire, or it might have been her presence, but his colouring was brighter than usual.

He's such a bonny lad, thought Chrissie, studying her clasped hands, the pain of being so near him suddenly acute. She listened as his voice flowed over her.

'It was like this,' he began. Within minutes, he had the room in stitches with his tale about how he had fought a sea serpent off Hoy Head. Everyone knew the 'sea serpent' was little more than a large seal which had surfaced too close to the boat, scaring the seal as much as it had done the fishermen. Charlie acted out the scene, putting on a gruff voice to portray the thoughts of the seal, and the hilarity in the room filled Chrissie up and melted the ice inside her. Without being able to help herself, she was soon laughing as loud as the others, tears spilling from her eyes. It was good to be able to laugh again.

That night, unbidden and unwanted, Charlie's face crept through the darkness of her dreams like a saving light.

Chapter 7

'It's no use,' Alexina Laird kicked at the limpet with the heel of her tacketty boot, knocking it off its rock. She bent down, picked it up and threw it into the pail. 'Charlie Rosie is never going to notice me. Who would with these?' She indicated her thick glasses.

'Don't you give in so soon,' said her sister Ruby. 'You're a bonny lassie. It is a pity you've got to wear them, but once he gets to know you, they'll not matter.'

'He's known me since we were at school!' Alexina kicked off another limpet. She loved it when Ruby came home a visit. Since she'd gone into service on the other side, as the islanders called mainland Scotland, she seldom had time off. Ruby's mistress was good to her, gave her clothes she no longer wanted. The result was that Ruby and Alexina were the best dressed lassies on the island.

As the second daughter, Alexina had had to leave school at twelve to take care of her ailing mother. No one seemed to know what exactly was wrong with mam, only that she either lay in bed or sat on a chair all day. 'It's all these bairns,' she would say when asked. 'Fourteen bairns have ruined my body. Six of them already in the graveyard.' Then she would cry, so the girls had long ago stopped asking.

'Come on.' Her frustration spent on the shellfish, Alexina indicated to Ruby to follow her. She needed to lift herself from this mood. Together they carried the bucket home and into the back kitchen.

'You're pretty.' Ruby came up behind her and smoothed the curls back from her face. 'Why don't you wear it pinned up?' she asked.

''I've never tried,' admitted Alexina as Ruby guided her into the main room and turned her to face the mirror. She had to acknowledge the face staring from the mirror was more attractive like this. 'I'm never going to be as bonny as you though.'

'You have your own kind of beauty.'

Easy for Ruby to say that. Anything would look good on her. Still, it was fun when Ruby was here. She pinned Alexina's hair up, pulling down a few strands to hang along the jaw line.

'Now for some colour.' She took a red book from the shelf, licked her finger and rubbed the cover. She turned Alexina to face her and applied the dye to her cheeks and lips. Then she removed a small amount of soot from the fireplace and transferred it to the back of her hand. 'Close your eyes,' she said. Alexina obeyed. This was some sort of joke; she was going to look like an idiot. She giggled at the thought.

Ruby's fingers dotted along the length of her eyelid. 'Open.' she commanded. Ruby turned Alexina's head left and right, and patted along the corner of her eyes. 'Stand up, shoulders back.'

Alexina sniggered but complied.

Ruby picked up the mirror so Alexina could admire her reflection.

Alexina gasped. Even in the distorted reflexion from the cheap glass, the Halloween face she had expected was not there. Her rosy cheeks and cherry lips camouflaged her normally pale complexion. The hair pulled back made her face more defined. If only she didn't have to wear these glasses she might even be bonny. She hated them. They ruined everything. Not wanting to hurt her sister, she laughed as if she was pleased.

Ruby applied the same colour to her own skin. If Ruby had looked bonny before, she looked radiant now. Her eyes had never seemed so enormous. Her skin was flawless. Compared to Ruby, Alexina felt dowdy.

'What are you two up to?' Her brother Don came into the room. He went into the back porch and washed his hands. 'I came back to get the pieces for the men.'

Alexina clapped her hand over her mouth. 'Oh, I forgot!' She scurried to the larder and began to slice the bread. 'Ruby, get me some lard.'

'Ah, dinna rush,' said Don. 'You deserve a wee break. You work hard, lass.' He touched her reddened cheek. 'What's Ruby been up to now?'

Don was the eldest and her favourite brother. William had joined the navy, and Sam had married and gone to America. Frank and Hugh were both at the herring fishing in Kirkwall. Dolly and Robert were ten and eight and both at school.

Alexina finished the sandwiches, wrapped them in a dishcloth and handed them to her brother.

'Aye, you'll make some lad a fine wife,' he said. She blushed beneath his gaze and thought of Charlie Rosie.

***

Winter came with screaming gales, starless, overcast skies and wild north winds; with lashing seas, storm bound boats and shipwrecks; with still, snow-covered moonlit nights and sharp fresh mornings. Winter was a time of boots and coats and shawls, of frozen fingers and chilblains and depleting food supplies. Winter was a time when women spun the wool into yarn and knitted ganseys and stockings; mended clothes that were more mending than cloth; struggled to dry washing hanging from lines strung from rafters and strove to provide their families with substantial meals when nothing was left of their stocks but salt-herring, smoked pork, potatoes and oatmeal.

For the men it was a time to make lead sinkers for the hand-lines; to knit twine nets; to make and repair creels and yoles; to build model yachts to race in the stretches of inland lochs and to carry out what maintenance was needed on houses and outbuildings.

A time bairns trailed through snowdrifts to reach the school where, with running noses, numb feet and wet clothes, they sat around a tiny stove and scratched out their letters in a box of sand. And when school was over, they would run home and line their bellies with a slice of cold, congealed porridge, which had been left to set in a drawer the night before. Then, depending on the weather, they sledged on snow covered braes, played hide and seek among the haystacks or swung on ropes tied to rafters in the barns, and icy fingers, numb toes and dribbling noses took second place to the joy of youth.

Winter was also a time of warm get-togethers; a time to sing, tell tales and laugh around blazing fires; to dance in the empty hay loft of the Mains to self-taught musicians, and to gather at Lottie's wee shop by the crossroads, where the men smoked and played cards while the women exchanged gossip and drank tea. And Chrissie met with them. She laughed as loud as any at the good-natured banter, enjoyed the familiar smells of paraffin, dried fish and pipe smoke and wished she could stay there forever.

At other times she heard laughter as young folk passed on the road, boys and girls, flirting, giggling and joking. It hardly seemed possible that just over five years ago, she was one of them. Music frequently flowed from an open cottage door as the islanders enjoyed off-chance visits. She was always welcome. Doors were open to all comers. Yet whenever her natural exuberance bubbled forth, it was immediately damped down by the cold image of Jack's twisted face and the scrape of the spade against bone. Yet Chrissie refused to be beaten down by her memories. She danced and sang as loud as any. And she tried not to notice the way Charlie's eyes still followed her, or feel the clench in her stomach every time she saw him.

The sick still needed tending to and bairns delivering. Chrissie loved this part of her work. Hearing the first cry of a brand new life, knowing she had played her part in bringing this soul into the world and witnessing the joy of grateful parents as she laid the infant in the mother's arms. In every successful birth there was something magical and beautiful, something that gave her hope that her world would eventually set itself to rights once more.

There was sorrow too. No matter how tired she might be, at every death, Chrissie was available to clasp a hand for as long as she was needed. Sometimes no words could bring comfort, but holding a sobbing mother, listening to reminiscences from a grieving son or daughter, or simply helping in practical ways, gave Chrissie a sense of purpose. Every time someone told her what a good person she was, she closed her eyes at her own hypocrisy. *If only you knew,* she thought.

The winter passed. As early spring breathed new energy over the land and shoots of corn and bere pushed up from the earth and the high thin cries of new lambs filled the air, Chrissie's ghosts gradually faded until they became no more than a scar on her mind.

Jack's name was rarely mentioned; he had joined the ranks of the few young men who had disappeared from the island. Some returned months or even years later with tales of their adventures. Some never did.

Chrissie rarely saw Charlie now, but when she did and their eyes met, the secret they shared flashed through air charged with mutual attraction and in spite of herself, her heart lurched. But, she swore, never again would she let a man rule her, either emotionally or physically. She had done the right thing by sending the lad away. Not only for her own salvation, but also for his sake. She could never be his wife and he deserved more than that.

Chapter 8

On a bright March morning, when the dry wind ruffled the crocuses growing along the wall of her cottage and the air was fat with sunshine, Chrissie pulled the washtub from where it leaned against the wall and dragged it to the green. Returning to stoke up the fire, she set the pans of water on the stove-top. On such a day, when the weather made a grand drought, she could finally wash away the grime of guilty secrets. It was still a bit early for spring-cleaning, but hers would be so thorough the ghosts of her past would be, if not banished completely, at least severely disabled.

Thank God for work. She started to sing again. She sang a lot these days.

Once the steam rose from the pots, she began to fill the tub outside. Geordie, from two crofts away, came slouching along the road. The bonnet hung sideways on his head and his navy gansey had holes in the elbows. He chewed a piece of grass which he moved to one side of his mouth when he spoke.

'You want a hand?' He grinned, showing yellowed teeth with spaces. A widower of eight years, the whole island knew he'd always had his eye on Chrissie. Now with Jack gone, she had wondered how long it would take for Geordie to come calling.

'I'm managing.' Much as she did need a hand, she did not want to give the man any encouragement. He was fine enough, slim with a bit of muscle and a load of money behind him so she had heard. But he was several years her senior and always sported what looked like a two day growth on his chin. Not in her wildest dreams could she imagine him in her bed. He followed her into the kitchen. The smell of old tobacco clung to his clothes and drifted with him into the room. Picking up the largest pan, he said, 'You're filling out a bit Chrissie. A man likes a bit of meat on a woman.'

Her cheeks burned. 'Are you going to empty that pot or stand there giving me cheek?'

'You need a man round the house, Chrissie.'

'Charlie and Angus help out, and old Dan, when he's able.'

'The lads'll take wives and they'll no' want you in their way. I tell you, lass, you'll not have a hand to do a turn. I've a fine croft and a boat and I could do with a woman to take care of me.'

She thought of the holes in Geordie's jumper and sniffed the air wafting around him. 'I don't doubt your words for a minute.'

'Then how about it? You and me.' Slanting his head a little to the right, he raised one eyebrow.

'I'm not interested. Away you go to another island and get yerself a wife. I'll do a wash and a mend for you if you give me a hand with the harvest, but you'll not put your boots under my bed and that's all I have to say.'

'Awe but Chrissie, I'll never get a wife as bonnie as you.' He carried the pot outside and emptied the water into the tub.

'What if Jack comes back?' She was surprised at her own ability to frame the words.

'Ach, I doubt that. He's been gone a fair while. Even if he does, you'd be better off with me. And how do you cope at night? You're a woman with needs like any other.'

She lifted the brush leaning against the outside wall and raised it over her head. 'Get away with your dirty talk.' She waved the broom in a mock threat.

With his palms held towards her and a look of pure innocence on his face, he said, 'Beat me if you will, for I'll take whatever you dole out if only you'll have me.'

'Away with you, you old fool.' Jack's face suddenly flashed before her. She lowered the brush as her smile froze.

'Are you all right?' Geordie asked, suddenly serious.

She forced the brightness back into her voice. 'I'm none the better for your asking.'

He gave a deep sigh. 'Well then, I'll empty the rest of the pots for you. Did you mean it when you said you'd do a wash for me?'

'Aye, but that's all you'll be getting here.'

'Right then.' He pulled off his boots and began to unbutton his trousers.

'Geordie!' Her voice rose. 'What are you doing?'

'This is my only pair and they sorely need washing'.

'Enough.' She raised the broom again.

'I'm going, I'm going. By, but you're a hard woman.' Geordie spread his arms in a helpless gesture before turning and walking up the field. She smiled to herself. With a wife to keep him in order, Geordie would make someone a fine man. But that someone would never be her. She shuddered at the idea and leant against the wall, closing her eyes. The memory of Jack still had the power to shake her. Back to work. Thank God for work.

Later that day, Chrissie arrived at Scartongarth. The smell of boiled herring filled the kitchen and made her nauseous. Mary-Jane's twins lay sleeping in the box-bed. Tyna stood by the table wiping her hands on a tattered dishcloth. Silvery scales covered her apron and fluttered to the ground where they lay against the black flagstone, iridescent in the sunlight shafting through the window. She bent down and wiped the floor and her hair fell out of an untidy knot and floated like cobwebs around her shoulders. When she stood up, her breath came in short, fast gasps. 'It's – pain - worse.' A bunched fist pressed against her chest.

Chrissie quickly set her basket on the table and guided the old woman to a chair. 'How long have you had this pain?' she asked.

'Days – weeks.' Her face had turned grey, like paper.

'Why didn't you say?'

'Ach, I didn't want to be a bother.' Tyna was failing. Death was in her eyes and in the lack of meat on her bones.

'I'll just be back,' said Chrissie. She hurried up the field to her own house where she collected a few herbs, then back to Scartongarth. Tyna sat where she had left her. After putting herbs in a cup and pouring boiling water over them, Chrissie allowed the mixture to steep for a minute. She then handed the cup to Tyna and watched until some colour came back to the cheeks. 'You rest,

I'll get the food.' Chrissie moved the large pan of potatoes from the heat. 'Where is everybody?'

'Give me a minute, lass.' Tyna placed a hand on her chest and spoke slowly. 'Mary-Jane's... at the shop.' She closed her eyes.

'Come on,' said Chrissie, 'Lie down. I'll help you to bed.'

'In... a wee while.' Tyna's chest rose and fell several times. 'I want to say something... about Jack.'

'Jack?'

The chiselled lines of Tyna's face stood out. Her lips and the skin around her eyes held a bluish tinge. She clutched Chrissie's hand. Her breath became more even. 'If he... ever comes back... don't be too hard on him.'

'I was never hard on him. Come on, I'll help you to bed.'

'No. I'm fine now. He... he was hard on you. We women... we have to make the best of our lot in life.'

'What do you want to tell me?'

Tyna took a few deep gasps. 'You must promise... never to tell a soul.'

'I promise.' Chrissie's body tightened.

Tyna's voice became stronger. 'My time on earth will not be long. Have I not seen death himself waiting by the door? But he won't take me, oh no. Not until I rid my soul of the burden I carry.' She fell silent again.

Chrissie waited. 'Take your time. I'm listening.'

'I never loved Jack. It was because of what his real father did to me.' Tyna's eyes closed and she sank back in the chair as if she had collapsed beneath the folds of her clothes. When Chrissie thought the old woman had fallen asleep, her eyes flickered.

'That black hearted factor. He left the island after that. Thank God. But Jack had the bad blood in him.'

Tears pooled in Chrissie's eyes. 'Oh, Tyna,' she whispered as the meaning of the words sank in.

'I tried not to show it, but he knew. Jack knew I had no love for him. And Dan – Dan... he must have had his own thoughts though he never said.'

Chrissie had always wondered why Jack was so different from his two brothers; dark while they were fair and why he was such a tortured soul. Yet she never suspected the pain Tyna had hidden. She stroked the old woman's hand. The skin was thin and mottled, the veins showing through. 'Don't upset yourself.'

'When we lost Jamsie – aye, he was the only one with any time for his brother – God forgive me, but I wished it had been Jack on the boat that day.' A tear formed at the corner of one eye, trickled down her face and sank into the wisps of hair gathered around her neck. 'It's maybe my fault... the way he turned out.'

'Don't blame yourself,' said Chrissie, her voice soft. 'Blood will out, so my granny used to say. And I did him a wrong too, for I loved Davie first.'

'But he was an innocent bairn. Tell him... tell him I'm sorry.'

'You'll tell him yourself, when he comes back.'

The old woman opened her eyes and turned to stare into the fire. The front door opened and Mary-Jane came in. 'The shop was fair crowded the day.' She looked at her mother-in-law and dumped her basket on the table. 'Are you all right?'

'I'm fine. A wee bit tired.' Tyna rested her head on the back of the chair.

'She had a turn,' said Chrissie. 'I've given her something to drink.'

'Don't make a fuss,' Tyna whispered urgently, as the sound of men struggling out of oilskins filled the front passage. She sat upright and twisted her hair behind her head knotting it tightly.

'I'll be getting off home now,' said Chrissie, grabbing her shawl.

'No, no, lassie. You'll stay for a bite to eat,' said Tyna. 'We don't see enough of you.'

'So what grand feast have you got for us the night?' Charlie walked into the kitchen. He took his seat and sniffed the air. 'Ah, herring for a change.' His eyes met Chrissie's and he smiled.

'Aye, and it's all you'll be getting 'til you get yourself out and set a few more rabbit traps,' said Mary-Jane jokingly. She poured the water from the potato pan into a basin and replaced the pan over the flames to dry. That done, she emptied them into the centre of the table on the newspaper spread there. 'Have you all washed your hands?'

'Aye. We did. We knew you'd be wanting to inspect them. The water in that barrel is turning green and as cold as the firth in winter,' said Angus.

'Do you want to look behind my ears?' Charlie held out his head.

'Get on with you.' Mary-Jane swatted him with the dishcloth.

Tyna gave a weak laugh.

'I'll try and get to the traps tomorrow,' said Angus. 'And I've got some shot for the gun. We'll maybe get a few birds.'

'I'll look forward to that.' Chrissie ladled out the fish, two for each person. She put Tyna's on a plate and handed it to her where she sat. 'You stay where you are.'

Tyna smiled. 'You're a good lass,' she said. 'A good lass.'

'What's wrong with her?' asked Angus.

'Been overdoing it a bit,' replied Tyna. 'Chrissie's making a fuss.'

'If Chrissie says you're to sit, you'd better answer her.' Charlie's eyes flicked to hers and just as quickly flew away.

'She'll be fine after a wee rest.' Chrissie patted Tyna's hand.

'If you're sure.' Angus hesitated, then closed his eyes and pressed his hands together before saying grace.

Avoiding Charlie's eyes, Chrissie began to pick at the flesh of the fish with her fingers. It was the only way to eat herring.

The following day, Mary-Jane met Chrissie at the door. 'Thank goodness you're here. It's Tyna. She's taken bad again. I was just away to put the sheet over the peat stack.'

Fear sliced through Chrissie. The sheet on the peat stack was a sign that a doctor was needed. From the mainland, the doctor would see it and know that a boat would be over for him before long.

She said nothing but hurried to the bedside of her mother-in-law.

Tyna's eyelids fluttered open. 'Did Jack come back?'

'He would have been right here if he had.'

'Would he? Mind... what I told you. Not a word. Not even to Jack. Just say. . . I'm sorry.' Tyna's breath faded, grew weak, her eyes widened and she stared at the corner of the ceiling. 'Jamsie?' Bloodless lips parted in a slow smile, and she lifted a shaky hand as if reaching for someone. Her eyes brightened for a flash then all the light fled from them, and her hand dropped onto the bed and the fingers curled inward. Then, with an outward rattling of air, Tyna lay still.

Chrissie passed her fingers over the glassy eyes, closing them. She rose, moved slowly to the window and opened it wide to let the soul fly free. 'Tell Jack yourself when you see him,' she said. 'May the good Lord grant you that, though I doubt Jack'll be in Heaven.' Then she pulled the curtains closed lest the devil saw the body and pursued the soul.

After a few minutes silence, she walked into the other room. Dan half rose from his chair, questions in his eyes.

'I'm sorry,' she said.

Shrinking back into his seat, he covered his face with his hands. His shoulders began to shake.

Chrissie looked at Mary-Jane. 'I'll do what needs to be done.'

Mary-Jane, eyes red rimmed and swimming with tears, wiped the moisture from her cheeks and nodded. 'March is a bitter time to die; a time when the earth grows hungry. She always said she would die in March.'

It was a fine clear day when Tyna Reid was laid to rest. Dan seemed to have withered overnight, so that his clothes appeared a size too large. He stared at the mound under which his wife lay. Chrissie clasped his hand. 'We'll all be here to look after you,' she said.

'Ach, lassie,' he replied. 'It won't be long afore I'm in beside them.'

Chrissie said nothing. Because the shadow that passed over him carried the certain knowledge that what he said was true.

Four weeks later, when the morning bleached darkness into submission, Chrissie, who had unsuccessfully tried to snatch a few hours' sleep, rose from her bed. She shivered against the chill that filled the room. In spite of the rough twine slippers she wore, the cold of the flagstone found its way to her feet and up into her legs.

The oatmeal, steeping since the night before, sat on the bricks beside the fire she had dampened down with coal dross and tea-leaves. She heaped some sticks on the still glowing ash, unfolded a sheet of newspaper, stretched it over the open fireplace and held it in place. A draught shot up the chimney from below and sucked the paper so it caved inward. After a few minutes, the flames caught, leapt and roared, and the centre of yesterday's news browned and blackened. She snatched the paper away, scrunching it up before it too, caught fire. After adding more fuel, she swung the porridge pan over the flames.

Once the oatmeal was ready, she spooned on some treacle. There would be no milk until the cow calved. She ate slowly and without appetite.

After washing the pot, plate and cup, she banked up the fire. Her black blouse and skirt from her kist hung over a chair. The scent of mothballs filled the air. She dressed slowly. The skirt wouldn't tie around her waist and she had to leave the zip open. These last few weeks she had been forced to acknowledge what she had hardly believed possible, that after all the barren years with Jack, she was going to have a bairn. It was a discovery which should have filled her with joy, instead she had cringed inside. Guilt about the death of her husband had struck her with renewed force. *The sins of the fathers will be visited upon the children.* The biblical phrase rang in her head repeatedly. As she had done every morning and every night since she suspected her condition, she pressed her hands together and prayed with all her heart. 'Please, God, make my bairn healthy and I'll never sin again.'

Still the dread plagued her. Was this child conceived by violence and rape? Would he be born ugly and deformed, carrying the mark of the devil who was his father? Or would he have red hair, making it all too clear who the father was and forcing her to bear the sly glances and no doubt a new wave of gossip about the disappearance of Jack? If it was only herself, she would suffer and bear it, but she had to protect the unborn child. She remembered too well old Jessie MacKenzie who'd had a bairn while unmarried. The lad grew to be a bitter adult who despised his mother and she turned to the drink. That would never happen to her, Chrissie vowed, because this child, this precious life she carried beneath her rib-cage would not have cause to feel ashamed of its birth, not if she could do anything to prevent it. From now on it was her and her child against the world, and however much the truth tore at her, the islanders and Charlie had to believe this child was Jack's. Her father had had a red tinge in his hair, maybe she would get away with it – as long as Charlie stayed away.

She covered her shoulders with her shawl and stepped outside. The early light slanted on the still colourless landscape and sparkled on the surface of the firth; the wind swept round the house in sporadic bursts, seagulls shrieked and the moan of the foghorns on distant islands threatened a dismal day. Without any urgency, Chrissie walked over the field and down the slope towards Scartongarth.

Mary-Jane stood in the kitchen, a teapot in her hand. Her soulful eyes were pink rimmed and puffy, her skin, pale. She looked like a ghost. Her children slept, tangled together on the bed in the recess of the wall. The smell of baking scones thickened the hot air.

Chrissie tried not to think of the coffin in the other room or the body lying within. She tried not to think of how much she would miss her father-in-law, his kindness, his wisdom. And most of all, she tried not to think of the secret Tyna had entrusted to her.

She lifted the best cups and saucers from the pine dresser against the back wall, and set them on the table. From the iron range, she picked up the kettle. 'I'll fill this and take the scones from the oven. The minister'll be here soon.'

'Move in with us, Chrissie. Then you wouldn't have to make the trip every morning. I do what I can, but. . .' Mary-Jane dropped her head and stared at the floor. 'Dan was a good man. He never complained. How was I to know he was ill?'

Chrissie crossed the space between them and rubbed the other woman's shoulder. 'Dan didn't have the will to go on after Tyna died. I think he just gave up.'

'I should have known, for I was the same after I lost Jamsie. If it wasn't for the bairns. . .' Mary-Jane's voice faded, then her eyes opened wide as if a new thought struck her. 'The croft and house will be Jack's now – that is if he isn't...' Her hand flew to her mouth. 'Me and my brothers and the bairns – we have no place here – we have no place at all.'

'Where else should you be?' said Chrissie. 'Your man was the oldest son – by rights everything should go to your wee boy.'

'But Dan made no will. Jack won't see it like that. He could still come back. I mean he could be anywhere... gone anywhere... oh.' Tears spilled from her eyes and grasping the tail of her apron, she lifted it to her face. 'He would throw us out – you know he would. And you couldn't stop him.'

'You'll always have a home here.' Chrissie set her hand on Mary-Jane's arm. 'I'll make sure of that.'

A sharp rap at the door. The collie shot up from the rug with a bark that echoed round the walls. The children stirred on the bed. Mary-Jane smoothed her apron, patted her hair, wiped her cheeks and straightened her shoulders.

Her eyes met Chrissie's. 'Ready?'

'Ready.'

Reverend Donald Charleston stood on the step, fingering the brim of the hat he held in his hands. The wind filled his coat, lifting up the tails so they fluttered like the wings of a great black bird.

'Come away in, minister,' said Chrissie to the young man. Within the liquid brown eyes she saw a deep sadness that mirrored her own. He followed her into the kitchen.

The door opened and Sanny the Post, his wife and two sons, traipsed into the kitchen and nodded at the minister. As more mourners arrived, Chrissie led them through to the best room, where, with discreet coughs and downcast eyes, they shuffled around the walls as if they needed to find themselves a space as far away from the coffin as possible.

After the men had left for the graveyard, the womenfolk sat around the long, white-wood table in the kitchen, drinking tea. Maggie from two crofts up folded her arms beneath her massive bosom and pursed her lips. 'Sad day right enough. Three sons and not even one to take a cord of the coffin.' She placed her arms on the table; her bosom slipped and came to rest on her bulging stomach.

Chrissie wished Maggie would go home. She wished they would all go home and leave Scartongarth to mourn the death of its oldest resident in peace.

Conversation drifted round the table, moving on to lambs and shop prices and Chrissie barely heard what they said. She busied herself washing cups and making yet another pot of tea. Mary-Jane's wee girl, Bel, toddled over the flagstone floor and grabbed the end of Chrissie's skirt. The bairn appeared thin and undernourished unlike her boisterous brother, Jimmy. Chrissie bent down and picked up the child. 'How you doing, peedy lasgie,' she said.

'I need to wash and change the bairns,' Chrissie said, grabbing Jimmy's hand and nodding at the women round the table. 'Go ben the house to the good room. Be more comfortable there.' In the back porch, she washed the children with water from the rain barrel. She took her time.

From the other room Maggie's voice grew louder, deliberately, Chrissie thought. Jack's name had not been mentioned at Tyna's funeral, but now, with Dan gone, people like Maggie could be free with their tongues. 'Wonder what really happened to Jack. He was no angel; the whole island knew his faults, but his poor mother. Not even a body to grieve over. She never stopped hoping he would come back, you know.'

Chrissie cringed. She hugged Bel, felt the baby curls soft against her cheek, the small fingers clutching the front of her blouse and she thought of the child growing in her own body. At this second, she hated Maggie for her words but in her heart she knew, that in spite of her ignorance, the woman was right. Innocent and unloved by his mother as a child, Jack at least deserved a Christian burial.

At the top of the rise, black dressed figures trailed along the road and turned down the cart track leading to Scartongarth. The men had returned and none of them kin of the old man they had just buried.

'I'm away, Chrissie. I'll not wait 'til the men get back.' Maggie's voice shrilled through the air as she wobbled from the front door and down the flagstone path. Chrissie willed her not to mention Jack again; funerals always filled her with a sense of dread without further comments.

Inside she found Mary-Jane seated in the rocking chair, crouched over the stove holding out her hands to the flame. From the best room, she could hear the murmur of voices as the womenfolk waited for the men.

'Please Chrissie, move in with us. Our Charlie likes you and you like him. My health might be failing, but I've got eyes in my head.' Mary-Jane's voice was low.

Chrissie opened her mouth to deny her involvement with Charlie: to say their connection had never progressed beyond the point of friendship. She hesitated, not wanting to lie, and said nothing, knowing the proof of her infidelity might soon be born for all the islanders to see. Nevertheless, the idea of moving from her house began to take hold. Flit into the larger, roomier Scartongarth. Get away from her cottage and the ghosts that dogged her. She couldn't change the past, but she could try to make the future better.

'I'll move in and help care for you and the bairns,' she said. 'But I'll use the store at the far end.' She spoke of a building once used as a salt store and attached to the house, but with its own door. Cleaned out for Mary-Jane and Jamsie when they first married, it now lay empty.

The ben room, or 'parlour' as Tyna had called it, was seldom used and kept clean and shining for distant family should they ever return. Tyna had wanted it that way, Chrissie knew, in hope that one day, Davie and Isa might sleep there again.

'The store room is green with damp. It'll take weeks to dry out. Maybe it's too soon for you and Charlie, but Jack's been gone a whole winter,' said Mary-Jane.

'Charlie should find himself a lass his own age. I can't be what he wants. I can never be his wife.' Even as Chrissie said the words, tears pushed behind her eyes. Charlie was a young lad. He deserved a wife and he deserved respect. She should have never allowed that night to happen. She would do anything to make sure her bairn was healthy.

'He's a good man, Chrissie. I pray you two will get together when the time is right.'

'He's a lad. He doesn't know his mind,' Chrissie said. 'And I'm fine on my own. I don't need any man.'

Mary-Jane opened her mouth, but before she could utter a word, the door opened and a tide of male bodies tramped into the house. Chrissie set another tray of scones on the table and spread them with butter and rhubarb jam. This conversation would have to wait for another time.

Chapter 9

'Be careful with that – it was my granny's,' Chrissie yelled, as Angus and Charlie staggered under the weight of the dresser. She grasped the horse's halter to keep him steady as the boys hoisted the remaining piece of furniture onto the cart.

'And what do you keep in it – your peats? It's heavy enough.' Charlie eased the dresser along the cart and dusted his hands together. 'Are you taking the curtains?'

'No for they're nothing but rips and holes. I've a wee bit money left after last year's lamb sales and the floating shops are due today. I'll surely be able to treat myself to something bonny for my new home.' Not many Raumsey homes boasted the luxury of curtained windows, but it was something that Chrissie had always insisted upon.

She looked up at the sky. The raw, wintery cold of the last few months had given way and the early sun rippled over the fields and the firth. Hardly a whisper of wind stirred the air. Maybe the clement weather was an omen for the rest of her life. She tugged at the horse's rein, urging him forward. 'Hold on to the dresser, now,' she shouted over her shoulder. 'I don't want it falling over, mind.'

'And you watch your feet in case you fall over,' said Charlie with a dry laugh, as she stumbled on a tuft of couch grass.

Half-way down the field, she glanced back at her cottage. She was glad to be leaving, but saddened the place where she had lived since birth no longer held wholesome memories.

She had started to work on her new home weeks before. The old salt store next to Scartongarth had to be swept, scrubbed, lime-washed and aired. Now a clean, dry room waited for her.

Once they had moved the few sticks of furniture, the boys would return for her cow, her hens, her pails of eggs and small barrels of salt herring and pork.

She stood in the doorway and looked up at the sky. The sun was bright but the wind was a bitter blade. She allowed the breeze to cool her cheeks. She watched birds riding the air currents, dark shapes against the sky. When she was a child, her schoolteacher had taught her their names. Herring gulls, black-backs, terns, guillemots, auks, puffins, oystercatchers, fulmars, curlews, peewits and skuas. She had been surprised how her classmates had no interest. To the islanders, all they needed to know was which birds were good to eat and which tasted tough and fishy.

If God spared her, she would pass her knowledge on to her child and to Jimmy and Bel; bairns she loved as her own.

The sun was high in the sky when the sail of the *Endeavour*, the first of the floating markets, sailed into the bay and sent its small boats ashore to pick up the waiting customers. Mary-Jane had written a list of things she wanted and between her and Chrissie they had a basket full of eggs, a pail of salt herring and a box of lobsters with which to trade.

Clusters of women gathered by the shore, gossiping, clutching baskets and waiting for their turn to be ferried to the larger vessels. Children too, allowed to take the morning off from their lessons, scampered about like spring lambs.

'Chrissie,' someone called. 'I see you're moving into Scartongarth.'

'It's for the best.' Chrissie joined the group. 'With Mary-Jane ailing and all.'

The women exchanged a sly glance. Had there already been gossip about her and Charlie, she wondered.

'Will you be selling your house?' asked one. 'My Billy's getting wed come summer and they've not got a place.'

'No, not for now.' Chrissie's hand tightened on the handle of her basket. A bead of sweat trickled down her side and settled around her waist. No, much as she needed the money, she would not, could not, sell her house. There must be no chance of anyone finding out what lay beneath the flagstones in the byre.

'Maybe you could rent it, then.' The woman jutted her face towards Chrissie, her small eyes black and shrew-like. Several hairs protruded from her chin.

'What if Jack comes back?' Chrissie's voice became sharp. 'How can I make up my mind so soon?'

'Ach.' The woman stepped back. 'It's been a fair while. I thought I was doing you a favour.' She muttered something to her neighbour.

Chrissie turned away, the wind a sharp nip against her fiery cheeks. She stared at the boats bobbing towards the shore and tried to think of the cloth she would buy for curtains. Something gay and bright. Something to lift her mood. 'I'll away, then.' She spoke hurriedly and picked her way over the shingle and onto the sandy slope.

'Come with me. I'll get you out right now – no waiting.' Meeting her, Charlie took the baskets and set them in the boat before offering her his hand. For a heartbeat their eyes met and held. She slipped her hand into his and immediately he steadied her then helped her aboard the *Christina*. The calloused warmth leaked through her skin. Neither spoke. He pushed the boat into deeper water and leapt aboard. Without meeting her eye, he grasped the oars and pulled the yole clear of the surf.

'You've settled in, then?' he asked, glancing over his shoulder.

'I've made it comfortable, yes.'

'Are you keeping all right?'

'I am, yes.' She studied the strong fingers grasping the oars. The well-bitten nails, the blunt thumb. The way his hands and arms moved, muscle rippling under skin as he manoeuvred the boat. Her eyes travelled up to where cotton strained over shoulders too broad for the size of his shirt. The seam was beginning to split. There were times it was hard to remember how young he was. She lowered her head, trying not to think about the hour she had spent in his arms. A few droplets of spray hit his skin and he wiped his face on his shoulder. The stubble on his chin made a rasping sound.

He pulled the oars in as they drew alongside the *Endeavour*, threw out the buffers and grabbed the side of the larger vessel. A wiry seaman bent forward and grabbed both Chrissie's hands. 'Chrissie Reid. I declare, you get bonnier every year.' He hoisted her aboard.

'And you get more brazen.' She laughed and shook her hands from his. 'How's the wife and bairns? Are you all still in Kirkwall?'

'Aye and they're doing grand. Me youngest has started school.'

'Tell the wife I'm asking for her. I'm off to have a wee look around.'

'Has that man of yours no come back yet? A fine looking woman like yourself is wasted on the likes of him. I'd never have left if you was me wife.'

'No, he's not come back and, yes, I know I'm wasted.' Chrissie spoke lightly enough, but her heart skipped a beat. She would have to get used to this – folk always asking.

'You'll be the draper,' she said to a stocky man she had not seen before who was helping with the incoming lobsters and fish. 'I'm after a piece of cloth.'

'Right you are, lass,' he said, 'Come away and see what we've got.' The drapery was the least busy and the draper was expected to help out wherever he was needed.

As she followed him down the boat, past the bulkheads and the shelves of groceries, she steadied herself against the swell by holding on to the bars of wood nailed along the shelf fronts to stop the goods tumbling off in heavy seas. It was over-warm inside the shop and the smell of old wood, tar and oatmeal filled the air. Mid-ship was used for the meal and feeding stuffs. She edged her way around a large weighing machine which stood in the centre and the sacks of flour, oatmeal, bran and corn which were built up along the sides.

At last they reached the stern and the drapery. Shoes, boots, rolls of wax cloth, oilskins, overalls and other items of clothing sat out on a bench, as well as on barred shelves and hanging on lines overhead.

'It's for curtains,' explained Chrissie.

The draper pointed to a shelf where several rolls of cloth were stacked. 'Anything take your fancy?'

There wasn't a wide selection and it did not take her long to find the material she wanted for her curtains.

'Can I get you anything else,' he said as he measured the cloth. His face creased into a grim smile as she paid for her purchases. 'Dinna mind Will up front. He's just an old fool from Kirkwall. I hope he didn't upset you asking about your man. Jack'll be back right enough.'

'Ach, I'm fine. And I'm all the better for your concern.' With a forced laugh, she thanked him. He hadn't upset her, but she did not want to discuss Jack. She did not even want to think about Jack. Life was so much easier with him gone, but that was something to which she could never admit. At least in public. A widow was supposed to be in mourning. With a farewell smile, she returned to collect the rest of her groceries.

She was disappointed to see the *Christina* had gone. What was she thinking? Charlie would be waiting for her? She had made her feelings clear on that score and she had been right to do so. He would have better things to do than sit around waiting for her.

Later that night, Chrissie stood at the window of her home. She adjusted her newly made curtains of red roses on white material and watched as the low sun painted a blush across the sky.

The room was fine enough with the normal bed in the recess of the wall, faded screens pulled back and a stone water bottle sitting atop the patchwork quilt her grandmother had made in her youth. Her armchair, her table and two chairs, her dresser and the rag rug sat in almost the same position as in her old house. The smell of fresh lime wash and burning peat mingled.

Through the wall, she could hear the children's laughter as Mary-Jane got them ready for bed and Chrissie set her hand on her stomach. Soon she would not be able to hide the truth from the islanders. A curlew cried outside, a forlorn flute that echoed a hollow place in her heart.

Charlie came up the path and her heart picked up its pace. The door opened.

'Settling in all right?' He came into the room and looked around. 'You've done it really bonnie.'

'I'm trying.' She forced nervous lips into a smile and pushed a lock of hair behind her ear. This was the first time they had been alone together since she had told him to leave her be.

'Do you feel better now – about things?'

'This is a new start for me.' Unable to meet his eyes, she turned her back on him and continued to stare through the panes. The setting sun had turned the windows of the cottages to fire and slanted golden rays over earth that guarded immature crops. In the bay the sea headed towards the land in long, white capped rollers that surged over the rocks and sent broken spray several feet into the air.

'Have you not got yourself a girl yet?' said Chrissie.

'What?' Charlie came up behind her.

'You're a fine looking lad. All the lassies have an eye for you, I'll be bound.' The words were difficult to say. She kept her gaze firmly on the window, although the scene outside blurred as tears filled her eyes.

'I've accepted the way things are. But I do have feelings for you Chrissie – I'll wait...'

'Wait for what? I wish I had never behaved the way I did. I was frightened and upset and... I don't know. I wasn't in my right mind. Dead or alive, Jack will always be between us.' She blinked her tears away and swung round to look at him.

'No. I won't let him. It will work out,' he said.

'You're young. You'll get over me and marry a lass your own age and have bairns.' She bit her lip and stared at her feet. 'With Jack gone – folks will soon talk if you come round here too often. Especially with me moving in and all.' Taking a deep breath, she lifted determined eyes to his. 'Stay away from me, Charlie – it's for the best. I do not want you, or any man in my life.'

He said nothing and the seconds stretched.

To avoid his gaze, her eyes flitted to the chipped mirror on the wall, to the dresser, to the newly painted rafters across the ceiling, to the black flags beneath her feet.

'Tell me there will never be a chance for us, then I'll go – but look me in the eye when you tell me,' he said finally.

She glanced up, willing her tears to remain where they were, stuck in the battleground behind her eyes. Could she love him? Could she ever love again? True she felt a flutter of excitement when he walked into the room, but she had felt that before and much more. What had men ever done for her but bring her heartache and pain?

He reached for her hands, but she snatched them away. She lowered her lids. 'Please. Charlie, please leave me alone.' She turned her back to hide the traitorous quiver of her lip. All that was important now was this precious life she nurtured in her body. Thoughts of the unborn child consumed her – she had no room for anyone else in her heart.

'What can I do?'

Stay away from me, she wanted to scream. *Leave me alone with your sea-bleached hair and your grey-green eyes.* Instead she said, 'There's a box social on this Saturday. You go with your friends. Bid for what some lassie's prepared and walk her home. You're missing all the fun a young lad should be having.'

'I want no one but you.' He put a hand on her shoulder.

She jerked away. And then the words were out before she could stop them. 'I'm having a bairn. Jack's bairn.'

Silence fell into the room. The ticking of the clock filled the space. Charlie cleared his throat before he spoke. 'Are you sure? But... but it could be... '

'It's Jack's.'

'I don't care if it is Jack's.'

'Charlie, I don't want a man in my life. My child is all that is important now.' A child whose father had died at sea would be treated with respect; a child whose mother had slept with another man while her husband was no sooner out of the door would be tormented and shunned.

'Are you sure...'

'The bairn is Jack's.' Her voice rose and grew strong. 'Leave me alone.'

Charlie's face swam before her, white, stricken. 'I... I love you. Like I said before, we can leave the island. I could get a job on the mainland.' He looked so vulnerable, she was reminded how young he was. She suddenly felt years older, as if he too was a child for whom she carried responsibility.

'No,' she said with renewed resolve. 'No more of this – you following me around with hope in your eyes.'

The door opened and Angus burst in. He looked from one face to the other. 'Come away to the house,' he said stiffly. 'We've visitors.'

'Not now,' said Charlie.

She heard the break in his voice, saw suspicion gather in Angus' eyes. 'No, no,' she said. 'I want to go.' She needed to get away from the boy with the salt of the sea about him, with his green trusting eyes, with his gentle lips and strong jaw line. She needed to make him go away. She did not know if she would ever want a man in her life again, she only knew that, right now, she wanted none of this.

In the ben-end of Scartongarth a couple of neighbours chattered like chickens over a fresh worm. Jeanag Bremner from the crossroads, thin as a knife, rushed to Chrissie and enveloped her in a hug, crushing her against a flat bosom.

'We heard you'd moved in.' Her voice reminded Chrissie of a hen's cackle. 'I hoped you'll no mind. Donnal said you'd be too tired for a wee sing-song the night, after moving in and all, but I said, Chrissie'll not be too tired for old friends – you're not are you?' Pushing the black tammy to the back of her head she tucked a few straggling wisps of grey behind her ears.

'No, I'm not too tired to have a wee song from yourself and Donnal.' Chrissie pulled the ends of her shawl across her stomach.

Donnal, belly hanging over trousers tied with string, carried a battered melodeon under one arm. With the other he reached out, grabbed Chrissie's hand and pumped it up and down. 'We were that sorry about Jack,' he said without feeling. Half a head shorter than her and twice the width, he had a face that reminded Chrissie of a smiling turnip.

'Sit yourselves down,' said Mary-Jane. 'Looks like you're going to give us a wee tune.' She turned from them, tossed a peat into the stove and put the kettle over the flames.

'Come on woman, howld your wheesht. We'll give the lass a wee bit o' music. Aye, you'll like this one, Chrissie, it's new.' Donnal sat on the armchair and began to play the melodeon. Jeanag moved to his side, set one hand on his shoulder and sang a song called *Kissin' in the Dark*, her voice occasionally hitting the correct note.

The clock had already chimed eleven by the time they left. Chrissie avoided Charlie's eyes as she said her goodnights.

Chapter 10

'Maggie's Billy is still looking for a house. Why don't you sell?' Mary-Jane gathered the breakfast plates, scraped the bacon rind and breadcrumbs into a dish and set it on the floor. Remnants for the dog. He wolfed it down instantly and whined for more. 'A bit of money would make things so much easier for all of us.' Mary-Jane picked up the dish.

Reaching for her shawl, Chrissie said, 'It was my granny's house – I'm not ready to let go of it yet.'

'Then why not let the lad live in it – he'll pay rent.'

'No!' Chrissie's voice was sharper than she intended and Mary-Jane's eyes rounded in surprise. 'Ach, I don't mean to snap. I can't think about it now,' said Chrissie.

'What ails you?' Mary-Jane touched Chrissie's arm. 'Have you fallen out with Charlie? He's going round like a pup with a sore tail.'

'What – he's biting his backside?' Chrissie forced a laugh, but the laugh was too hard and it was obvious Mary-Jane was not fooled.

'There's something you're not telling me and that's a fact.'

Chrissie pressed her eyelids together. 'I'm going to have a bairn.' Would this explanation be enough to satisfy Mary-Jane?

'A bairn... but that's grand, isn't it? After all those years – you must be delighted! I know it's a bad time with Jack gone... Chrissie what's wrong?'

Chrissie had burst into tears.

'Nothing. It's...'

'Do you miss Jack?'

Chrissie shook her head. 'I'm just weepy. Being in the family way, it does that to a body. And I'm scared – I've wanted a bairn for so long. What if it's not right?' She gave a wan smile. 'And bringing a bairn up with no father... '

'I was the same myself when I was left to bring two bairns up. And well do I remember the worry before the birth. But it's something to look forward to – a new life.' Mary-Jane started to stack the dishes in the enamel basin. 'Every bairn brings its own blessing.'

Aye, thought Chrissie touching her stomach. Her fingers closed on the material of her overall, gathering it in her hand. She had said those very words to many a mother who despaired of having another mouth to feed. She wondered what Mary-Jane would say if she knew the truth. After five barren years with Jack, it was highly unlikely the bairn was his. And she so wanted Charlie to be the father – whatever the outcome. Her love for this child was already strong enough to overcome any adversity, and always would be, she vowed fiercely.

'Is that what's wrong with Charlie?' said Mary-Jane.

'It's upset him, yes.'

Mary-Jane still looked doubtful. 'You'll not make a fool of the lad?'

'Why would I do that?'

'I've seen the way he looks at you. He loves you, the way a man loves a woman.'

'He's too young. He doesn't know his own mind. A girl his own age is what he needs. Oh, Mary.' She grabbed the edge of the table and leaned forward as the tears thickened in her throat.

'Don't get upset. It's not good for the bairn.' Mary-Jane wrapped her arms around her.

'But Jack's dead, and without a body, I'm not even a widow.' For a mad moment she was tempted to pour out the whole story, to lay her burden on her friend's shoulders. She looked into the sad, gaunt face of Mary-Jane and her voice faltered. Was it fair to burden this ailing woman with even more worries? And if her family knew what really happened to Jack, would that make them accessories if the murder should ever be uncovered? She knew so little about the law and she didn't trust it. None of the islanders did. No, it was better this remained her secret.

Chrissie turned away and wiped her eyes, eager now to change the subject. 'Don't mind me. I'll be fine. The cow's pretty near calving. It'll be good to have milk again. And with both our cows, we'll have more than enough. I won't need to sell my house, you'll see.' She clasped Mary-Jane's hand, 'I'll away up to Lottie's shop. Anything you need?'

'If you're sure you're all right.' Mary-Jane's eyes remained worried.

Chrissie sniffed and forced a smile.

Mary-Jane opened a small wooden box sitting on the mantelpiece and took out some coins. 'Get me some flour and a tin of treacle.'

Lottie's shop sat at the crossroads amid a clutch of cottages, some with the thatch already replaced by slabs of slate quarried from the north side of the island. The shop sold a little bit of almost anything, but it was here where the women acquired most of the gossip, the old men met up to play cards or dominoes, and the young folk gathered after the day's work was done.

Chrissie pushed the door open and a bell tinkled above her head. A sudden hush descended on the occupants and Chrissie guessed she, or at least Jack, had been the subject of discussion. The air, thick with the scent of paraffin, pipe tobacco, oatmeal and dried fish, filled her nostrils with suffocating warmth. Three old men, sitting at a wooden bench in the corner wrapped in a haze of smoke, raised their eyes.

'Aye, Chrissie,' said one. The others nodded before returning to their game of cards.

Lottie leaned across the counter, her heavy arms folded over her breasts. Her frizzled hair, bleached by age, sparsely covered her scalp. 'If it isn't yerself, Chrissie. I'm right glad to see you. What can I do for you the day?'

The two other women moved aside. 'How're they faring at Scartongarth?' asked one. 'Sad days for them right enough.'

'Aye. But we do what we can.' Chrissie set her basket on the counter. 'I need some wool. Some of that bonny soft stuff. I want to knit a cardigan for Bel.' Her pregnancy would remain a secret for as long as possible. It was the island way.

'I've just the thing,' said Lottie. 'Pink. Got it in last week.' She reached up to pull a hank down from the shelf above her head.

'No, no,' said Chrissie quickly. 'White. Be bonny, white, for the summer.'

Lottie reached further across and pulled down some white wool. 'Will two hanks do? It's all I've left.'

'Two's fine,' said Chrissie. She fingered the wool. Soft enough for a baby's shawl not like wool she spun herself, the colour of the sheep or the mute colours of the grasses or flowers used to make dye.

'Will you have a cup o' tea?' said Lottie. The kettle sang gently on top of a paraffin stove.

Chrissie shook her head. 'I'll not wait.' Eager to get home and wind the wool into balls, she gave Mary-Jane's order. It would be good to see the shawl take shape beneath her fingers. Excited about the bairn, she had imagined the foetus at each stage of development, little arms and legs already forming. Each time she hugged her expanding waistline or felt the minute stirrings of life, a warm fuzzy feeling enveloped her. She, Chrissie Reid, was going to hold her own child in her arms at last. Yet in her dark moments, she was still plagued with a deep sense of dread, a fear she would be punished for her sins and that punishment might be visited upon on the child she carried. Her guilt was her secret and hers alone.

Chapter 11

The following Friday night Charlie, leaning against the wall in the hayloft of the Mains, watched the folks gathered in the hall. Long wooden benches sat against the white-washed, stone walls. A makeshift table, fashioned from upright barrels and planks of wood and covered with a white sheet, groaned under the weight of a tea urn and home baking. Tonight was the first box social of the year and many of the islanders had turned out, dressed in their best clothes. A fine dusting of slippery powder covered the floor, and bairns, shrieking with delight, slid across the wooden boards. Three old men sat in the corner, for there was no stage, and with a melodeon, a fiddle and a mouth organ, they produced a grand sound, but not quite drowning the chatter of the women as they greeted each other. The female voices reminded Charlie of so many yapping sea-birds on the high cliffs.

Beside the band was a pile of biscuit boxes. Each box, containing baking for two, was wrapped in bright paper and tied with a ribbon. Whichever young man won the bid for a box spent the evening in the company of the girl who had donated it. Bottles of whisky traded from steamers were being passed between the men.

'Come on, Charlie,' said Angus, handing his brother a half bottle of Johnny Walker.

Charlie took a swig, wiped his mouth on the back of his hand and passed the bottle back.

'Alexina Laird's been eyeing you since we came in.' Angus rubbed his wrist across the bottle top and raised it to his own lips.

'Well... can you blame her? She's only human. Not that it'll do her any good.'

'That'll be because you've never taken your eyes off Chrissie. What's the matter with you, man? The woman's married and expecting a bairn.'

'Aye, but her man has gone.'

'He could come back. You know how it is.'

In spite of himself, Charlie's eyes were once more drawn to where Chrissie and Mary-Jane sat on a wooden bench with a few other women, sipping tea and eating home baked scones. As if she sensed his stare, she looked up, and as quickly, turned away. Charlie grabbed the bottle and took another long swallow.

'For any sake, what on earth is the matter with you? There's a roomful of bonnie lassies and you could have any one of them for the asking,' said Angus.

Charlie handed the bottle back and pressed his eyes closed. He leaned back against the wall, grateful for the solidity of cold stone. The whisky burned its way to his belly.

'The bairn might be mine.'

'What?' Angus rounded on him. 'You mean you and Chrissie? You're havering, man.'

Before he could respond, the auctioneer stood up and banged his gavel on the small table before him. 'Time to auction the boxes,' he shouted, and a cheering and clapping erupted as all the lassies huddled to one side of the loft, giggling.

With no desire to spend the night partnered by any of the single girls, Charlie climbed down the wooden stairs, went outside and lit a cigarette. Someone else lurked in the shadows.

Alexina Laird stepped into the light that spilled from the open door. 'Are you not bidding on Ruth's box, then?' she asked. Ruth Manson was the prettiest girl on the island.

Charlie removed the cigarette from his mouth and flicked the ash. 'What?'

'Ruth. She made sure all the lads knew which box is hers. Don't tell me she didn't tell *you*.'

'I couldn't care less.' Charlie dropped his cigarette and ground it out with the toe of his boot. 'What about you – why aren't you in with the others?'

Alexina looked away. 'I didn't make a box.'

'Why not?'

'No one would want to walk me home, not with these.' She

pointed to her glasses. 'My eyes are bad 'cos I had measles when I was a baby, my mam says.'

'You're not that bad looking,' Charlie mumbled. He didn't think she was one way or the other, but it seemed the kindest thing to say. He turned to go back inside.

She grabbed his arm. 'Look at me.'

With a sigh, he turned around. She had removed her glasses. At least in the faint light she did have a nice face. Her lips curled at the corners, ready to laugh. Her eyes, which had seemed enormous behind the spectacles, were dark, shadowed in the meagre light. Her nose turned upward slightly. She smelt of rose water and heather. 'You are a bonny lass,' he said, and meant it.

'Who have you got your eye on then?' She tilted her head sideways. 'Maybe it's a married woman, is that it?'

'Of course not!' Without knowing why, he bent down and kissed her quickly on the lips. She stepped back, stumbled and fell, her backside thumping on the earthy ground.

'Alexina!' He reached out to her, but she was laughing so hard she could do nothing to help herself. He grabbed her hand and jerked her to her feet. She fell against him and he held her to stop her falling again. 'Have you been at the whisky?' he asked.

'A wee drop. Don't tell.'

She felt warm and soft and womanly and the whisky had fuzzed his mind. When her arms went round his neck and her lips sought his, he was tempted. It would be so easy. Hit by a sudden pang of guilt, he grabbed her wrists and gently put her hands at her sides.

'Aw, Alexina, sorry,' he said.

She scrabbled in her pockets for her glasses. 'Ah, don't worry. I wouldn't let you go too far. It's only a bit of fun. Just friends then?' Something in her laugh failed to convince him.

'Just friends,' he repeated.

'Aye, I know you don't have an eye for me, and for that I wouldn't blame you. Who'd want a half blind wife?'

'Don't be daft. You're a fine looking girl. But I... '

'You don't have to explain.'

'I like you well enough, Alexina, but not in that way. I shouldn't have kissed you... don't know why I did.'

She stared at the ground. 'Maybe you'd keep company with me now and then? I don't want anything – just a laugh.' Although she smiled there was a wistfulness in her voice that shamed him. He had been as guilty as the other lads for not giving her the time of day.

'I'd like that fine,' he said.

'Do you want to go back inside?' she asked.

No.' He fought the desire to say yes, for Chrissie was like a magnet drawing him towards her.

'Neither do I. Come on, I've an idea.' She spun round and ran to the road. A misshapen moon smirked down on them, turning the road into a bright ribbon. Alexina looked back at him. 'Come on.'

Hand in hand, they ran along the road until she stopped so suddenly he stumbled against her and once again she was in his arms.

'Where are we going?' he asked.

'Ida Sinclair's house.' She pointed to the cottage, at the end of a long garden. Ida was middle aged, unmarried and a stanch church goer.

'It's a lark I've always wanted to play. Help me. Weems Mackie sneaks up to her house at night. Thinks nobody knows. Old fools, so they are. His wife's aye going on about the long hours he works. Ha, it's not with her, that's a fact.'

When they reached the cottage, Alexina crept along the wall and pressed her ear to the windowpane. 'Although the curtains are raggedy, you'll not see through them.'

Charlie joined her. They heard a man's voice and the high pitched giggle of a woman. Alexina grabbed Charlie's hand and pulled him a little way from the window, where they both covered their mouths to stop the laughter. Prim, po-faced, bible thumping Ida, giggling like a schoolgirl.

'A fair sized roll of rope's coiled behind the door in the barn and there's a cart by the side of the house,' whispered Alexina.

'You've come here before,' said Charlie.

'Lots of times. My sister, Ruby, and me. I never take the younger ones.'

'I think I know what you've got in mind.' This would be a rare prank right enough. Together they felt their way around the darkened barn until they found the rope.

'Wait 'til they start making a fair bit of noise,' said Alexina, then they'll not hear us.' Holding in their mirth, they pressed their ears to the window again. The giggling stopped and the bed began to creak.

'Now,' Charlie said, as the incredible image of pot-bellied Weems and the skinny, hawk nosed Miss Ida Sinclair flossing about on the bed filled his head. They knotted the rope tightly on the door knob, stretched the rope around to the side of the house and secured the other end to the horse cart. Then they slipped back to the window to listen. The creaking had now risen to a crescendo and the gasping and muttering made Charlie and Alexina hold their stomachs with suppressed mirth.

'Give him ten minutes and he'll be out that door and back up the road,' whispered Alexina, as they slipped away and hid behind a scroo of hay. 'Except he won't be – not tonight.'

'Why don't we lads know about this? We could have played a prank before now,' said Charlie.

'Like the time you built all that snow in front of Beenie's house when the doctor was paying her a visit and he couldn't get out. That was cruel. What if someone was ill?'

'That was a wee bit stupid, him being a doctor an all. Still, she did seem to take ill an awful lot and was fine with a smile on her face after the doctor had gone. Anyway, the men dug them out before the tide turned.'

'And no one ever knew it was you and Angus, except us. Aye, funny Beenie never asked Chrissie for medicine.'

The mention of Chrissie's name sent a small jolt through him. The front door jerked, stuck and jerked again. Weems' oaths were not loud enough to be heard from the road, but the two young people heard every word. 'For the love of God, something's stopping the door.'

'Can't be.' The panicky voice of Ida.

'It's... it's tied, someone's tied the knob.'

'You said no one would know.' Ida sounded near to tears. 'Don't make a noise – don't make a noise.'

'How the hell am I going to get out? I'll have to break a window.'

A bark of laughter escaped Alexina's lips. Charlie put one arm around her and clamped the other hand over her mouth.

'Who's there?' shouted Weems. 'Untie this door or there'll be hell to pay.'

Charlie and Alexina ran behind the barn and fell on their hands and knees in young corn. They crawled to the edge of the field then raced to the Mains, where they slipped discreetly into the dance hall.

'Take your partners for an old time waltz,' said the announcer.

'Come on,' Alexina removed her glasses, slid her arms around Charlie's neck and pulled him onto the floor. She stumbled over his feet and he caught her in his arms. Aware of her body against his, he looked down into her upturned face, her flushed cheeks and eyes the colour of soft brown sugar.

He let her go and they stood awkwardly. 'Okay, he said. Let's start again.'

She giggled. They moved together watching each other's feet and laughing at their own clumsiness.

Once they had established a rhythm, Charlie lifted his head. His eyes met Chrissie's and she immediately turned away.

'Ow watch out!' Alexina cried as he trod on her foot. He glanced at her pained expression and laughed, realising how much he was enjoying her company. Being with Alexina was easy.

'Can you get me a whisky?' she asked him as the dance finished.

'Whisky? But your sister....'

'...Will think the drink's for you.' Alexina ended the sentence for him.

'All right. I'd better go while you still have two feet to stand on.'

A grin spread across her face.

Within minutes, Charlie was back. He handed her a can. 'Ruby didn't catch me,' he whispered.

'Thanks Charlie,' she said. Crinkling her nose, she turned her back to the revellers and swallowed the whisky. She pressed her hand to her mouth stifling a cough and with the other shoved the can back into Charlie's hand.

'More?' he asked, surprised at her ability to swallow the burning liquid so quickly. Island girls were not expected to behave like that.

'Better not,' she said. 'Da' would kill me if I came home drunk.' She giggled and covered her mouth with her hand again. Her eyes sparkled. 'I enjoyed myself tonight.'

The last waltz was announced.

'So did I,' Charlie admitted and gazed round the hall. Women were gathering their wraps and shawls. He took Alexina's arm and led her outside where they waited for her sister.

'Charlie,' she whispered. 'Have you ever done *it*?

He took a quick step backwards. 'Wha...t?' he spluttered.

'Don't be daft. I didn't mean that I wanted to do *it* with you. I wondered – that's all.'

'I wouldn't... I didn't mean...' he stammered.

'I didn't mean to make you feel daft,' she laughed.

'Och, Alexina, you are a case,' he said, and bent down to kiss her gently on the cheek.

If he had looked around, he would have seen Chrissie watching them from the barn doorway.

The next day, it was said, Ida Sinclair had been standing on a chair when she fell and knocked a jug through the glass. It was lucky she had not cut her hand. She mended the window herself with nails and a square of wood. As far as Charlie knew, she had no more nightly visits from Weems.

***

Angus said nothing until the following day, when, under the light of early dawn, they sailed the *Christina* into the fishing grounds. 'About Chrissie's bairn being yours. . . ' he began.

Charlie wiped a dash of spray from his face and the sleeve of his jacket felt rough against his skin. He had been waiting with dread for this moment. Having heard part of the secret, Angus would not let up until he had the lot. Charlie knew that well enough.

'I'll tell you what I know,' he said, 'but you must promise never to breathe a word to a soul.'

Angus crossed his heart. As he pulled in creels and removed the lobsters and crabs, Charlie told him how he had found Chrissie outside the byre half dead and how she had behaved with him several nights later.

'Dash it all, man,' said Angus. 'What are you going to do?'

'What can I do, for she'll hardly speak to me now? I think she hates me. But I don't think badly of her. I can't forget her.'

'Your first experience little brother,' said Angus. 'Gone to your head. Roll a few more lassies in the hay and you'll soon get Chrissie out of your mind.'

'That's what she says.' Charlie baited a creel and dropped it over the side. He watched as it sunk below the green water. The yole rocked slowly on the swell. 'Told me to have fun.'

'She's right. Do you want the responsibility of a wife and bairn when we can hardly feed ourselves? Can't say about you, Charlie, but I don't want to stay here all my life. I've a mind to join the navy – see a bit of the world. Thought you had too.'

'I did, once.' Charlie lifted another creel. 'But we're the only men in Scartongarth now. We've already got responsibilities. And it doesn't seem to me the men who join the navy or chase the herring are any better off.' He looked towards the shafts of sunlight spilling between clouds and dappling the wide expanse of ocean.

'At least they see something of the world.' Angus hauled in a creel and removed the lobster. 'Whatever Jack was, he provided well; we can't deny that. If he was here we'd maybe be free to go.'

The water boomed and roared in the lee of the Skerries. Birds shrieked above their heads, the sharp smell of excrement that whitened the cliff face caught in their breath.

'There's something else I have to tell you,' said Charlie. He set his creel down and sat on the crossbar. His hands dangled between his knees. He began.

Chapter 12

1907 was a good year for the islanders. The weather was clement and the crops grew well. Chrissie remained healthy throughout her pregnancy and yet the fears often plagued her.

When her time to give birth came, she did her normal work as long as possible. When she felt she could no longer hide the pains, which had plagued her since the night before, she made the excuse of being tired and went to her own room.

After pouring boiling water into a basin holding scissors, cotton and a needle, she barred the door and banked up the fire. She spread a bedding of straw on the floor, covered it with towels and set the basin within easy reach. Then she stripped off her clothes and knelt on the towels. No need for help. She wanted to be first to see who this bairn looked like. Give herself time, if necessary, to prepare her story.

She bent her knees and, supporting herself against the chair, she squatted. The sweat rolled down her face and body. She did not cry out. With her eyes shut, she grunted, sometimes rolling her head from right to left. When she felt the undeniable urge to bear downwards, she held her breath, using her remaining energy to push the child into the world. In this position she could watch as the blue wrinkled crown appeared. Suddenly, she felt as though she was being torn apart and when the baby's head thrust its way from her, she reached between her legs, catching the slippery body as it slid into her hands. She laid the child face down over her thigh and rubbed the back. It was a fine sturdy boy and he was already making gurgling noises in his throat. After the first lusty cry, she laid the infant on the towel beside her and she pulled a length of cotton from the water by her side. She held the umbilical cord between her finger and thumb until the pulsing ceased then tied the cotton in two places about an inch apart. With the scissors, she cut the cord between the bits of thread. This child was now a separate being.

Love and desire to protect this scrap of humanity surged through her. She curled up on the blankets already on the floor and placed the precious infant to her breast. He immediately latched on. Wrapping a quilt around her shoulders for warmth, she studied the little face, and the eyes opened and stared at her with that wise, uncanny, all-knowing way new-born babies had. 'Yes, peedy manny,' she said, 'I'm your Mammy.' She touched the tiny hand and the fingers immediately wrapped around her own. The deep blue eyes continued to stare unblinkingly into hers.

'But who's your Da' – do you know?'

Sparse white lashes slowly closed. Little fingers relaxed their grip. The mouth continued to make sucking motions; milk dribbled from the corners. The baby fell asleep. For a long time Chrissie lay like that, gazing at this tiny miracle, the button nose and round face so like her own. Try as she might, she could not find any resemblance to either Charlie or Jack. The black fuzz covering his head meant nothing – birth hair fell out within a matter of weeks.

When she felt sufficiently rested, she rose, reluctantly laid the infant in a drawer, which had been prepared as a make-shift cot, warmed some water and washed and dressed, first herself and then the child. She wrapped the placenta in newspaper and placed it on the fire. That done, she wrapped the child in the shawl she had knitted, kissed the wrinkled brow and made her way to Scartongarth.

'Chrissie! Goodness. The baby – why didn't you call me?' Mary-Jane rushed over and guided her to a chair.

'Meet Peter Adam Reid,' Chrissie said. 'And why would I be bothering you? I'm the howdie am I not?'

'You might have needed help.' Mary-Jane parted the shawl. 'Oh my. But he looks just like you. Can I hold him?'

'He came quickly. He was no bother.' Chrissie kissed the small head and passed him to the other woman, immediately feeling the emptiness in her arms.

'He doesn't look like Jack at all.' Mary-Jane rocked the infant.

'He'll be none the worse of that.' Chrissie fought to keep her voice light.

'Should you not be lying down?'

'Not me. My granny said she went straight back to work in the fields after she birthed hers and she had eleven.'

'I'll make tea.' Mary-Jane handed the baby back and lifted the teapot.

Suddenly weak, Chrissie sat down and her head tipped against the back of the chair. 'Thank you. Then I'll go to my own bit. I am tired.'

'Leave wee Peter with me,' said Mary-Jane. 'I'll manage fine for an hour or so.'

'No. I'll take him to the bed with me.' Chrissie couldn't bear the thought of being parted from him, even if it was only for a short time. She didn't want to share him with anyone – even Mary-Jane.

Later that night, Charlie came to her door and the air from the sea and the moor clung to his clothes.

Chrissie stood back and allowed him to enter. She watched the turn of his body and the way his shirt stretched over the breadth of his shoulders. It was right he should be here, she thought – here for her and for this child, who was, in all probability, his son. On the night of the box social she had noticed him leave the loft, noticed his return, noticed too the flushed animated state of both him and Alexina and the caring way he had kissed her cheek goodnight. Something had happened between them, she was sure, and in spite of her resolve, the suspicion ripped her heart.

Charlie stared at the infant. She watched as his eyes pooled.

'He's real bonny. Are you certain...' His voice trailed off as he lifted his head and met her gaze.

'Of course I'm certain,' she said with difficulty. 'How's Alexina?'

'She's fine.' He avoided her eye.

As she knew he would, he had found a girl his own age. She turned from him. 'I'm tired out. I need rest.' Close to tears, she opened the door and stood aside. 'Leave me now.'

'All right. But I'll be back tomorrow; see if there's anything you need, like.' He stopped and gazed at her. 'I've never seen you look more beautiful, Chrissie.'

With an awkward laugh, she touched her head. 'I'm sure I'm a bonny sight, right enough.' She had not long given birth. Her skin was blotched, her hair unwashed, her breasts ached, her eyes were heavy for want of sleep. She felt anything but beautiful. But his words warmed her. The baby stirred in the drawer and gave a wavering cry.

'I'll need to feed him,' said Chrissie. 'You'd better go Charlie.'

'I had hoped... ach, what's the point? But you know, anything you need...' He left the sentence unfinished.

Chrissie walked to the window and watched as Charlie disappeared into the night. 'Well, go and leave me, then,' she said as the tears filled her eyes and trickled down her cheeks. She had treated many women who suffered from what they called the 'baby blues'. *That's all it is*, she thought, *all that's wrong with me. That's why I want to cry now.* But she had never expected to feel so emotional. 'Charlie,' she called, running to the door, wanting him back. Needing him with her.

Charlie didn't hear. He had already gone into Scartongarth. She sat down, hugged little Peter to her and cried until her body was sore.

***

Charlie could not settle. He went outside, sat on the stone bench and lit a cigarette. Above his head, the sky was a navy dome, studded with pinpricks of light and the wind was still. The sea constantly whispered as it washed up the sand, and seals mourned and barked as if their hearts were aching. From distant islands, lighthouses threw out intermittent flashes, and the dark shapes of ships glided silently across the river of moonlight. The scent of fields and sea and burning peat filled the night.

If Chrissie really wanted none of him, if the child really was Jack's, Charlie thought, perhaps it would be better if he left the island. It would not be through choice, because he was a man of the soil and sea. It was rooted in him – part of his very soul. But without Chrissie, what was here for him? He might marry Alexina, for she was a fine girl, get a croft of his own, raise a family. He liked her a lot, and they got on well. Although no words had been spoken, he knew the offer would be accepted were he to make it. But he wanted more. He wanted the blood to pound in his veins the way only Chrissie could make it. And then Chrissie and Peter would always be around, a constant reminder of what might have been; a constant ache without a cure. Stubbing out his cigarette, he came to a decision. Tomorrow he would go to the mainland for information. He would join the Merchant Navy.

'Damn you, I was the one who wanted to get out of here,' Angus said in mock horror when Charlie announced his plans at the table the next night. 'But good luck to you, boy. I'll take care of the women until you get back.'

'But how will we manage? There's more work than we can cope with as it is,' said Mary-Jane.

'We'll be fine,' said Angus. 'And no doubt Charlie'll send money back when he can.'

'Aye, I will.' Charlie sought out Chrissie's eyes. If she asked him to stay, he would, willingly. But, with her gaze averted and her face set, she picked up the empty plates and turned away.

'I'll be gone at first light,' he said awkwardly, still watching Chrissie. When there was no response, he rose from the table. 'I'd better see Alexina and the lads. Say goodbye, like.'

'I'll bake some fresh scones, for the journey,' said Mary-Jane. She looked at him with sorrow in her eyes. 'We'll miss you sorely.'

Chrissie rose early the following morning. Charlie's words had startled her the night before, but at the time she dared not respond. She needed time to think. All night she had lain awake, remembering his touch, remembering his eyes as they looked into hers. Unsure if her need for him was love or the same desperate emptiness that had driven her to Jack many years ago, she decided it was good Charlie was going. It would put the much needed space between them – give them both time to sort out their true feelings.

She fed the baby then stood by the window until she heard the front door of Scartongarth open. Charlie, a lone figure in the misty dawn walked along the path. She stood back lest he saw her. To bid him goodbye would be harder than she had imagined. As he passed her window, he hesitated. Her heart raced and for a minute she thought he would come to her door. Then, as if he changed his mind, he turned and walked up the path; his haversack bounced slightly against his back. She touched her lips and set her fingers against the glass. 'Goodbye, my love,' she whispered.

Chapter 13

At his next visit, Chrissie handed the Reverend Charleston a cup of tea. 'I'm glad to see you looking so well,' he said. 'This baby is certainly a blessing. I will be glad to dedicate him to the Lord next Sunday.' He set his hat on the wooden table next to his tea cup.

Wondering if the minister would be so keen to do the christening if he knew the child could be illegitimate, she stroked the baby's head. Eyes cast downward, she nibbled at her lip.

'Is something bothering you?' Donald Charleston asked.

'I'm worried,' she began carefully. 'It says in the bible the sins of the father will be visited upon the children. Is this true of the sins of the mother also?'

'You're worried about the child? The Reverend leaned towards her. His voice was soft and deep. 'You spoke to me before about your concerns. Have you been truly repentant of your sins?'

'Yes. I have.' She thought of what she had done to Jack. And yes, she was truly, truly repentant. Yet she could not see, even now, how there could have been any other way out of her situation. Her child had been born healthy; surely that is a sign of forgiveness.

'I'm sure Peter will be a blessing to you.' He took a sip of his tea.

'But the words, *sins of the father* – what do they mean?' she said.

The Reverend looked thoughtful for a minute. 'Imagine a man who loves the drink more than his family. Would the children not suffer by the father's actions?'

She grasped at this explanation. 'Yes I suppose... do you think that's what it means – God won't punish the children?'

'Once the baby is christened he will be a child of God. And would a loving father harm his own child regardless of what the earthly parents have done?'

'No, no, he wouldn't.' She so wanted this to be true.

The Reverend looked uncomfortable. 'I cannot tell you for certain what the Lord would do or what that scripture really means, but I do not think my God would harm an innocent child.' The minister shifted his weight, making the chair creak. Chrissie stared at the floor.

'If I was sure Jack was dead, loving another man – that wouldn't be a sin then, would it?' she asked, leaning forward.

He reached out to clasp her hand. His fingers were warm and soft. When his eyes met hers, dark brown liquid pools, she was amazed at the sadness in them.

'It's sometimes very hard to do the right thing. Listen to your own conscience, Chrissie,' he said. 'For I cannot advise you.'

She wondered what hurt he had suffered to prompt his words. Had there been truth in the rumours about him and Isa after all? If a minister could be tempted... then why was she so scared of the wrath of the Almighty?

One week later, Peter was christened in the ben end of Scartongarth with only immediate family present.

***

As the months passed, Chrissie tried not to think about Charlie. She wondered how he felt now. Did he love his new life – would he ever want to settle back on Raumsey? Whatever direction he chose, she wished him well. He wrote to Mary-Jane once to say he had a berth on *The Empress of Britain* sailing between Liverpool and Quebec and he probably wouldn't get a chance to write again for a while. His letter had sounded cheerful and full of anticipation. He had asked about her and wee Peter, but to Chrissie herself, he had not put pen to paper.

She first heard the news in the shop. She heard it in the whispers of the women, the knowing looks and the self-satisfied smugness of mothers with chaste daughters at home, weaving and knitting.

'Alexina Green. They say she's expecting.'

'Aye, she's that poor looking in the face.'

'It'll be Charlie Rosie's. They were aye together.'

'Sure enough. Never seen her with anybody else.'

'Her poor Ma'. Never been out of bed since she had the youngest.'

'Don't know how she'll cope without Alexina. But the lass'll have to get wed now.'

Chrissie's scalp grew hot and her body cold. Her stomach knotted.

'Ah, Chrissie. You're the one to ask. You know about such things.' Lottie leaned over the counter and eyed her shrewdly. 'Would you say the lass is expecting?'

Chrissie opened her mouth, but it was as if a wad of dry cotton stopped up her throat. Act normal. Whatever you do, act normal. She set her basket on the counter, keeping her fingers tight around the handle. Anything to stop the tremble.

'Are you all right, lass?' Someone asked.

'Aye, aye,' Chrissie gave a shrill laugh. 'I... I think I left a pot on the fire. Here. . here's my linie. I'll come back.' She handed the shopping list to Lottie and hurried out of the shop, barely aware of the curious eyes that followed her.

She rushed down the road, blind to anyone who greeted her as she passed. Alexina having a bairn! Charlie would have to come home and marry her. The shock of the news made her, for the first time, fully realise what she had lost. For the first time since that dreadful night she knew for definite that she could love again, and that the only man she could love was lost to her. Why oh why had she not given him hope? Why hadn't she asked him to wait until she was ready?

Before she realised where she was she had walked past Scartongarth. Not wanting to face anyone, she carried on past the lighthouse to the furthest point where the rocks jutted into the sea. What had she thought? That he would wait for her anyway? She lowered herself down on the hummocky ground and wrapped her arms around her knees. A scuffling noise made her glance around, straight into the eyes of an otter. For a moment he regarded her solemnly before darting away. She looked to where the horizon was broken by the outline of a large ship. Did he already know? Was he at this time travelling home to take his bride? But what if it wasn't true? The gossips didn't always get it right. There would be no rest for her until she saw the girl for herself. She lowered her head into her hands and allowed her tears to flow.

It was a week later that she noticed Alexina collecting driftwood on the shore. She tucked Peter in his shawl and made her way to the beach. As soon as she saw the girl, she knew that the rumours were true. Her waistline was already thickening, and her eyes puffy, sad testament of many tears.

Alexina came over and touched Peter's head. 'He's lovely,' she said softly.

Chrissie took the girl's hand and led her to a rock where they both sat down. Alexina offered no resistance. She bit her lip and her magnified eyes met Chrissie's. 'You know,' she said. Her mouth quivered.

Chrissie nodded. 'Charlie's a good man. He'll stand by you.' Every word tore at her.

Alexina withdrew her hand and burst into tears.

'He will, won't he?' A cold shiver passed through Chrissie. Charlie was a man of honour. Would she be able to feel the same about him if he shirked his responsibilities now? Was that the real reason he'd left to join the navy? No, not Charlie. He wouldn't do that.

'I love Charlie – I really do,' the girl said through her tears. 'But he'll never want me now.'

Chrissie felt her heart lurch. 'What do you mean?'

'The bairn's not his! It's my own fault. I started to like the whisky. Too much.'

Chrissie put an arm around Alexina's shoulders. 'Who is it?'

'Allan More. I don't even like him! But I couldn't stop him.'

'He's not a bad lad. Does he know?' Chrissie angrily thought of the ineffectual, pimpled faced youth who undoubtedly took advantage of a girl who had drunk too much whisky.

Alexina shook her head. 'Don't tell anyone. Chrissie, is there anything I can do? I don't want this bairn.'

Chrissie shook her head. The girl before her was little more than a child. 'You have to marry the babe's father. It's the right thing to do.' Chrissie stood up, pulling Alexina with her. Was it? Would she have said the same words if she was sure Charlie wouldn't marry the girl to save her reputation?

Alexina burst into tears. 'Mam and Da' doesn't know.'

'I'll come with you. We'll tell them. Then I'll go and see Allan.'

***

Just before Christmas, Charlie came home.

From the high rigs where she was forking hay from the cart to feed the sheep, Chrissie saw him. He was striding up the road, his kitbag flung over one shoulder. Her heart leapt. Pushing her shawl from her head, she stood upright. The sky was gloomily spitting hail and, although the wind was light, it had a bitter edge. To the east, bruised blue and brown clouds with scarlet-streaked underbellies bled into each other. It was only three o'clock in the afternoon, but darkness fell early in the north in winter.

She grabbed her horse's bridle and led him towards the road. The animal snorted, his breath fogging in little clouds before him.

Charlie turned to face her, lifted a hand and swung his bulging kitbag from his shoulders. 'Hey, lass,' he said and his eyes held hers.

'You didn't let us know you were coming.' She marvelled at how he made her tremble.

His smile was awkward. He threw his kit bag into the cart and the horse snorted and stamped his feet. With a slight laugh, Charlie fell into step beside Chrissie as she started to walk. 'How are they all?'

'We're doing fine, Charlie. You'll not recognise wee Peter, he's grown so well. How long are you home for?'

'Well, 'til after New Year. I'll have to get another trip. I've applied for a berth with *The White Star Shipping Line*. They build new ships all the time. If I get on with them I'll be set for life.' They both fell silent. Scartongarth came into view, smoke escaping from the chimney like a ghost in the frosty sky. 'What a grand sight,' said Charlie, stopping, removing his sailor's hat and rubbing his hand over his head. His hair was short and bristly. 'I know I've not been gone all that long, but I've missed this place.' He turned to look at her. 'And I've missed you.' His eyes found hers and the hunger still sat in them.

'What, not a girl in every port?' She laughed to hide the racing of her heart.

'Not a one.' His eyes crinkled at the corners. 'And what of Alexina? I heard she got wed.' His face fell solemn. 'I was surprised. How is she, anyway?'

'She seems well. But you, Charlie? You must have so many yarns.'

'Aye.' The snow crunched beneath his boots. The familiar yapping of geese filled the sky. He lifted his head to watch them. 'I'm glad to be home.'

Her hands tightened on the horse's reins as she pulled the animal to a standstill and turned to face Charlie. Breath feathered into the air between them.

'And I'm glad you're home too.' She spoke barely above a whisper.

The horse nudged her impatiently, jolting her forwards and breaking the spell. 'They'll be right glad to see you at Scartongarth,' she said, her eyes turning to the cottage.

Charlie laughed. 'Not half as glad as I'll be to see my own bed.' They turned down the track leading to the bay and the welcome she knew would be provided for the returning sailor.

That night it was a merry crowd that gathered in the ben end of Scartongarth. Charlie had them in stitches with his tales of life on an ocean going liner although no one believed he had fought a whale single handed. He had brought presents too. Headscarves for the women, several twists of tobacco for Angus, a china doll for Bel, a model liner for Jimmy and a rattle for Peter.

'When are you going back?' Angus asked.

'I'll stay a couple of weeks to help you out. I told Chrissie, I've a good chance of a berth with the *White Star Shipping Line*. Oh, Angus, you should come too. You should see some of their liners.'

Chrissie's heart sank. He sounded so enthusiastic. She had never heard of *White Star Shipping Line*, but she had lost him, as sure as the sun would rise tomorrow.

After Christmas, Chrissie helped prepare for the New Year. She had not seen Charlie alone since he had returned. The young folk on the island, hungry for his news, had taken up much of his time. Then there was the work that had mounted up in his absence and he had applied himself immediately to the making of lead sinkers, the mending of nets, and the repairing of the thatch where age and winds had loosened it. She had waited for him to come to her door at night in vain. Finally, she was forced to accept the possibility he was no longer interested in her in the way she now wanted.

That Hogmanay, as she had done on many others, Chrissie sat alone as the first footers traipsed over the countryside with bottles of whisky, pieces of black bun and peats, bringing luck for the New Year to every open door. Since only the menfolk were out this night, it was unlikely they would call on a woman alone. Peter lay asleep upstairs in the attic space above her room, in the bedroom she had fashioned for him in the eaves.

She knew she would be welcome to take in the New Year with Mary-Jane, but with the woman's failing health, it was unfair to expect her to remain awake until the clock struck twelve.

Turning her gaze to her bed, she remembered the way the firelight had glistened over Charlie's naked torso. She ran her hand across her breasts, touching her nipples. They tingled and the tingle ran all the way through her body and to her thighs. She tilted her head back, surprised by the heat of her own desire. After Peter was born, she never thought she would yearn for a man's body again, but these last months that yearning had returned tenfold. A knock came to the door. She tensed, heart beating so hard she felt it in her stomach.

'Chrissie, it's me, Charlie.'

'Wait a minute.' She dragged herself upright, wrapped her shawl over her long flannel nightgown, lit the lamp and quickly checked her reflection in the pockmarked mirror on the wall. Her cheeks were flushed; her curls a wild mess around her face, her eyes appeared large and dark. Smoothing her hair, she padded to the door.

Flakes of snow rested on Charlie's head and shoulders, his cheeks and nose were red. He held up a whisky bottle. 'So you won't go thirsty.' With his other hand, he held out a peat. 'So you won't go cold. Will you let me in? You know it's bad luck not to accept wishes from a first foot.'

'And you know it's bad luck for a man with red hair to put a first foot over the threshold.' She looked him in the eye and let her tongue slide over her lips. Her erect nipples tingled against the cotton of her nightgown.

'Ha, but the clock hasn't struck twelve yet.' He smiled; his eyes held some of the old sparkle. The scent of whisky lay thick on his breath. His gaze slipped down the length of her body and back to her face.

The wind froze her bare feet, rippled the edges of her gown and made the flames in the fireplace shoot up the chimney. 'Come in,' she said, stepping back.

He kicked the wall to rid his boots of snow before he entered. Behind him, the flakes fell thick and silent, filling up the space where he had been. After pulling the door closed, he set the bottle on the table and threw the peat on the fire. From his pocket, he drew two pieces of black bun wrapped in a dishcloth and set them beside the whisky. 'So you won't go hungry.'

She watched him shake the snow from his jacket and hang it over the back of a chair. She studied the ripple of muscle beneath the too tight gansey. He rubbed his hands together. His nails were short and bitten. Fine golden hairs sprinkled the backs of his fingers.

'Will I turn down the lamp?' he said. 'In case the others see the light and come to your door.'

She nodded, although the lamp was already low.

The clock whirred and struck twelve. Their eyes met in the shadows and held. She swallowed, felt her throat restrict and drew in a breath. 'You're a rare looking lad.' She reached out and grasped his hand.

For a time they stood like that, neither moving. Then, with unspoken agreement, they leaned towards each other. His lips touched hers, briefly. 'Happy New Year,' he whispered and moved away.

Chrissie studied his face. His strong jawline, clean-shaven, his sculpted lips slightly roughened by frosty air and his eyes. The firelight danced in his eyes. With a wild rush of emotion, she placed a hand on either side of his head and pulled him towards her, pressing her lips firmly against his.

He allowed the kiss then drew away as if in surprise.

'Do you not want me anymore?' she said, horrified.

'Oh, aye.' The red glow of the fire glittered on his wet cheeks and shimmered on the droplets of melted snow on his head.

'I want you now,' she said.

A smile stretched his mouth.

She ran her tongue over her lips and began to unbutton her nightgown, taking her time. Once her breasts fell free, she pulled the garment over her head. 'Now you,' she said, and watched him hungrily as he struggled out of his clothes. Slipping her arms around his back, she pulled him downward until they both fell onto the rag rug.

'Are you sure,' he gasped as their lips found each other's again and again.

'I'm sure,' she whispered.

He moved slightly away and stroked her face. His hands travelled down her neck, across her shoulders and over her breasts. She closed her eyes and gave herself up to the wonder of his touch. This was not the hurried, desperate need that had driven her into his arms before. This was a time of discovery, a time of gentleness and of mutual desire.

Later, as they lay entwined, Chrissie cried, and her sobs were for a sadness that had surfaced from deep down inside. Charlie's kisses had been slow and tender and his touch swept her away on a wave of emotion she had never before experienced. For the first time since her grandmother died, she felt loved.

'Do you want me to stay the night?' he asked into her hair.

'Yes.' Her voice was little more than a whisper. And, in case he hadn't heard, she nodded against his neck. He picked her up and carried her to the bed. They would hold on to each other through this night, regardless what tomorrow might hold.

Chapter 14

Charlie woke to the sound of the clock striking six times. By the fireside, Chrissie nursed the baby, her head bent, her hair covering her face. For a while he lay watching the picture she made; the stoop of her shoulders; the way she held Peter in the crook of her arm. He watched the little hand waving in the air, grasping at the collar of Chrissie's blouse. Shifting his weight, he heard the bed creak.

Chrissie looked up. 'You're awake,' she said.

Charlie sat and swung his legs over the side of the bed. His feet hit the floor and the cold solidity of the flagstone jolted him. He padded across the room, knelt beside Chrissie and grasped the baby's hand. 'You're not going to send me away again, are you?' he said, his voice low.

Chrissie shook her head. 'No. Never. But we have to keep this – us – a secret, for Peter's sake.'

Charlie knew she was only echoing the voices of the many women before her, and though it was a bitter cruelty and hard to bear, bear it they did. A woman's life had rules. She was expected to work with her hands and cart peats and take her turn in the fields, but no matter what the circumstances, the vows of marriage were sacred. He nodded. It was not the way he would have chosen, and secrets were hard to keep on an island this size, but he too feared how their relationship would be viewed by the islanders. He and Chrissie could weather the brunt of gossip, but an innocent child could not.

A few days later, Charlie and Angus leaned against the shop wall, surrounded by another two lads and a handful of lassies. The snow lay a crisp covering on the ground and crunched under their feet. The boys lit their cigarettes, blowing smoke into the icy air.

Reverend Donald Charleston came out of the shop. 'And what mischief are young folk up to today?' he asked.

'Going to bring our yachts out now. The first race of the year,' said Angus.

'I'll come along and watch,' said the Reverend. 'You lads are dab hands at making model yachts. I'm impressed.'

'The best yachts in the north. You still got that wireless thing you was telling us about?' Charlie referred to a conversation they had had before he left for the navy. The Reverend knew lots of things with his reading and his connections in Glasgow, and Charlie was always hungry for information. The young minister was full of enthusiasm for what he called *the latest invention*. And in Charlie and Angus, he found willing students.

'Yes, you're welcome to come and help me put it together when I get all the components. So much is going on in Europe, it'll be good to get the news without having to wait for the papers.'

'It doesn't seem possible, voices sent through the air.' Angus threw his cigarette down and ground it with the toe of his boot.

'Oh, it's true, I can assure you,' said the minister, turning to leave.

Charlie fell into step beside him. Used to communicating by Morse code with a lantern in the night, flags or a mirror during the day, he found this new invention fascinating.

'Where are you going?' said Angus. 'I thought we were getting the yachts out.'

'Ach, it doesn't take the two of us to get one boat ready. You can have the yacht anyway. I'm back to the navy soon and I want to hear more of this wireless thing.'

'My brother in America sent me a list of instructions. All I have to do is get the parts.' Excitement glowed around the young Reverend. 'An Italian sent and received his first signal in Italy in 1895. Someone managed to telegraph a message from England to Newfoundland in 1902.'

'Fancy that,' said Charlie.

'I've ordered everything I need.'

'And it will really work?'

'I'll be most disappointed if it doesn't. I'll put my shopping away and I'll come with you to the loch.'

What he wanted was to tell the whole island he and Chrissie were together. He did not like sneaking to her room after dark. It barely bothered him what folks thought, but the bairn had to be considered – and Chrissie put a lot of store on her reputation.

'Reverend,' he said. 'I read if a body disappears for seven years or more, they can be declared legally dead. Is that true?'

'I don't know. But I'll find out for you. What are you thinking?'

'I know it's too soon, but if Jack was declared dead, would you marry myself and Chrissie?'

The Reverend looked at him for a minute. 'So that's the way of it. Of course I will, and I must say, I'm not surprised.'

'Chrissie wants to keep this a secret for now – for Peter's sake. But I'm willing to wait the seven years if it means we can be together.'

The Reverend nodded slowly. 'But you don't know Jack is dead. What if he comes back before then?'

'She'll divorce him. Will you marry a divorced woman?'

'I will. But not in the kirk.'

Convinced both he and Chrissie were now strong enough to stand up to Jack, Charlie hoped he *would* return. Then it would be ended once and for all. He realised he had been foolish to confront Jack the way he had. Chrissie had been right; he should have gone to the law, been a bit more underhand and humiliated Jack by telling the whole island about the letters. But then again, imagining what the shame, the pain of knowing what Jack had done to their beloved Davie and the disgrace of having a convict for a son would have destroyed Dan and Tyna. Maybe, after all, things had happened for the best.

'And what if Jack comes back in - say, eight years' time, what then?' asked the minister.

Charlie hadn't thought of that. He shrugged his shoulders unhappily. 'We'll deal with that if it happens, I suppose.'

Charlie and the minister joined the others at the banks of the loch. The water shone a flat silver in the sunlight, ice clinging to the edges. Many of the islanders were there, every family who owned a model yacht. The weather was bright but cold. The breeze, barely strong enough, ruffled the heads of the reeds and the tufts of grass poking above the scant snow which covered the flat landscape around the loch. To the north, clouds hung heavily, bruised blue with purple underbellies. Snow would fall before night.

'Go on Angus.' Charlie shouted his encouragement, as men wearing rubber boots waded into the water and held their yachts at the start line.

Ready, steady,' shouted Jondy the linesman, and blew on his whistle, a sharp sound that rent the air. The yachts were released, and, with the wind in their sails, sped across the water. With long poles, the men guided their crafts away from the edge of the loch. Children, scarfs tied around their necks, crossed over their chests and knotted behind their backs, raced along the bank and shouted encouragement to their fathers, brothers and uncles. Their breath misted before them.

Angus' yacht reached the finish line a nose ahead of the others and the cheers intensified. He had won the silver cup for the last season and already his name was engraved on the base. That cup sat proudly on the mantelpiece of Scartongarth, where it would remain until the end of the season. Charlie hoped his brother would not have to surrender his prize to a new champion at that time. If he won it three years in succession, he would be allowed to keep it, and that would mean a lot to the folks in Scartongarth.

By three o'clock in the afternoon, Angus was still ahead. The day was drawing to a close and the setting sun burned the sky pink and purple. Cold, wet but jubilant, the men returned to the Mains, carrying their precious boats. There the women served them hot stovies, potatoes with chunks of mutton and lashings of gravy, and cups of tea with oatcakes.

Charlie met Chrissie's eyes and they shared a secret smile. He had not yet told her he had received notification today he had been accepted as a crew member by *The White Star Shipping Company*. Anticipating her disappointment at his leaving, he decided to explain later, when they were alone, how much this post meant to him.

That night, as she lay in his arms, Chrissie stared into the darkness, unable to sleep. The navy meant more to Charlie than he had let on, she thought. Although she said she understood, she clung to him, dreading the time when he would go away again. For some reason his news had filled her with a dread. 'Are you sure this is the right company for you,' she whispered, unable to put her fears into words.

'They're a great company. I'll be set for life,' he said, and then, as if to placate her, 'There's a law, Chrissie. I've heard. If someone is missing for seven years, they can be declared legally dead. If Jack doesn't come back, we can marry then.'

Chrissie's heart contracted. Tears threatened so she was unable to speak. Could this really be possible? Did she deserve such happiness? For a brief moment she imagined how it could be. She and Charlie running Scartongarth until Jimmy, who was surely the heir, came of age. As many bairns as God sent them. And all with the blessing of the kirk. Then the hand of dread that constantly lurked below the surface of her contentment sneaked its way around her heart. 'Oh, Charlie, that would make me so happy,' she whispered, and closed her eyes against the anxiety and the pain of his leaving.

Chapter 15

As a regular employee of *The White Star Shipping Line*, Charlie was never short of a berth. Two or three times a year he returned home, sometimes for a few weeks, sometimes for several months. It was a time of excitement, Charlie's homecomings. He always brought gifts; food and clothes, toys for the children. He and Chrissie fell into an easy rhythm, but he didn't mention marriage or having Jack declared dead again. Each time he went away, she missed him more than she could say, and each trip he promised would be his last.

'I wish you and Peter could move to the mainland,' he said one night after bad weather had kept him in Huna at the other side of the firth for almost a week.

'I can't leave Mary-Jane and the twins,' she said. 'But you could afford to give up the navy now. People are leaving the island. There's more land for those of us who are left. '

It was true. Families were usually large and with not enough land on the island to accommodate more crofts, many of the young men joined the navy or fishing fleets of Wick and Scrabster, moving their families to the mainland. The herring were thick and plentiful and with their reputation as seafarers, a Raumsey man could always be sure of a berth. Life, although never easy, had improved for the people of Raumsey by 1911.

'I will, soon.' He kissed her forehead.

***

The following April, Charlie returned home on leave. Peter raced to meet him and he swung the boy in the air. 'Look what I've made for you,' Charlie said, and handed him a model version of the *Christina* that he had carved from a chunk of driftwood. Peter gave a little shriek of delight and Charlie turned to hug Chrissie.

'I'd better go and give them in Scartongarth a shout,' he said as he released her. I'll see you later.'

Chrissie nodded, her heart singing.

'I like this boat,' Peter said happily, holding up the model. 'Can I sail it now?'

'I'll take you to the beach a little later.' Chrissie ruffled his hair. 'Want to go now.' His mouth turned down.

'I'll fill the wash tub. How'll that do?'

'I want Jimmy to play with me.' His lips parted in a smile that lit up his face. 'Or can I go to the loch with Charlie?'

'Jimmy will once he's checked the traps for rabbits. Charlie's just home. You be a good boy now, play in the tub and we'll go down to the rock pools for a wee while before bed. I've got to help Mary-Jane with the tea.'

Peter trailed after her as she brought out the tub and filled it with water from the barrel. He clapped his hands and laughed as the boat sailed across the surface. Chrissie watched him with indulgence, studying his chubby face as she had done so often, searching for any clue, any likeness to either of the two men who might be the father, but all she saw was a mirror image of herself; the hair corn-coloured, the eyes smoky blue. Not a day passed she did not give thanks for his birth. He was bright and funny and above all, healthy. Such a sunny natured child could be no offspring of Jack's, she had told herself long ago.

She would have loved to be married to Charlie, she would have loved more children, but given her circumstances, she had to be very careful.

Charlie shared her bed at night sneaking in once Peter was asleep and leaving before he rose. But in spite of how careful they were, she knew people wondered and whispered. Nevertheless, she hoped, as she did on his every leave, that this time he would choose to stay at home. But that hope was shattered when he announced over the evening meal that he had been accepted as a crew member on the *Titanic*, one of the newest and most modern of the passenger liners. He had spoken about this ship before, and she knew this was a dream come true. The *Titanic* had been under construction for the last couple of years.

'I've seen pictures,' he said. 'She's the largest liner I've ever had a chance to sail on. I'm so lucky, Chrissie. This will be my last trip, I promise.'

Chrissie shivered and she didn't know why.

Later, as they lay before the fire in Chrissie's room, he whispered, 'You don't mind me going, do you? This really will be the last trip.'

'I've a bad feeling,' she started, setting her hand on her chest. 'In here.'

'Afterwards,' he promised, and kissed her cheek, 'we'll talk about me settling down.'

A few days after Charlie left, Chrissie came down with a chest cold. Pressing her hand against the flannel that covered the bread poultice she had applied, she closed her eyes and leaned back against the bed head. She had been up all night for the last three nights. Whooping cough was sweeping across the island and had already claimed one young life. Last night she had sat up with both Bel and Jimmy, boiling kettles and pans of water to try and keep their airways clear. Jimmy, in particular, vomited after every coughing fit and had developed a fever. Today Peter's nose was constantly running and he had started with a slight cough. Soon he too would succumb.

Chrissie herself had a thumping headache. She felt hot then cold alternately. She was not afraid of whooping cough, since she had had it as a child, but Jimmy also had a fever and since he was already low, it could be fatal.

A hammering at the door made her lift her head. 'Who is it?' she called.

'It's me. Jimmy's really bad.' The voice of Mary-Jane, high and near hysterical.

Closing her eyes against her own pain, Chrissie rose and staggered to the door. 'I'm ill too,' she said. 'I can't risk giving the bairns more germs.' She did not add, it could very likely kill them. 'Has Angus gone for the doctor?'

'Aye, over an hour ago. But bairns are sick on the mainland too.'

'I'll come, but you have to do what I tell you.' She swallowed and her tonsils met and parted painfully.

The kitchen of Scartongarth was overwarm. Jimmy, wrapped in a blanket, lay shivering before the fire. Forgetting her own illness, Chrissie picked him up. His skin was dry and hot, his body limp. His eyes rolled back in his head.

'He took some kind of fit,' Mary-Jane cried.

'He has a bad fever.' Chrissie threw the blanket to the floor and hurried outside, the child in her arms. 'We have to cool him down. She had seen children take fits and die when in the throes of a fever and keeping them warm only made things worse. Her grandmother had learnt this through experience and passed the knowledge on to her.

'But he's shivering. It's cold outside.' Mary-Jane ran after her tugging on her arm.

Chrissie shook her off. 'If we don't cool him down he could die.'

Mary-Jane stumbled against the wall, sobbing. 'I'm sorry, Chrissie. I do trust you, but if I lose him too. . .'

Chrissie said nothing. Jimmy was not responding. 'Keep him out here, and strip off his clothes.' She ran indoors and brought out a flannel and a basin which she filled from the barrel. As the cold water slapped against the burning body he began to shiver more violently.

Mary-Jane turned her head away and pressed the heels of her hands to her eyes.

Finally, when the chattering body felt cooler to the touch, Chrissie carried him indoors and laid him on the bed, on top of the covers.

'He's in God's hands,' said Chrissie. 'All we can do is pray. I have to go and see to Peter.'

Outside, she wiped her head and her hand came away damp. Her clothes clung to her back and the world swam. To the north the sky was beginning to brighten. A man's silhouette appeared over the rise and came towards her. Angus, thank God. But he was alone. Where was the doctor? She knew no more. The force of her own fever overtook her and she sank to the ground.

She awoke to a cool cloth being pressed to her head and the sound of Peter's noisy whoop as he struggled with the cough. A pan of water boiled over the fire, and steam fogged the room.

'Chrissie, you scared me.' Angus was leaning over her.

'The doctor...' Her voice rasped painfully through a dry, hot throat.

'Too many patients. He said he could do nothing anyway. The cough has to take its course.'

'Jimmy?'

'He made it through the night. Mary-Jane's not well herself, but she won't leave his side. Bel seems to be improving.'

Peter began to cough again. 'Mam,' he cried hoarsely between spasms. Angus picked him up and carried him to the bed, laying him beside his mother as the dreaded whoop shook his body.

'Charlie'll be home by night,' said Angus.

'Charlie? But isn't he sailing today?'

'I sent him a telegram last night. You're not fit to do another turn. Mary-Jane has the bronchitis herself and most of the islanders are ill too. We need him here.'

'Go see how Jimmy is,' said Chrissie. She turned to attend to Peter as the fit of coughing subsided and with a grumbling cry, he fell back asleep. 'Hurry now,' she said, as Angus went out of the door. She hoped Mary-Jane had enough sense not to cover the child with blankets again.

Chrissie shivered. The blankets around her were damp from her sweat and had turned clammy. Where was Angus? She glanced at the clock. Not yet eight. Each tick reverberated in her head. Unable to lie still any longer – not when Jimmy could be... she made to rise, but the room spun around her and she sank back. Charlie was coming home. Thank God. She looked at the clock again. Hardly five minutes had passed since Angus had left, yet it seemed like hours.

The door opened. Chrissie tried to pull herself upright. Angus dropped to his knees before the bed. His eyes swam with moisture.

'Jimmy?' she whispered as fear shook her voice.

Angus grabbed her hands and started to cry.

'No!' The word burst from her, but before she could draw another breath, Angus spoke again, hurriedly.

'The fever's broken. He's sleeping normally. Oh, Chrissie, he's going to be all right.'

Without enough strength to rise, Chrissie spent the day in bed, Peter beside her. Angus ran around, carrying out her instructions. Mary-Jane also had no strength left.

Before dark, the door creaked back on its hinges. Chrissie moaned and opened her eyes to a gathering dusk. She had no knowledge of how much time had passed. She was aware of Charlie dropping to his knees beside her bed. A sense of relief flowing through her, she grabbed his hand. Everything would be all right now.

'You're hot,' he said, his hand on her forehead. 'Just stay there. Angus and I, we'll see to the others.' He picked Peter up and carried him into Scartongarth. For the first time in ages, Chrissie fell into a peaceful sleep.

She awoke to find Charlie stirring something in a pan over the flames. He turned when she moved. 'I'm making porridge,' he said. 'It's the only thing I can cook, that and fried ham.' He gave a feeble laugh.

Chrissie suddenly realised she was ravenous. 'Porridge is grand,' she said hoarsely.

***

Five days later, with the occupants of Scartongarth on the mend, Angus returned from the mainland where he had gone to buy cough medicine for Chrissie and Mary-Jane who still struggled with the bronchitis. White faced, he rushed into the kitchen. Chrissie looked up from where she sat at the table peeling potatoes.

'Charlie, where's Charlie?' Angus spun around, eyes searching every corner of the room.

'He's away in the fields,' said Chrissie. She stood up quickly, the knife falling to the floor clattering against the flagstones. 'What is it, Angus?' Her gaze fell on the newspaper curled up in his hand.

'This.' He slapped the paper on the table and it rolled open.

At first Chrissie couldn't comprehend what she was seeing. Again she read the bold black headlines.

1,500 TO 1,800 DEAD.

The words *Titanic* and *disaster* and the grainy picture of the large steamer spun before her. 'God brought him home,' she whispered, as the breath rushed from her lungs.

***

For once, Charlie said nothing as they sat around the table that night. He had known many of the crew members on board the *Titanic*, had sailed with a few of them.

'Isn't it the hand of God that brought you back,' said Mary-Jane into the silence as she sliced the bread.

'It wasn't his time,' Chrissie agreed. She was still shaken. The bairns were thin and pale, both she and Mary-Jane were still suffering the effects of the bronchitis, but it was worth it all to have Charlie safe at home with them.

'You'll surely stay with us a while now.' Mary-Jane said. 'We need another hand on the croft.'

Charlie stared at the newspaper curled up on the chair. 'I still can't take it in,' he said, and reached over and grasped Chrissie's hand. 'If ever there was a sign, this is it. I'll stay for as long as you need me.'

Chrissie closed her eyes and said a silent prayer of thanks.

***

Long after darkness had fallen, Charlie found himself unable to sleep. Finally he rose and walked to the end of the house and sat on the stone seat, where he stared over the bay. It was a still night and the seals cried, loud and morbid. Water whispered up the sand and washed gently across the shingle. Looking at the still ocean and the sparkle of moonlight on the surface, it was hard to imagine the tragedy of which he could have so easily been part.

He remembered the excitement when he and his crewmates had gathered at the dock in Dublin, and the subsequent disappointment at being called back to Raumsey, and how he had considered ignoring the call. Then he had re-read the telegram.

Jimmy seriously ill. Stop. Chrissie and Mary-Jane sick. Stop. Come home. Stop.

He had no choice. For Chrissie to take to her bed, she would have had to be pretty serious herself, especially with Jimmy's life in the balance. Raising his eyes to the great liner, he had crumpled the telegram and shoved it in his pocket, then turned and pushed his way through the excited crowd on the quayside, his heart simultaneously weighed down with disappointment and worry.

'Never you mind, laddie,' said his friend Tommy. 'You'll be with us on the next trip.'

Charlie picked up a stone and hurled it as far as he could. And then the tears began. No, he would not go back to the navy. He was not a devout believer in God, but something had brought him back and this was a sign he was needed here on this island with his family.

Chapter 16

For the next two years Charlie remained on Raumsey and he and Chrissie carried on as they had done. They were more careless now, since Jack had been gone over five years and the islanders were more accepting of a new relationship. However, no one apart from Mary-Jane and Angus, knew for certain that Charlie spent the night in Chrissie's bed. It was wrong, without the marriage vows, Chrissie knew, and yet her feelings for Charlie had overcome her religious beliefs. However, her strong desire to protect her son from wagging tongues, remained.

Then one day, Peter asked the question Chrissie knew she would eventually have to answer.

'Is Charlie my dad?'

Chrissie took him by the arms and sat down, pulling him onto her knee. She smoothed the hair from his brow. 'Your Dad was lost at sea before you were born,' she said. He must never know what she suspected and talk about it outside. A bastard child in 1913 did not have an easy life.

'Like Jimmy and Bel's dad?' he asked.

'Yes, just like that.'

'But Mary-Jane talks about their dad all the time. Why don't you talk about my dad?'

'Sometimes it's better not to talk about things that hurt too much.' She didn't know how else to answer. Telling him otherwise would only confuse him. Maybe she would tell him about the kind of person Jack really was someday, when he was old enough to understand.

'What did he look like?'

'Not like you. He had dark hair. He would have loved you though.'

Peter looked thoughtful. Afraid he was going to ask another question, Chrissie eased him onto the floor. 'Come on,' she said. Let's go and look for eggs.'

Peter's face lit up. 'Bet I find all the brown ones. Do brown hens lay brown eggs?'

The questions about his father were forgotten for the moment.

She caught Charlie as he washed his hands in the rain barrel after work. 'He's started asking about his dad,' she said.

Charlie chewed on his bottom lip. 'It had to happen. What did you tell him?'

'The only thing I could. That Jack was his dad and he was drowned at the sea.'

'I wish it were different.' He shook his hands to dry them.

'So do I.' Chrissie handed him a towel.

Charlie reached for the towel and his hand closed over hers. 'I wish we could tell him the truth.'

'What – that I slept with two men in the space of a couple of weeks?' She pulled her hand away slowly.

'I'm his father, Chrissie. He looks nothing like Jack.'

'We can't talk about that.' Not out loud, she thought, and said nothing as they went indoors.

The next evening, in the kitchen of Scartongarth, Charlie picked up his newspaper and bent low. Reading was difficult with only the light of a small oil lamp. 'There's more unrest in Europe,' he said.

'And why would that bother us?' asked Mary-Jane.

'If there's a war, we'll all be pulled into it.'

'Ach, we're far enough away. London's never bothered with us before,' Chrissie shouted through the open door from the back porch where she was washing dishes.

'Ah, but they will. They'll need all the fighting men they can get. They're building a naval base at Scapa Flow.' Charlie spoke to her over his shoulder. He pushed the paper towards his brother. 'See here Angus.'

'My goodness. Surely the Germans are not going to come all the way up here?' said Mary-Jane pausing. With the kettle in her hand she turned to look at him.

'It's to hide the British fleet,' said Angus. 'It's the navy for us lads, aye?'

'You're needed on the land. They surely won't make you go.'

'It's best to get it done and over with. More of us who join up, sooner the war will be over. They can't let the Kaiser march all over Europe, doing whatever he wants.'

'Well, I doubt if he'll be interested in Raumsey.' Mary-Jane poured hot water into the teapot. 'Get that paper out of the way so I can set your cup down.'

'Hey, see this. Here's an article here about the new radio thing, you know, the one the minister was talking about a few years ago,' said Charlie.

'The receiver, like the one he tried to make himself?' said Angus. 'It didn't work.'

'He had the idea. Maybe not the right parts. There's more in the news about it now.'

'Aye, says you can hear people talking in London. That would be good. We'd know all about the war then.' It was a nuisance waiting for news when they couldn't get the papers for the bad weather.'

'What nonsense you lads talk!' said Mary-Jane. 'You mean a telephone. I read about that. It won't be for the likes of us. No, only for the king and the prime minister. Asquith, he'll be getting one.'

No it's not the telephone. It's like, like a box with knobs and you put these things on your head. Look, here's a picture.'

She peered over his shoulder. 'And you can make one yourself?'

'Aye, so the minister said. I could hardly believe him, and when he couldn't get it to work... but look, there it is.' He stabbed his finger on the page. 'He'll be having another go at it, as sure as eggs is eggs.'

'What lads for dreams.' Mary-Jane shook her head.

'Ach, well, if the war gets me out of Raumsey for a while, I'm all for it.' Angus leaned back in his chair. 'They say it'll be over by Christmas.'

'Owld Archie was in the shop this morning, says he can't understand why we're joining the French against the Germans when it was always the other way round.' Mary-Jane turned back to her tea making.

'The Germans have invaded Belgium. What does a doddery old fool like Archie know?' said Angus.

'Archie should know what he's talking about. He's over ninety and his mind is as sharp as a whip.' Chrissie returned to the kitchen. 'The war'll not affect us. You don't need to go. The men of Raumsey won't make much of a difference.'

Charlie reached for his cup. 'I wouldn't mind going. I never thought I would, but I do miss the navy now and again. I wonder what the other lads are doing.'

'There might not even be a war.' The hairs on the back of Chrissie's neck prickled; a chilly shiver ran the length of her spine. Somehow she knew there would be a war, and with just as much certainty, she knew it would not be over by Christmas.

Chrissie's instincts were right. On the 28th of July, 1914, Britain declared war on Germany.

Charlie did not mention joining the Royal Navy again. He knew Chrissie would use his escape from the *Titanic* as a sign that he was meant to be on the island. Charlie himself had once believed as much, but that was two years ago, and time had blunted the edges of his superstitious beliefs. Although he loved Chrissie and Peter so much they were part of his soul, his country needed him, and the call of adventure was strong. When they were alone, he and Angus often discussed the possibility of going to war.

On a mild summer's evening, the boys leant against the shop wall. Above their heads, Lottie had stuck up a board with a picture of Lord Kitchener pointing a finger. *Your country needs you*, said the slogan printed beneath.

'What do you think?' said Charlie.

Angus inclined his head. 'Sooner or later we'll have to go – maybe we'll have no choice. The women can say nothing then.'

'Aye, I feel bad staying here while all our friends go. Guilty even. But it won't be for long, they say.'

Reverend Donald Charleston walked out of the shop, stopped and looked at the lads. His eyes were bright – excited. 'I think I've finally got a signal on my wireless,' he said.

'What – you're still working on it? I knew you would. Didn't I say that, Angus?' asked Charlie.

'It was crackling, but I heard it. Why don't you lads come along tonight – see what we can get.'

'I'm up for that,' said Charlie. 'Do you think this war will last a while?'

'It seems very likely.' Charleston's brow furrowed as he looked across the firth.

Charlie's eyes followed his gaze. The water lay like a grey blanket shot with red beneath the sinking sun. 'The sooner we get over there and give them a good hiding, the better.'

***

Donald Charleston stared at the distant hills of Flotta. The scent of honeysuckle and heather lay heavily in his nostrils. A bee buzzed lazily around a purple headed thistle. Here in the shade of the shop, the midges were thick and bothersome. His enthusiasm about the radio was dampened by the prospect of war and the subsequent excitement of the young men. They seemed to view it as no more than an adventure. His father had fought in Crimea and had never recovered from the horrors he had witnessed there.

'It'll be over by Christmas,' Charlie said, breaking into his thoughts.

'I pray to God that you are right.' Donald Charleston closed his eyes against the image of the screaming men and broken bodies his father had described in sickening detail and made a mental note to pass some literature on to Charlie. 'I pray to God you are right,' he repeated, quietly.

Chapter 17

It was October of 1914, a grey day, and Chrissie had been working since dawn. Flexing her shoulders to relieve the ache, she glanced at the sky. She still had the potatoes to gather in the high field before darkness inked out the daylight. Standing up to stretch, she placed her hand on her aching back. Peter and Jimmy were at the other end of the field, racing each other to see who filled their bucket first. Peter was competitive and keen to win. That bit older, Jimmy, his cousin, was always patient.

Charlie jumped over the dry-stone wall and came striding towards Chrissie. He did not wear his dungarees and patched gansey, but his Sunday clothes and he looked so striking her breath stuck in her throat. The wind picked up the tails of his jacket and they rose and flapped. His ginger hair stood in tufts and his arms swung as if he was marching.

'Where've you been all day, lad?' she called, but he did not answer immediately. As he approached, her fingers closed tightly around the spade handle, and the tension ran up her arm. With her eyes on his face, she waited for him to speak.

A bead of moisture quivered on his long, almost white eyelashes, and his sprinkling of freckles seemed lighter, camouflaged against the wind-stung redness of his cheeks. Dry skin flaked on the bridge of his nose, and a muscle twitched along one cheek. 'We went to the mainland today, me and some of the lads.'

Gulls screeched above their heads, eager for whatever morsel the freshly turned earth might yield. The wind sighed within the young grass in the nearby fields. Somewhere a cow bellowed.

'I've signed up. I've taken the King's shilling.'

'No.' The word exploded from her and she dropped the spade. Knowing how restless Charlie had been since the outbreak of war, she had dreaded this day.

'Two soldiers were in the town. What they said made sense. The other lads are going.'

'Angus too?'

'Angus too.'

'How will we manage without the men?'

'It'll be over soon enough. When these Huns get a glimpse of the brawny island lads they'll run, tail between their legs.'

A sudden cold gripped her body. It lasted for no more than a heartbeat, but it left her with a feeling of dread. 'Please... no. I need you here and farmers don't have to go they say.'

He stepped forward and grabbed her earth covered hands. His skin was calloused yet his touch, gentle. 'I need to do this. Anyway I've decided on the navy. I'll like as not be stationed in Scapa Flow – just across the water.' He nodded towards the hills of Flotta.

'And you'll be back before Christmas?'

'As sure as eggs is eggs.'

'Don't go, Charlie,' she said, but in her heart she knew he would go, just as she knew he would not be back so soon.

'Charlie... I won look.' Peter came running up the field, his small bucket held in front of him, his bare feet sliding between the dreels of earth.

'Well done, man,' Charlie looked into the bucket and lightly punched the boy's arm.

'Chrissie, Chrissie.'

The thin voice of her niece, Bel, tore Chrissie's attention away. Pale golden hair flying backwards in the wind, the girl ran up the field towards them. She clambered over the wall, staggered forward and stopped in front of Chrissie, bent from the waist as she fought to regain her breath.

Chrissie grabbed the child's shoulders. The bones were sharp beneath the thin fabric of her dress. 'What is it?'

'Mam... she's bad.'

'Don't worry, pet.' Chrissie took the child's hand in her own and, followed by Charlie, she hurried back to Scartongarth.

Mary-Jane sat in the fireside chair, her breath coming in short gasps, her lips tinged blue. 'The pain,' she said, clutching her chest, 'it's awful bad this time.'

Chrissie lifted her bag from the corner, opened it and brought out a small vial which she uncorked. Mary-Jane tipped it to her lips and drank.

'Come and lie down, now,' said Charlie, helping her to her feet and into the box-bed. 'You shouldn't be doing so much with a bad heart.'

Mary-Jane lay back, covering her face with her forearm and closing her eyes. 'Angus told me. You boys are going to war.'

'Aye, we are.'

'No. I can't stand it,' she whispered.

Chrissie held Mary-Jane's wrist counting her heartbeats. 'Was it the news of them going to war that brought on this attack?'

'I've been feeling dizzy for days. Now with the men going, how are we going to manage? If only Jack was here.'

Chrissie's insides shrivelled. She had not thought about Jack for a long time. 'Thank God he isn't,' she said.

'Whatever he was, he could work like the devil. Do you ever wonder what happened to him?'

No, I don't wonder, Chrissie wanted to shout. *I don't wonder because he's dead. Dead and buried in my byre.* Instead she shook her head. 'No point in wondering that.' She turned to Charlie. 'She'll be fine.'

'If you're sure.' He hesitated and looked at his sister for another minute. 'Then I'll go and change my clothes.' He left the room.

'You stay in bed Mary. I'll need to get back to the tattie picking.' Chrissie laid Mary-Jane's hand back on the bed and patted her arm.

Outside, Bel and Peter sat on the dyke.

'Why are you not helping in the field?' she asked Peter. 'Bel, go and make your mam a cup of tea.'

'I finished my dreel. Don't want to do any more. Bel doesn't have to and she's ten! I'm only seven.' Peter looked at the ground, pouted and scraped his feet along the dusty earth.

Chrissie sat beside him. 'Bel has to watch her mam. Jimmy's up there, so are the other bairns.' She cupped his chin in her hand and turned his face to hers.

'Picking tatties is boring.'

'If we don't work we don't eat.' She gave him a hug.

'Don't like picking tatties.' A tear formed at the corner of his eye and rolled down his face.

'Don't cry.'

'Can I stay here? Pleeeeese. My back's sore.' His tears always brought such a rush of protective love she could deny him nothing.

'This time, then.' She stroked his face and kissed his cheek.

Jimmy came running up. 'Peter kicked my bucket over,' he said. 'Just cos I was winning.'

Peter stamped his foot. 'Didn't.'

'Oh Peter,' said Chrissie.

'Why do I always get the blame for everything?' Peter jerked away from her.

'Nobody's blaming you for everything, boygie. But you can't always win.' Charlie came up behind them. He turned to Chrissie. 'You spoil him. How's Mary really?'

'She's over the worst, this time. But she needs proper food. We had little enough before the war. Look now, the shop is running out of everything. And you're leaving.'

'I might have to sooner or later. Best go and get it over with. Don't be wild with me,' he said.

'For going to war, or for leaving us to fend for ourselves?' She shook her head. 'I can't stop you.'

Charlie's lips tightened. 'We're leaving in the morning. And the night, all the lads – we're having a do in the Main's loft, to say goodbye, like.'

Chrissie stared at him. 'So soon?'

'You said yourself, sooner we go, sooner we'll finish it.'

'How are two island lads going to make a difference?' Emotion filled her up, and a tremor ran through her body. She wanted to plead with him not to go, to yell and shout, to grab him and physically stop him, but she knew that that would be useless.

'Please, Chrissie, try to understand.'

She turned away. There was nothing more she could do.

Later that night, after spending a few hours in the Mains, Charlie, carrying a sleeping Peter, followed Chrissie back home and put the child to bed. As music wafted over the hill on the evening breeze, Charlie took Chrissie in his arms. 'It won't be for long,' he whispered, his lips soft against her ear. She didn't answer. She couldn't. The sense of dread had become a tight knot in her stomach. All she could do was to wrap her arms around him and bury her face in his chest. If only she could hold him this way forever. That night they did not sleep, but clung to each other, breathing in as much of the other as possible

In the morning, he disentangled himself from her arms and crossed to where his trousers hung on the chair. 'I've something to give you.' He fumbled in the pocket. 'This is my grandmother's ring. When I come home we'll use it as a wedding ring.'

'But... Jack,' she started.

'Ach, he's been gone long enough. We can see about having him declared dead. Then we can marry.'

She flung her arms around him. 'I'll wear it around my neck, next to my heart. I'll keep it safe until then.' Pray to God he would be safe, she thought. 'Go on and finish the war so you can all come home.'

As the boat carrying the young volunteers left the quay, Chrissie felt as though her own soul had been torn away, leaving only a dark void in the shell of her body.

Chapter 18

The men had been gone for over five months and the peat stack was running low. 'Not a week's worth of peats left,' said Chrissie, setting the bucket at her feet. 'We'll never have fire 'til April.'

'Geordie MacIntyre offered to take you over to Mey tomorrow. A few boatloads are going,' Mary-Jane replied. 'I wish I could help... '

'Stop apologising for being ill.' Chrissie wiped her forehead on the back of her hand. Her empty stomach rumbled.

'I can't help it. I feel bad.' Mary-Jane wiped her eyes.

'There might be something left in the peat bogs in Raumsey.' Chrissie was desperate to avoid Geordie's attentions. Since most of the men had gone, he had become attentive again, using the opportunity to 'help out' as he put it. She felt his eyes creep over her like a black, heavy beetle.

'But Raumsey peat'll hardly burn and doesn't give off the heat. An Eday man was in Lottie's shop last week. Both islands of Harray and Eday have plenty of spare peat. He was trying to sell them. Said he would deliver them and all,' said Mary-Jane.

'He's taking advantage of this bloody war. What will we pay him with – answer me that?' Chrissie walked to the window. She pressed her palms to the sill. 'I'll have to go with Geordie to Mey to cut our own, though the man can't keep his hands to himself.'

'Chrissie – you swore.'

Chrissie pushed her eyes closed. 'I work as hard as any man and Lord knows, work's been even harder with them gone. I have the right to swear.' Pressing her hand to her head, she lowered her voice. 'I'm sorry; I don't mean to be sharp. I'm so tired and worried about the boys – this war and all.' She was doing the work of three, and there was still seldom a bit of fresh meat for the table.

'You shouldn't have taken Bel out of school to look after me; she was so good with her letters.' Mary-Jane's voice took on a whining edge as she turned away.

Chrissie closed her eyes. *I had no choice*, she wanted to scream, but what was the point? She heard Mary-Jane sniff and fought the irritation that welled up. Lately Mary-Jane's illness had changed her in her mind as well as her body. Now she spent her days alternately crying or complaining and apologising for both. With her nerves stretched to the limit and her stomach constantly crying out for food, Chrissie found herself increasingly irritable and was ashamed because of it.

'I'm off for the tools,' Chrissie said, knowing she needed to get away.

From the back of the barn she collected the tuskar and the luggy, the implements she would need for cutting the peat and wiped them clean of cobwebs. Then she went to see Geordie MacIntyre.

Geordie's mouth stretched at the sight of her. 'You know I'll help you out any time,' he said with a leer. 'With anything.' He winked.

Chrissie shuddered. 'If I could sail a boat, I wouldn't be asking for your help.'

'Don't be like that. It's a hard life without a man in your bed.' He winked again.

I wouldn't have one that stinks, she thought and wrinkled her nose. 'When we go with the others tomorrow, I hope you'll be wearing that shift of clothes I washed for you. And shove the ones on your back round to Scartongarth. They're going to need a fair amount of steeping, and that's a fact. And don't even think of stripping now,' she shouted, as he fiddled with his belt.

'Ach, well. I thought you could've taken them home with you. Saved me from visiting the night. But maybe that's what you want, eh?'

'Leave them outside the door. I'll be at the lambing.'

'Well, we'll be leaving for the peats early. I'll even have a bath the night. Sure you don't want to come round and wash my back, make sure I do it proper, like?'

'Get on with you. And I'll have the bairns with me tomorrow, before you get any ideas.'

Chrissie left his house, slammed the door and took a long slow breath of fresh sea air.

***

The next day, with Peter and Jimmy carrying the tuskar and the luggy, they climbed aboard Geordie's yole. The sky and sea were leaden and seemed to merge into one on the horizon. As they approached Mey, the water rippled softly across the pebbled beach, calm and somnolent for once. Up on the hill, mainlanders in caps and heavy jackets worked their own peat banks, silhouettes against the glancing rays of sunlight. As spring gained strength, the early flowers would turn this wasteland into a blanket of yellow, purple and green, but for now, only the white heads of bog cotton dipping in the sea breeze broke the flat brown landscape.

Once the boats had been beached, the islanders made their way across the bog. The children, bare footed, laughed as brown water squished between their toes. Bairns and women. The only men there were either too young or too old to go to war, but they all had one thing in common, they could sail a boat. A sudden dazzle of sunlight sliced its way through the clouds, bounced over peat lands and highlighted dark disfigurations crisscrossing the land. Generations of peat trenches.

Geordie's booted feet pushed the tuskar through the soft damp earth and it crunched through roots. One by one he lifted oblong slabs oozing with brown water and dumped them by his side. Chrissie and the boys laid them flat to dry out. After a few days, they would return and bring the peats back to the island where they would build them beside the individual crofts. Triangular piles that allowed the wind to blow between them.

The day was long and back breaking and by the time they relaxed to eat their bread and dripping, their feet and hands were frozen and their clothes were wet and stained.

Thankfully the sun had burned away the mists and fell lightly on their faces.

'You'll be needing your bath the night,' said Geordie, lowering himself down beside Chrissie.

She closed her eyes. A warm bath after a hard day's work was no more than a dream, for her muscles already ached too much to even think of lugging pails of water from the well to heat up. Others had folk at home who would have all that ready and waiting, but with only Mary-Jane and Bel in Scartongarth, there was no hope of any such luxury.

Finally the day drew to a close, and weary workers made their way back to the boats.

Chapter 19

A week later, with the peat home and stacked by the side of the cottage, Chrissie watched the children trail up the rigs towards the school. The wind was warmer this late April day, blowing from the south and carrying the scent of heather and peat-smoke on its back. She returned indoors, where Mary-Jane still lay in the box-bed.

'I'll put the kettle on,' said Chrissie. 'You take your rest.'

'I wish I could help you more.' Mary-Jane raised herself on one elbow. She had grown even thinner since the barrels of salt fish and pork were almost empty. There was no bread, as the shop had run out of flour, and the Main's farm could barely grind enough for their own needs.

Picking up the kettle, Chrissie realised it was dry. She fetched the pail from the back porch and went outside to the well. The sharp bite of the wind caught her breath.

Geordie MacIntyre came up the path his fingers hooked through the gills of a cod. There had been an unseasonable flurry of snow and it lay like soft paper on his hair and shoulders. 'You'll be short of fish now, with no a man to help you.' His eyes crept over her.

'I'll not deny that,' said Chrissie. 'Thank you kindly. Have you any more washing for me to do?' Avoiding his eye and trying not to let her hand make contact with his, she took the cod from him and went to go back inside.

'Hold on a minute,' Geordie grabbed her arm. 'Are you not going to ask me in for a cup of tea? It's a fine way to treat a man who comes bearing gifts – turning your back on him.'

She mentally shuddered. 'Mary-Jane is still in bed.'

'At least spare me the time of day.' His grip tightened.

'I'm sorry, Geordie, but I'm busy, can you not see? I'm hoping the floating shops will have more supplies.'

'Na, I just heard word. The shops won't be coming 'til this war is over. Scared, see. Since the naval base set up at Scapa, these waters are too dangerous. And Lottie's shop will not be getting many more goods – not with things no better on the mainland – worse in the towns. But me now, I'm a man of means.' He winked.

Chrissie winced. 'We're fine for now, Geordie.'

But his grip did not slacken. 'I've means of getting food. What about it? Come to the barn with me for a wee while, you'll not be sorry.'

He grabbed her round the waist, pressed his body against hers and rotated his hips. She dropped the cod and tried to push him away, but he held on tighter, his slack, wet lips searching for hers.

'Get off me,' she yelled. 'Or so help me...'

'You'll do what, Chrissie?' She was against the wall now, his rough, unshaven face searing hers. 'There's no a man around here now, and a woman has her needs.'

'Well, it's not you I'll be needing, Geordie MacIntyre, and that's a fact!' She brought her knee up sharply.

'What...' He staggered back gasping. 'There was no need for that. Can't a man give a lass a cuddle now, for any sake?'

'You cannot give me a cuddle, now or any time.'

'You could have a share of all the fish I catch, aye and rabbits too. Maybe I did come on a bit too heavy like, but Chrissie, there's little enough to go round on this island – you should be grateful.'

'Go, just go,' She bent down, slipped her fingers beneath the gills of the fish and thrust it at him. 'I'll do without your hand outs, if it's payment of that kind you're wanting.'

'Keep the fish. But it's the last help you'll be getting. I'm not good enough for you, is that it? You think we don't all know about you and young Charlie? It's plain what kind of woman you are.'

'How dare you!' She threw the cod at him and it slapped him across the shoulder. 'I don't want your fish. And get someone else to do your washing!' She had tried to keep her relationship with Charlie a secret, but nothing was a secret in an island as small as this. Suddenly, she realised she didn't care. What were a few wagging tongues in comparison to what was going on in Europe?

With a final glower, and leaving the fish where it fell, Geordie marched up the path. He stopped and shouted over his shoulder. 'I'll go, but you'll be begging me to catch fish for you before this war's over. Mark my words. I've got money put by. Money buys stuff when none can be found.'

'Oh, go away, will you. I'll do my own fishing. I don't need you or any man.'

'A woman on a boat? You know how unlucky that is?

'You're daft. Living on an island, how can a woman not go on a boat her whole life? How do you think we get to the floating shops?'

'The Lord turns a blind eye when there's good reason.'

'Well I've got good reason. I'll not be beholden to you.'

She watched him storm up the road, and knew what he said was true. The diet was more limited than ever. And they needed money for other things. But summer would soon be here, and with it the food the season brought. Once the cow calved, there would be milk, and the hens would be laying better. The ditches would be lined with sorrel leaves, greens until the vegetable garden matured. But there was no saying how long this war would last. Without lobster and crab to send south, there was no money to be made. She thought of Mary-Jane's sunken eyes and the thin limbs of the children, and she knew what she had to do. If a woman could turn her hand to a plough as well as any man, she could also learn to fish. She picked the cod from the path. 'No need to let the gulls get you, is there,' she said to the fish, and went back indoors.

The first time she put to sea she took Jimmy and Peter with her. They knew more than she did for they had been in the boat with Angus and Charlie many a time. It was a fine day, and she had no fear as she helped the boys run the *Christina* into the surf before jumping in themselves. 'Hold fast to the tiller, Mam,' said Peter. 'First you have to unfurl the sail.' She said nothing, but the wet tails of her skirt clung uncomfortably around her legs. Tomorrow she would face the disapproval of the good women of the parish and wear a pair of Charlie's trousers.

'You show me how, pet,' she said, not wanting to admit she had seen it done many a time.

With a look of concentration on his face he began to untie the ropes. The sail bulged out as the wind caught it, and the sea swelled beneath them. Jimmy set his hand beside hers, and he put his weight against the tiller so that the boat met the next wave head on. 'Face her onto the breakers,' he said, as the yole rose and then dipped in the trough.

Chrissie felt a rare thrill as the wind caught the sail and the boat surged forward, ploughing its way northward. The wind strummed in the rigging and the water splashed against the sides, occasionally throwing up a handful of spray. Although the breeze was slight, it blew stronger out here and gusted over Chrissie's face, loosening her hair from her braid and nipping her eyes.

Her cheeks burned with the salt of the wind and a wild exhilaration filled her up. For the first time she understood how a man with the sea in his blood could never leave it.

'We'll pull into yonder geo. It's a good place for pitching the creels,' said Jimmy, 'Are you finished baiting yet, Peter?'

'Aye, aye, captain.' Peter saluted the older boy and then started furling the sail. 'The tide'll take her the rest of the way.'

'You didn't need to come with us, Chrissie,' said Jimmy proudly. 'We can do it ourselves.'

'Aye and a fine pair of seamen you are too, but I enjoy it.' She didn't say that at five and seven years old she could never allow them out on their own.

After pitching the creels, they sailed into deeper waters and pulled out their hand lines. The boys surprised Chrissie with their knowledge. 'Watch for the meezes,' shouted Jimmy. 'Level her up with the Haven Road.'

Chrissie had heard the men talk of the 'meezes' before, understanding them to be landmarks on the shore to pinpoint a particular spot at sea where the cod was plentiful. The lads, young though they were, had learned well. When they sailed home that night, it was with a boatload of fish.

With a lighter heart than she had set out with, Chrissie helped the boys to winch the boat ashore. 'Who needs Geordie MacIntyre now?' she said, with a laugh. And with a barrow load of fresh food, the trio walked home, singing.

***

Reverend Charleston had finally managed to get his crystal receiver to work, and he listened to the news every night. Each day, he turned up at Lottie's shop to give out the latest bulletins. Then one day he brought the radio into the shop. 'I'm leaving,' he said. 'I'm young and fit and I should be helping my country.'

'Surely they don't expect a minister to fight?' said Lottie, a look of horror on her face at the very idea.

'The men need spiritual support more than they ever needed it at home. I'll be an army chaplain, doing what I can.'

Chapter 20

'No letters for us the day?' Chrissie asked Sanny the Post as he pushed his bike up the rutted track.

He shook his head. 'The boys wrote home regularly at first, but yer not the only ones on this island waiting for news. And the letters that do come give out less and less.'

'It's been months now without anything from the lads.'

'No news is good news.' Sanny pushed his bonnet to the back of his head and scratched his hairline. 'I just now delivered a telegram to Consty and Jock.'

'No! Does that mean...'

'It's not my place to go asking questions.' Then he nodded and his eyes became liquid pools. With a sniff, he turned his back and walked away, his steps slow, his shoulders hunched. He stopped and looked over his shoulder. 'Don't go near them though. They don't want visitors. I'm erecting a flagpole by the post office and when a telegram comes, I'll fly the Union Jack at half-mast. I'll no surprise another family again.'

After that, when the flag was hoisted, the islanders watched, their stomachs in knots, as Sanny the Post mounted his bicycle and made his way to one house or another with the latest sad news.

Then one day he came towards Scartongarth.

In the doorway, Chrissie and Mary-Jane linked arms and watched as the old man dismounted, set his bike aside and walked towards them. Each step he took lasted a lifetime. The wind was uncannily still, not even the tall grasses by the garden wall whispered their secrets. From somewhere a peewit emitted its high pitched call, and it was the loneliest sound in the world.

Mary-Jane slipped her arm from Chrissie's. 'You go,' she said, her voice barely above a whisper. 'You open it.' She watched as

Chrissie moved forward, watched as the hand lifted from her side and took the telegram from Sanny. A sudden breeze sprung from nowhere and stirred the weeds that grew between the flagstones beneath her feet, rustled the corn heads together and then died away. She watched as Chrissie read the paper. Heard the brief animal cry.

'Oh merciful God,' said Mary-Jane, grasping the door frame.

Before her, Chrissie sank to her knees and bowed her head, the telegram fluttering to the ground.

Sanny set his hand on her shoulder. His words came from a distance, sitting on a non-existent wind. 'I'm sorry about Charlie, lass. But at least Angus will be coming home. The war is over for him.'

***

Several months later, a silent group stood on the shore as Angus was helped from the boat. Chrissie ran towards him and clasped his free hand. The other was swathed in bandages. Although she had been warned what to expect she still fought not to recoil. Nothing could have prepared her for the horror of his actual injuries. The left side of his mouth dragged upwards; skin stretched over the cheekbone causing a veined shiny surface, still livid red, to pucker under his eye, which was mercifully untouched. Where his ear should be, there was nothing at all, and the right side of his head, where thick red hair once grew, was blistered tissue.

Grasping his arm in both of hers, she felt the hot sting of tears as they tumbled unbidden down her cheeks. 'Angus,' she said, 'Oh my, Angus.'

'You recognise me?' His laugh crackled, split the air and hung in the momentary silence.

Chrissie found her voice and her words tumbled out. 'You...yes. Yes of course. 'I'm sorry; I didn't mean to react like that. They told me... what happened.'

'You had to see me sometime, lass. And the reaction – I've got to get used to it.'

'And... and Charlie. You were with him when...' Her voice broke before the words were out.

'Charlie wasn't the only one. A lot of good men died.' His voice trembled and he looked away. 'Don't ask me anything...' He shook his head and she could see he too was crying. She held him then, and as his thin body shuddered with sobs he clung to her, a sinking soul in a sea of pain. The fingers of his good hand clutched at her hair and he pressed her so closely to him she could hardly breathe. 'Oh, Chrissie.' The words seemed to choke him. 'Chrissie, Chrissie.'

'At least you're alive,' she said.

'I wish I wasn't.'

'Don't say that. We'll get you home. Mary-Jane has a pot of fish soup on the boil.' She turned and reached out to the children.

Bel came forward and hugged Angus tentatively, then with a gulp, turned and ran up the road, crying aloud. Peter, all the colour drained from his skin, stared, wordlessly.

Jimmy stood still, his lip trembling, the distress he felt written on the plains of his face. He glanced at Chrissie, eyes pleading for guidance.

'Help us,' said Chrissie, nodding towards Angus.

Bravely, Jimmy took Angus' arm and helped him to the waiting cart, but kept his face averted. He took the reins and Chrissie and Peter sat at either side of Angus as the cart jolted up the incline and across the island.

Mary-Jane met them at the door and burst into tears when she saw her brother. Together the women led him into the kitchen but he refused to sit, choosing instead to pace the floor.

'I don't want to stay here,' he said.

'Where else would you be staying?' Chrissie said. 'We want to look after you.'

'I have nightmares. I am sick in the night. I need to be alone.'

'We've made the ben room up for you,' said Mary-Jane. 'We'll not have you anywhere else. Sit down now. Have your soup.'

Bel opened the front of the stove and threw in a lump of wood. The flames crackled and shot up. Angus started back with a whimper and covered his face. Chrissie and Mary-Jane exchanged a look.

'Don't mind me,' he said quickly. 'It's the fire.'

Knowing how badly he had been burned and understanding his fear, Chrissie shut the hob and the stove door. 'Sit down and take your soup. You're safe now.'

Angus sat, but his hand shook so much he could hardly reach his lips with the spoon. Eventually he bowed his head. 'I'll away and rest, I need to get my sleep while I can. But tomorrow, I'm moving into your old house, Chrissie.'

Once everyone was in bed, Angus rose and went to the shore. He sat on the stone seat and stared across the firth. Silhouetted against the moonlight, warships glided silently, breaking the horizon, on their way to Scapa Flow. His whole body trembling and rocking slowly, Angus watched them. Then, covering his face in his good hand, he wept. Great wracking sobs that felt as though they would tear his body apart and, as he vomited the few mouthfuls of food he had forced down, he welcomed the pain.

Part Two

May 1920

Chapter 21

Chrissie emptied the ash bucket in the lavatory and was making her way back to the house when she spotted Sanny the Post cycling down the rutted track.

'Aye, Sanny, anything for me the day?' she said as he drew near.

'I have that, Missus Reid.' He leaned his bicycle against the fence and fumbled in his bag. 'Here we are.' He pushed his bonnet back, held an envelope close to his eyes and squinted. 'I can't make out the postmark.' He moved it a little way and squinted again.

'Don't think it's from your sister-in-law in Canada. Have ye got a secret admirer, Chrissie?'

'Secret admirer – hah, that would be the day!' She snatched the letter from his hand, laughing as she did so.

'Dinna be so fast to say that. There's many a man who would put his boots under yer bed. If I didna have my Nellie.... who's it fae then?' He blinked a few times and picked up his cycle, but made no move to leave.

'Get away you old fool. It's ... ,' Chrissie's eyes skimmed the address and ice chips filled her blood as she recognised the writing. 'No one... nothing...' She turned her back to Sanny and ripped the flap open.

'Be like that, then,' said Sanny and, realising no more was forthcoming, pushed his cycle slowly up the trail.

Chrissie lurched to the front of the cottage and her body folded onto the stone seat. The night before, the dream had returned. It had been years since the last time, and then it had been barely memorable. Now she understood what it had meant. A forerunner – a warning.

Dear Chrissie

You will be surprised to hear from me after all this time. I've been thinking about you and Scartongarth a lot lately. You and I were meant to be together for eternity. I'm coming home.

All my love,

Jack

'Are you all right, Chrissie?'

The voice startled her, bringing out of her stupor. Her niece Bel stood on the path, her hands curled around the handles of two water pails which were kept away from her spindly legs by a square wooden surround. She set down the pails, stepped out of the frame and ran to Chrissie's side.

Chrissie tried to speak, but the words stuck in her throat.

'What's wrong?' Bel cried.

Faced with the girl's anxiety, the anaesthetic of shock faded.

'I ... I... think I'm doing too much, that's all.' Chrissie's voice sounded alien to her own ears, fractured and broken.

'Come inside. I'll make you a cup o' tea.'

'What...? Oh, aye, aye.' She allowed Bel to lead her into the kitchen where she lurched against the table, causing the globe of the oil lamp to clatter in its cradle. 'I need to sit.' She pushed a cat from the cracked leather armchair and sank into the cushion.

'Did you see the coal I gathered from the beach this morning? The ship it fell from'll not be making good steam the day, I think.' Bel lifted a bucket, emptied it into the iron range and dragged the kettle directly over the flames.

Chrissie barely heard her. Somewhere in the distance a dog barked.

Dropping to her knees, Bel clutched Chrissie's shaking hands. 'Will we send for the doctor?

'Don't be daft. *I* cure the sick here.'

'You only know about herbs and things – maybe you need Doctor MacKenzie.'

'I don't need the doctor from the mainland.' Chrissie sat upright, faking normality.

'Come away, the work'll not do itself. Take bread and a can of water to the men in the high rigs. Then you'd better check if any ewes are about to lamb.'

'Are you sure – are you really sure?' Bel pulled a handful of her fine, pale hair forward and began to chew on the strands. Her skin appeared almost transparent where it stretched over cheek bones. Dark smudges lay beneath her eyes.

Chrissie reached out and stroked the girl's head. Poor lassie, she thought. Her mam, Mary-Jane, had died over a month ago. After years of declining health, her heart had finally given out. 'I'm really sure, pet,' she said. 'Now away you go.'

Bel brought two portions of bread from the back porch. That done, she picked up a knife, opened a dresser drawer and eased out a slice of cooked oatmeal left to set since the night before. Then she spread the porridge between the wedges of bread, divided the sandwich in two and wrapped the lot in a cloth.

'I miss Mam.' Bel filled a pitcher from the water pail.

'Aye, I miss her and all,' said Chrissie.

'You always told Mam what ailed you.' Bel lifted her soulful eyes, so like her mother's.

'And I would tell you as well, Bel, if there was anything to tell.'

'Any word from Aunt Isa?'

'No, but a letter'll take a while to get to Canada. She'd have come if she could. You're a good lass, Bel, a good lass.'

Chrissie watched from the window as the girl she loved like a daughter walked up the field towards the high rise. Bel's skeletal frame was visible beneath her threadbare shift. Thoughts tumbled through her mind. Decent food is what we need. The diet of salt fish and porridge is not enough for a body who can't keep meat on her bones. Chrissie touched the windowpane with the tips of her fingers. The glass was cold and damp. She considered the hens. Growing old they were, their laying days almost at an end. But when the cow calved, at least they would have milk and a fine calf to fatten up.

For the rest of the day she carried out her chores automatically, trying not to think. The clock struck five. The door opened, making her jump.

'Did I scare you?' asked Peter, mild surprise on his face. He set a pail on the floor. 'I caught these partans.' He went to wash his hands in the barrel outside the back door. In the pail, three large crabs crawled over each other.

'Get me a pan of water. We'd best boil them while they're still alive. We don't want to be poisoned,' shouted Chrissie. At the mention of poison, a word so carelessly fallen from her mouth, a shudder started at the base of her spine and snaked its way to her neck.

'Donkey on your grave?' said Peter, coming into the room.

Chrissie gave a sharp laugh, trying to act normal, but it sounded cracked and broken.

Peter did not appear to notice. He lifted the large pan onto the stove. At thirteen, he had shot up this last year and, although blighted by the gangliness of youth, his build promised a broad-set adult. He reminded Chrissie so much of her own dad, his gap-toothed smile, his corn-coloured hair, his wide eyes. Thank God he had not taken after his father – whoever that might be.

An hour later, she prepared the crabs. Carefully she removed the poisonous portion, the dead man's fingers, smashed the claws with a hammer, mixed both white and dark flesh with breadcrumbs, and served with potatoes and carrots.

After the meal was over, Bel glanced at Chrissie. 'You feeling better?'

Peter frowned. 'What's wrong?'

'There's nothing wrong. Can't a body get tired now and again?'

'Want a game of cards after we've washed up? Ina and Connie are coming later.' Bel was watching her. She had the uncanny sensation that the girl could read her thoughts. Knew her fears without her having mentioned them.

'I'm fine. You go ahead with your friends. I've a jumper to finish.' Chrissie nodded at ball of wool speared with knitting needles, lying on one of two padded boxes on either side of the fireplace. She had to keep busy; had to keep her hands moving;

had to occupy her mind. She was glad Bel's friends were coming; glad of the diversion youthful laughter brought into the house. There had been a gap since Jimmy left to serve an apprenticeship on the mainland. He was going to be a joiner – a fine trade. She picked up the knitting, looped the wool across her fingers and clicked the needles faster and faster until they snapped together like falling rain on a tin roof.

Much later, after Peter and Bel had gone to bed, Chrissie brought a basket of clothes for darning to the fireside, knowing there would be no sleep for her this night. With a fat pebble in the toe of a thick fisherman's sock, she weaved the yarn across the hole. The needle slipped and pierced her thumb. She scrabbled in the pocket of her apron for a handkerchief and her fingers closed around the letter she had received this morning. The letter from someone pretending to be Jack. Her hand jerked away like she'd touched venom.

A joke, that's what it was. A cruel, vindictive joke. But who hated her that much? Tentatively, she reached into her pocket again. Pulling open the stove's door with her other hand, she hurled the envelope and its poisonous contents into the fire. The edges curled and darkened. Only when the blackened remains lifted on the draught and floated away with the smoke, did she realise she had not done the most obvious thing. She had not checked the postmark. There was no point asking Sanny the Post. With his failing eyesight, he would have been unable to make it out.

To concentrate on the mending was now impossible. Unnaturally tense, she paced to the window and back again. The clock on the mantelpiece struck the hour. The fire settled. The kettle hummed. Outside, an April storm lashed against the windows with a fury. The dog slept on, making whimpering noises, his legs occasionally kicking as if he were chasing rabbits across the moors.

Chrissie returned to the window. Reflected in the glass, behind raindrops dragged sideways across the pane, she saw herself. Her eyes were dark hollows beneath her thick brows, her cheek bones visible, furrows emphasising the corners of her mouth.

With her hand on her chest, she felt the outline of a ring secured on a length of wool beneath her blouse. She pulled the ring out, the ring Charlie had given her before he left for war, and closed her fingers around it until the metal grew hot against her palm. She thought of Charlie.

Lovely, gentle, funny Charlie. His words floated inside her head. *This was my grandmother's. When I return we'll use it as a wedding ring.*

But he had not returned. He'd been killed at the battle of Jutland. Angus had survived but because of his injuries, both physically and mentally, some said he'd be better off dead.

She closed her eyes against her pain. She had never told a soul about what had really happened to Jack. If only Charlie were here now, she would tell him, aye that she would.

Opening her eyes, she leaned towards the windowpane until the reflections disappeared. Outside the moon smirked at her between scudding clouds. Angus' cottage sat third to the right along the road at the top of the rise above Scartongarth. No lamp lit his window. Tonight at least, she hoped *his* nightmares would leave him in peace.

The following morning, Chrissie pegged the last of the sheets on the line where they hung like wayward sails. The few moments' sleep she had been able to catch had been plagued by dreams, Jack's poison polluting her brain.

'Bel was worried about you.' The voice came from behind her.

She spun round. Angus leaned on the wall. Chrissie had become accustomed to the way he looked, familiarity blunting the edges of his deformity. He crossed the space between them. He smelled of carbolic soap and new cut grass – so different to Geordie MacIntyre who still hung around her at any excuse.

She removed the last peg from her mouth. 'Did Charlie ever talk to you about Jack?' She secured the end of the sheet.

162

Wariness flashed in Angus' eyes. 'Jack? Why should you ask about Jack after all this time?'

The desire to tell him was strong; the desire to spill everything and lay the words on the green. But remembering the weeks after Angus had returned from the war; how he had wakened screaming in the night, how he had vomited the sparse meals she had been able to feed him, how he had refused to talk of Charlie and how he finally persuaded her to rent him her old house so he could suffer alone, she decided against giving him extra pain.

'Did he?' She asked again, gently.

'No.'

'Nothing at all?'

Angus shook his head and turned his eyes to the sea. The hand he raised to his head trembled.

Chrissie watched as hope of sharing her burden slipped away. 'Come inside, I'll put the kettle on.' She lifted the empty basket and led him into the cottage.

'Something's happened, something about Jack,' said Angus, his voice unsteady.

'No. I got to thinking, remembering. That's all.'

'What made you think about *him*?' He grabbed her arm and pulled her around to face him. 'You have to tell me.' The urgency in his voice surprised her.

'Och don't mind me. I'm getting maudlin in my old age.' She forced a laugh.

'Chrissie, you're not yerself. The bairns are worried and so am I.'

Her fingers knotted in the material of her apron. Her eyes sped to the ceiling, to the far wall, to the floor. 'I got a letter,' she whispered at last.

'From Jack?' Angus dropped his hand. 'Let me see.'

'I ... burnt it.'

The colour drained from his face. 'You what? Did you see where it was posted?'

Chrissie shook her head.

'Don't worry... you mustn't worry.' Angus' fingers twitched.

He lightly rubbed his damaged cheek. 'What did he say – word for word?'

'Chrissie closed her eyes. 'Said he's coming home, that we were meant to be together.'

'Bastard!'

'Charlie did talk to you, didn't he?'

Angus placed his hand on his brow.

'Please, Angus. I know how much it pains you to hear Charlie's name, but I need to know.'

He turned away from her and walked across the room. Stopping at the window, he set his elbows on the sill and leaned forward. 'Yes he told me. About the fight, about how Jack came back and beat you up before he left.' His voice was a monotone.

Chrissie sank on a chair. Her fingers curled around the wooden arm. She bit down on her bottom lip and sucked air in through her nostrils. Then the words burst from her. 'Jack couldn't have written that letter. Jack is dead.'

'I know you want to believe that, but...'

'But nothing. Jack is dead.'

Angus spun around to face her. 'How can you know for sure?'

Something swelled in her chest. All those years she had found small comfort in the belief Jack could never hurt her again. All those years she had trapped the truth inside her to the extent that it was hard to let it go. Twice she tried to say the words and twice they froze in her throat. 'I'm sorry,' she whispered finally. 'Go home. I can't talk any longer.'

'Chrissie...'

The door swung open and Bel entered carrying a baby lamb in her arms. 'The last ewe birthed three. We'll have to make a pet of this one.' Her eyes flitted from Chrissie to Angus and back again. She blinked. 'What's wrong?'

'Nothing at all, lass.' Chrissie shot a look at Angus warning him to remain silent. She saw the control in the tight lines of his face, in the set of his jaw.

He squeezed her hand. 'I'll leave you to tend to the lamb. We'll talk later.'

'What's that all about?' asked Bel, as Angus closed the door behind him. She settled the lamb on the dog's blanket and began to rub him with one end.

'Ach, we were reminiscing. We got a bit weepy.' Chrissie wiped her eyes. 'I'll go wash the feeding bottle and get you some straw.' Bel did not appear convinced but Chrissie was glad of the diversion the lamb had created.

Chrissie stared at the fire while her family slept above her. She could not spend another night like the last, tossing while the tendrils of the past reached out and twisted her heart. She had to make certain; to see again the bones that lay beneath her byre – to prove that her brain had not been playing tricks on her all those years ago. With her shawl wrapped around her shoulders, she went to the cupboard for the storm lantern. Outside, the wind was scarce and a layer of gauze shrouded the moon. Clover, heather, the ozone of the sea and burning peat scented the night air. Before her the countryside lay in eerie shapes and shadows; in the firth, the seals continued their lonely dirge, small creatures of the night rustled in the grass. She pulled in a lungful of sea-salt air. Could she do this? Yes. She had to. 'Dear God,' she whispered, 'Give me strength.' Across the field, her old home stood like a sentinel, guarding her secret. The window was a black oblong in the shadowy building. Praying Angus wouldn't hear her, she crossed the field and skirted the house.

The latch to the barn door stuck. She hauled at it until it rose with a click, loud in the stillness. Inside, the air was fetid with damp earth, mouldy wood and bird droppings. There was a wild flutter of wings as birds, disturbed from their night's rest, rose and escaped through a hole in the rotten thatch of the roof. For a while she stopped, listened, until all she could hear was the thunder of her own heartbeat. The flickering light of her lantern cast shadows in the dust covered stalls, places where Chrissie tried not to look. She fancied the eyes of Jack's ghost, silent and accusing, watching her from the dark corners.

Wiping her palms down the sides of her skirt, she sucked air in between her teeth. She opened and closed her hand and reached for the spade, which still leaned against the wall. She began to clear away the old straw. Then, pushing the sharp end of the spade beneath the flagstone, she levered it up and eased it sideways. The waft of damp earth rose like an invisible cloud. Her legs threatened to give way.

Struggling against a desire to turn and run, Chrissie forced the spade into the packed earth and stood back, already scared. Scared of what she might find, even more scared of what she might not. She wiped the sweat from her forehead, pushed the spade into the earth again, once, twice. The blade struck something solid. She scraped the earth away and froze. The light flickered over the contours of a skull. There was no stopping now. A thin whine escaped her lips. She picked up the graip, pushed the tines through the eye socket and edged the skull upwards until she could fully see it. 'Oh my Lord,' she cried as her legs buckled beneath her and she fell to her knees. Still clinging to the graip handle, she pressed her eyes shut. The sounds of the night closed in around her. The interior of the byre grew thick and airless. Using the graip for leverage, she pushed herself to her feet and stumbled out into the night air. She staggered, fell against the door frame and stared at her earth covered boots.

'Why... Charlie... why?' She jumped as a mouse darted between her feet. 'Oh my God, am I going mad?' She took no comfort from the solid stone surface against which she stumbled.

Unshod footsteps whispered through the grass. 'What is it – who's there?' A man's voice startled her. A light from the cottage door lay in a rectangle across the flagstone path in front of the house. The flame of a lantern swayed and jerked as Angus walked towards her. 'Chrissie, what have you done?'

But words were beyond her. She allowed him to take her arm and lead her indoors where he swung the kettle over the flames. Kneeling before her, he covered her hands with his. 'You're frozen. What happened?'

Chrissie pulled her voice from deep within her, a soft whimper. 'Jack.'

'What about him?'

She couldn't answer.

The kettle began to boil. Angus brewed the tea, handed her a cup laced with whisky. 'Tell me what you were doing in the barn.'

But Chrissie only stared into the fire.

Chapter 22

As the first rays of sun washed night from the sky, Chrissie still had not spoken. Sleep had claimed her, a fitful uneasy slumber born of sheer exhaustion. In her dreams she opened the grave. Then the earth fell away and Jack rose before her, his flesh in tatters, black, rotting. Here and there white bone a sharp contrast, one eye missing. 'Where's my eye, Chrissie, I want my eye.' And she could see it, on the end of the pitchfork, staring at her. She flung the pitchfork from her and tried to run, but her movements were sluggish. Jack laughed, that evil laugh which had followed her down the years.

He caught her; she could feel his arms trapping her. She screamed herself awake. The room was familiar; the arms that held her were no longer those of Jack. She breathed in the scent of the body pressed against her own. 'Charlie,' she whispered. For the time it took to draw a breath, she was lost in the past. Safe. Back in Charlie's arms. And then she was fully conscious and the man who held her was Angus. She wrapped her arms around him, felt the thinness of his frame, pressed her face to his chest and allowed the tears to come.

'It's all right,' he whispered, stroking her back and adjusting the blanket around her shoulders. 'Everything is going to be all right.' She could hear his voice coming at her as if from a distance.

As words filled her mouth, she lifted her head. 'I killed him. I buried him in the byre.' Her voice had no substance. She stared past Angus into the flames licking up around the driftwood.

'You killed him?'

'I loved Charlie. He was just a boy, but he was more a man than Jack could ever be.'

'What do you remember of the night Jack left the island? Can you tell me?'

'I have to, for it's a bitter burden to bear alone.'

Angus inhaled deeply, paused a minute. 'You don't have to bear it on your own.'

Chrissie pressed her hand against her chest and felt the outline of Charlie's ring. A kaleidoscope of emotions tumbled through her brain.

'I don't remember it all. I never wanted to. I tried to put it out of my mind afterwards.'

'Take your time.'

'I remember putting poison in his whisky. I knew he was mad. And he would kill – aye – with not a thought. One of us had to die that night. And I've lived with the knowledge every day since. When Charlie was taken, I knew it was my punishment.'

'Oh God, Chrissie. You didn't kill anyone.'

She pulled away and looked into his face. 'But I saw him. He stopped breathing. And then I couldn't remember – I didn't want to remember.' She dropped her head and stared at the fire.' But that letter...'

'Don't worry. I protected you once,' Angus said. 'I can do it again.'

'You protected me?'

'I mean Charlie did. He told me.'

'You said Charlie didn't tell you a thing.' Chrissie took both his hands in hers and looked him straight in the eye. 'And you said *I* protected you. Angus look at me.' Her eyes never left his face, the face that had become so familiar to her, and she saw the pain there. She remembered when she had first woken up, how she had been sure she was in Charlie's arms. Sitting up now, she looked at him, really looked at him. Surely not – surely he would not do this to her.

Charlie had always been that bit heavier, his smile a fraction more ready. Yes, she had always known the difference. Would have known it even if it weren't for the half-moon shaped birth mark on Charlie's upper arm. But with a damaged face, his body skeletal by constant nightmares that wrenched the food from his gut, would she know? The brothers had been together when

Charlie was killed. It would have been easy... 'No, you wouldn't.' She shook her head.

His eye slid sideways, refusing to meet hers, and something about the turn of his head stirred an almost forgotten memory. Her breath caught in her throat. 'My God,' she said. 'You *are* Charlie.'

'No, no.'

'Then show me. Show me your arm.'

'Leave it be, Chrissie. Leave it be.'

'I want to know what you know. Who you are.' She reached forward, grabbed his sleeve and tried to pull it up.

He snatched his arm away. 'Charlie is dead. I'm sorry Chrissie.'

'Angus, I want to see your arm, now. I'm not stopping 'til you show me.' She grabbed his shirt sleeve and tore at the cloth with determination.

'No. Stop.' He tried to push her away.

'I want to see your arm.' Her lips pressed together, her eyes narrowed. 'I'm waiting.'

With a deep sigh, he began to roll up his sleeve. And there it was. The undeniable proof of his true identity. The dark half-moon shape.

She gasped. 'No – Charlie, why? Oh God.' She bent forward, her stomach roiling. 'Oh God in Heaven. Why... why would you do this to me?'

'Charlie and Angus both died in the war. This,' Angus jutted his face towards her and jabbed at his scars with his finger. 'This is all that is left of *us*. We were twins, identical, this, this monstrosity is us... *us*. Don't you understand?'

Unable to look into his lying eyes a moment longer, Chrissie turned her head away. With her voice raised and trembling, she said, 'I went through hell. My Charlie. Dead. How could you?'

'Seeing me like a freak, would that not hurt more?'

With difficulty, she looked at him again. He stared at the fire, tears gathering in his eyes and glinting in the light. The undamaged half of his face was visible, showing the mature, handsome man he was meant to be. 'I couldn't stand to have you look at me with pity or stay with me out of loyalty. I wanted to set you free.'

'You took Angus' name. Your brother's name.'

'You used to say I was a bonny lad. You used to gaze at me as if you couldn't take your eyes away. And to come back like this. It was easier for us both if you remembered me the way I was. As Angus, I could still be close to you and Peter. As Charlie I would never have come home.'

'All I wanted was Charlie. If you think I'd turn against you 'cause of the way you look, you don't know me after all.'

'*That* Charlie is dead, Chrissie. *That* Charlie will never come back.'

'I *should* have known. I should have recognised you.' Finally the tears came, pouring out of her with great gulping sobs.

He put his arms round her and held her until the storm had passed.

'I can't cope with this.' She pushed him away, emotions whirling through her. She loved him, she would always love him, she had mourned him and now he was here. How could she forgive the years of deceit? Yet she had to know everything. When she spoke her voice was cold, hiding the turbulence inside her. 'At first I thought Jack's letter was a joke – some cruel, sick joke. I had to see his body for myself. '

'And you found. . .'

'A sheep. Oh my God, I buried a sheep.'

'I'm sorry, so sorry,' he whispered. 'I thought you couldn't remember – didn't want to remember. That night, you were in such a state. You scared me.'

'Then tell me now. For any sake, tell me what you should have told me years ago.'

'I tried to. You wouldn't listen.'

'You should have made me.'

'You didn't want to know – I was young... I thought it was for the best.'

'I don't want excuses! Just tell me what happened that night.' She heard the ice in her voice; she felt the hardness of it in the words forced from between her lips. 'Come on, *Charlie*, tell me the truth, finally.'

Chapter 23

Angus began to speak, his voice splintered. 'I was scared. Hell, I was so, so scared. I wanted to help you.' He stopped and drew in a quick breath. 'Protect you from him and later, protect you from the truth. I thought you wouldn't cope. I waited for you to remember – to tell me when you were ready.' He paced to the window.

'You thought *I* couldn't cope?'

'You were a woman. A woman should be cherished, looked after, that's how I was brought up. I was so young.'

'Stop using youth as an excuse.'

He turned to face her. 'I tried to tell you – you wouldn't listen – didn't want to listen. If the truth be told, I didn't want to remember that night either.'

She was calm now, calm and cold and without emotion. She sat down by the fire. 'I'm waiting.'

***

Although he longed to hold her, to shed his own tears against the softness of her hair, Charlie did not attempt to touch her again. Recoiling from the anger in her eyes, he prayed he could make her understand. That was the most he could hope for. He threw some peat on the fire and stepped back. Although it was contained, a sudden burst of flame still terrified him. He stared at the wall as if the past played itself out on the whitewashed bricks. The years fell away and he saw Chrissie as she had been then, a young, lithe woman with flashing eyes and ready wit. When he was twelve and she was seventeen, he had played pranks on her just to be near her, and she had chased him and his brother with the broom, but with a smile on her lips.

He remembered his devastation when she married Jack. And then, an even greater devastation as he watched the meat fall from her bones, saw the bruises on her flesh and the sparkle fade from her eyes. The day she looked at him, looked at him as a man rather than a boy, he had sworn to never let her down.

'I'm waiting.' Chrissie's voice sliced through his thoughts.

'Give me a minute.' He directed his memories back to 1906, the night he had found her outside the byre barely conscious and she collapsed in his arms. The anger had flowed through him like a raging storm. He felt it again, tasted it in his mouth.

'The byre... a grave... for you,' she had whispered in a voice so weak he'd strained to catch the words. He had pushed what was left of the passage door open with his elbow and stopped. The smell of vomit and blood in that room was something he would never forget. Images flooded his brain and he could see it all again, as clear as if it had been yesterday. 'All right,' he said, with a deep, shuddering breath. 'I'll tell you it all...'

He had carried her into the house where Jack's inert body lay slumped amidst the devastation. Charlie laid her on the bed and covered her with the quilt. Her hand rose slightly, then fell on the cover and lay limp.

'Lie easy. I'll do what needs to be done,' he said. He stooped beside Jack and checked the pulse. The beat hardly registered. What had Chrissie done? He inspected the injury to Jack's head. The rough bandage had fallen away and the cut was deep, the flesh around bruised and swollen. The result of Chrissie's attempt to stop the fight by the shore. No, that blow was not how he came to be so near to death. Jack had recovered enough to come back here and almost beat his wife to mush. Yet this wound alone was physical evidence of her violence. Faced with that, would a jury believe her version of events? Indecision raged through him; should he send for a doctor, the constable, Angus? Surely no court in the land would convict her if he died? But he had heard stories of injustice, how the law always favoured the man. No, the risk was too great. He couldn't chance Chrissie being charged with murder; she could even be hanged.

He checked Jack's pulse one more time. The beat was growing stronger. Jack would survive. He looked again at Chrissie's battered body, heard her whimpers. He grabbed a cushion from the chair. His fingers clenched, digging into the softness. He poised over Jack. It wouldn't take long. A matter of minutes – Chrissie would be free and safe. They would all be safe.

Moaning, Jack rolled onto his back. Charlie closed his eyes. Tight. And began to shake. It was no use. Not for any of his emotions, horror, rage, love, hate, would he be able to commit murder on a helpless man. With a growl, he flung the cushion from him and ran outside, across the field and down the cart track to Scartongarth, not stopping until he reached the door. He flexed his fingers and turned the knob. Be careful. Don't rush. Open the door slowly – don't let it creak. Why hadn't he oiled it like he'd been planning to do for months? He stopped, steadied himself, listened. Soft snores came from the box-bed in the kitchen. Tyna had fallen asleep. Good. He had no excuse ready, no explanation for his dishevelled state or for his return. Knowing which step creaked and avoiding it, he crept up the stairs and into the loft space. Angus opened his eyes.

Charlie put his forefinger to his lips. He fumbled under his mattress and withdrew a pouch. The money he and Angus were saving to buy a boat of their own.

'What are you doing?' Angus raised himself on his elbow.

'Trust me, man,' Charlie whispered.

Angus threw the old coat that served as a blanket from him and slid his legs over the side of his bed. 'I'll come...'

'No.' Charlie raised a hand, palm outwards. 'Stay here. Please don't ask any questions.'

Their eyes met in the moonlit slanting through the narrow skylight. Angus pulled his legs back onto the bed and the coat across his body. There was no need for words – the brothers understood each other in a way only identical twins could.

On the landing, the stairwell disappeared into a black void. Charlie felt each descending step with a careful foot until he reached the passageway. From the cupboard, he removed the rifle used to shoot rabbits and birds. Once outside, he ran, a prayer in every step – a prayer that Jack had not already gained full consciousness. The night deepened. The dark was changing and thickening. Clouds blotted the moon and stars. At Chrissie's cottage, he stopped and listened, bracing himself. Only the sounds of the night. He cocked the gun and walked in.

Jack lay where he had been, eyelids fluttering, one hand lifting to his head. Charlie glanced at the bed. The soft bubbly snores of sleep rattled in Chrissie's throat. He turned his attention to Jack and watched as consciousness poured into him and his eyes opened, blinked and grew suddenly round. Dodging the gun barrel that was inches from his face, he struggled to sit.

'Get up. You and me, we're going for a walk,' said Charlie.

Jack's back rested against the solid armchair; his palm remained between him and the muzzle. His red shot eyes flashed with fear. 'What... what are you going to do?' His voice trembled and rasped. A wet stain spread across the front of his trousers.

A deep cold calm replaced the roiling in Charlie's body. 'I'm going to give you a chance, though God knows you don't deserve any. Get up.'

Jack put his hands to his stomach. 'I... I can't. My gut.' He doubled over, retching.

'Get up, or I warn you, I'll finish what Chrissie started.'

Jack struggled to his feet and staggered forward, grabbed a chair and fell over, taking the chair with him. 'I'm... ill. Doctor... please... The bitch poisoned me.'

So that was it. Charlie glanced at Chrissie again; she hadn't moved.

'For the last time, get up.' He indicated towards the front door with the rifle. 'And out.'

Jack rose. Supporting himself alternately on the furniture and wall, he reached the outside.

Charlie knew they had little time before the daily grind for the crofters began. 'The beach, now.' He poked Jack with the barrel of the gun.

Jack took a few faltering steps. Every second he was gaining strength.

'Come on.' Charlie prodded him again. 'Faster.' He grabbed Jack's shoulder propelling him forward. He believed Jack moved deliberately slowly in the hope the island would stir to life and rescue him from whatever fate awaited him.

Jack stumbled and fell over a hummocky mound of grass. 'God's sake, man.' He groaned and rolled over, clutching his stomach. 'I... can't... move.'

Charlie hesitated, waiting. He looked around. Sheep, frozen to ghostly shapes in the sporadic moonlight stood nearby, chewing, watching. He glanced back. Jack had risen to a crouching position. At that second, Jack sprang forward and grabbed the barrel of the gun, forcing it sideways. Taken by surprise, Charlie fought to maintain his hold on the weapon. The firearm discharged; a hollow explosion in the still night air. The bullet went wide. A ewe fell. With only one shot in the chamber, the gun was now useless. Charlie drew back his fist, bringing it with all his strength into Jack's face. He staggered, swayed and nosedived to the ground. Charlie straddled him, untied his kerchief and bound Jack's hands tightly behind his back, then dragged him upright. The shot had alerted some islanders. Lights glowed in one or two windows. A few doors opened and lights from lanterns swayed like landlocked stars. Charlie threw the rifle into a ditch and dragged Jack behind a wall where he held him down until the unsteady lights returned indoors. He then half carried, half pushed him to the beach where the *Christina* lay.

'What... are... you going to do?' said Jack, his voice hoarse.

Charlie put his lips close to the other man's ear. 'What you planned for me... well it's going to happen – to you.'

'Let... me go. I'll... I'll join the navy. You can have Chrissie. You can't do this.' Gone was the mad, threatening voice, instead his words came in a broken sob.

Charlie pushed him against the *Christina*, 'Get in.'

'Untie my hands, please. Give... give me a chance. You're no murderer.'

'More's the pity.' Charlie pushed Jack again, hard enough to make him fall head first over the side of the yole. He grabbed the feet and shoved them after the body so that Jack lay in a twist on the bottom of the boat. Charlie waded into the water and opened a submerged wooden box in which lobsters, their claws tied, were stored to keep them alive before shipping them south. He removed four lobsters and, after carrying them back to the boat, threw them in. Then he put his back to the hull, forcing the *Christina* down the shingles and into the sea.

'Help me, someone,' Jack cried. But his weak cries were lost in the worried shrieks of the sea birds. The dark helmets of seals poked above the water in silence, then disappeared as one, leaving only a settling ripple.

Charlie leapt into the boat and unfurled the sail. The stench of urine, blood, vomit and something even less pleasant rose from his captive. The sea was calm and the wind was just enough. Far in the distance, a slash of dawn streaked the eastern sky, breaking the horizon and outlining the islands to the north. Charlie turned the boat and sailed towards the sunrise.

'Come on, man,' said Jack, struggling to right himself.

Charlie stared ahead, trying not to hear.

'You don't know what she's like. She... comes on all innocent, but she was no virgin when we wed.'

'You almost killed her.' Charlie spoke through gritted teeth. Jack was a liar, he told himself. The only other lad Chrissie had courted was Davie. Was that why Jack hated his brother? Did it matter? Chrissie was still Chrissie. Lovely, volatile, funny Chrissie.

'She didn't, did she?' Jack's voice grew sly. 'She's using you – using you like she used me.'

Charlie's hand tightened on the tiller. He filled his lungs with the salt air. 'If you don't shut up, I'll dump you over the side right now.'

The wind snapped the sails and the yole sped along. Foam, painting lacy patterns on waves and rising along the sides threw flecks into the air, striking Charlie's skin. Jack leaned his head back and closed his eyes. In the fading moonlight his face was grey as slate. 'I was warning you, man, as a friend.'

A hoot of derisive laughter burst through Charlie's lips. 'God preserve us from friends like you.'

Neither one spoke again as the slash of light across the horizon grew, the moon lost its brilliance and the islands were flooded with the hazy, amber prelude to daylight. Sea traffic constantly navigated the Pentland Firth and this morning was no different. Charlie watched as a large ship materialised out of the mist where sea and sky blended. He unfurled the sail, steadied the yole with the oars and waited.

'What... are you doing?' The voice was hoarse and broken.

Charlie turned around. Jack's eyes were wide open. His back was hard against the side of the boat. *He thinks I'm going to tip him overboard*, thought Charlie, and grinned. The merchant ship drew closer. Charlie stood up in the yole and waved his arms, a lobster in each hand, until the steamer slowed and pulled alongside and a sailor's head appeared at the railings.

'You want to trade?' shouted the sailor.

'Where are you bound?' Charlie raised his voice above the throb of the engines.

'America,' said the man.

'Have you room for a passenger?'

The sailor vanished. A few minutes later, a man wearing a captain's cap poked his head over the side. Charlie repeated his request.

'You?'

'No, my friend here.'

The captain studied the bound man lying on the bottom of the yole. 'He looks like trouble.'

'I can pay,' said Charlie. 'And I've fresh lobsters here.'

'Can he work?'

'He'll work. You will work, won't you?' He nudged Jack with his foot.

Jack nodded desperately.

'Then I'll take him. How much money have you got?'

Charlie tossed him the pouch. The captain counted the coins. 'This and work will earn him a passage, but any trouble and he'll spend his time in the bilges.'

'Suits me fine.' Charlie hoisted Jack to his feet and lowered his voice to a hiss. 'If you ever return to Raumsey, I *will* kill you. No second chances.'

He watched as Jack was winched aboard the steamer and out of their lives.

***

Charlie sailed back to the island, skirting the quay, estimating the time to be almost six in the morning. He sailed to the most secluded bay he knew. Once near land, he jumped into the shallows and let the *Christina* go. Waste of a good boat, he thought, as he pushed her as far out as he was able, but this was necessary if folks were to believe Jack had left of his own accord.

He climbed up the embankment and looked over the fields to the pier. Yoles already dotted the bay, but luck had been on his side. He was sure he had not been seen. He flung himself on the heather where he lay staring into the early light. The horizon broke as the arc of a rising sun climbed from the sea. Pulling himself upright, he blinked the fatigue from his eyes. No one would be on the land yet. He skirted the houses and stacks of hay. Milking pails clinked and lamp-light gleamed out of byre doors. The island was coming to life. Time was precious.

First, he went to Chrissie's and marvelled at how she could sleep so deeply given her injuries. 'Please be all right, Chrissie,' he said under his breath, allowing his hand to rest on her forehead. She remained still. There was no time to tend to her now; morning was seeping into the world. He left the house and ran to where the dead sheep lay. Thankfully, she had not been tethered so it might be assumed she went over a cliff. He dragged her through the dissipating haar to the byre and tumbled the body into the shallow grave Jack had dug, covered the corpse with earth and replaced the flagstones.

His arms and chest ached, his shirt stuck to his back, his neck and head throbbed, but it was done. He would retrieve the gun later. Only then was he free to tend to Chrissie.

Chapter 24

Back in the present, Charlie lifted his eyes. Chrissie sat upright, staring at him. Her eyes cold, unforgiving. He reached for her hand, but she snatched it away.

'I tidied everything, mended the door, emptied the bath. You were sleeping so deeply. It was like... like you were unconscious, and then you moved. I thought maybe you did remember but didn't want me to know. Whichever it was, you wouldn't talk about it – I respected your wishes.' It was no use. He knew by her expression she wouldn't understand.

Chrissie rose to her feet. 'Have you any idea of what you've done to me? First allowing me to believe I'd killed Jack and then thinking you dead?' Her voice rose an octave. 'Have you any idea?'

'I'm sorry. If I'd known...'

'Don't blame me.' She shook her head. 'I want nothing else to do with you, Charlie Rosie, you hear?'

'I expected nothing less. My face...'

'It has nothing to do with your face!' Her voice rose further. 'It has to do with trust and honesty and... and simply being man enough to ... You're not the man I thought you were. And if you thought I'd turn you down because of your face, you don't know me at all.'

'Chrissie, I know I'm not the man I was. I don't deserve happiness. When I came back, I never expected a normal life and I never wanted you to know the truth. Believe me, I only did what I thought was best at the time. I can still protect you. We could sell up now, go to the mainland, go where Jack can never find you.'

'How can I ever trust you again?'

'No matter what, I'll be here if you need me.'

'Are you deaf? I want no more of you. '

Charlie stared at the floor and nodded slowly. 'You'll be better off. For my own demons still plague me. It's not just my face. I'm crippled in every way possible. I can never make love to a woman again – my injuries saw to that. You deserve more.'

She walked towards the door where she stopped and looked back. 'It would not have been pity, Charlie.'

'Do one thing for me,' he said. 'Don't tell anybody. Let them carry on believing I'm Angus.

'More secrets?'

He chose to ignore the sharpness of her remark. 'Jack is a real threat. The best thing you can do is move to the mainland. Say the word and I'll go tomorrow; see if I can get you a house and a job. I'll come back to the island, leave you alone, if that's what you want.'

She hesitated. What he said made sense. What else could she do? Much as she hated leaving Scartongarth, the only other option was the possibility of facing Jack. Jimmy was already on the mainland, and Bel could go into service. Chrissie herself would undoubtedly get a job at the herring gutting and rooms in the town. If she was lucky, she might even get a country position.

'Try and get a farm-workers cottage. You know how I can work.'

'I'll do my best for you, Chrissie.'

As she walked away, she experienced a greater loneliness than she had ever known before.

Chapter 25

Elbow deep in soap suds, Chrissie rubbed Peter's dungarees against the ribs of the board. The washing soda stung small rents in her fingers, but she was barely aware of the pain. Charlie's revelations had left her so shaken, she could not think of anything else. The memories of his body, his kindness, his gentle lips, which she had cherished all those years, had been destroyed. Destroyed by his deceit. Destroyed by her own inability to realise how innocent he had been back then. Destroyed by her own foolishness as much as his. Her thoughts were in a turmoil.

All this time, he had been here. And all this time she had accepted she would be damned to hell for Jack's murder, yet he was still alive. Slapping the trousers against the washboard again, she cursed silently. She cursed a lot in her head these days. Lifting her eyes, she looked at the horizon. Jack was out there, somewhere, perhaps on his way back right now. Her stomach roiled. She bit back her sobs but could not stem the tears. Wiping her eyes on the back of her hand, she blew away the suds that landed on her lips, sniffed hard and silently cursed some more.

For so long the memory of the day Charlie had bade her goodbye had been a bittersweet glow in her heart. The joy that had leapt there as he pressed his grandmother's ring into her palm and asked her to marry him. The anticipation of his return. Watching the warships break the horizon on their way to Scapa Flow, sharp reminders of the dangers of war. The heart-stopping minutes after the flag had flown at half-mast over the post office. The searing pain when that same heart was ripped to shreds by the news of his death. One minute she wanted to run to Charlie and fling her arms around him, the next she hated him for what he had put her through. Arguments chased each other round her head as she tried to put herself in his shoes. Had she not kept a secret too? Was she not as bad as him? If she had somehow been so badly disfigured would she have been able to face him? Then she remembered the nights she had longed for his arms, thought of how little he had trusted her that he couldn't give her the choice, and she would hate him again. How could there ever be any future for them now? Yet her eyes were drawn to the house on the hill. In her heart, she knew his suffering was as bad, if not worse, than hers.

'You're going to have a hole in those trousers.'

She had not heard Bel come up behind her.

'Could you hang that washing out for me, pet?' She tried to smile into the worried eyes of her niece.

'You're a big girl now,' she said hurriedly, before Bel could ask again what the matter was. 'I was thinking, it's time I taught you how to deliver a bairn.'

Bel's mouth fell open, her eyes brightened. 'Really? I'd love that. I want to be the howdie when I'm older.' Her voice faltered. 'Help you, I mean,' she finished lamely.

Chrissie gave a slight laugh. 'It's fine, lasgie. Has... I mean have you seen Sanny the Post the day?'

'Aye, a wee while ago. Nothing for us. Were you expecting something?'

'No, no.' Chrissie dreaded another letter. She loved Scartongarth, and the wrench of leaving would be severe. 'I wanted to talk to you about moving to the mainland. There'll be a better chance for Peter as well,' she said.

Bel, pegging out the washing, twisted her head in Chrissie's direction. 'The mainland? What about Scartongarth – Angus?'

'Angus will be fine.'

'We can't leave Scartongarth.'

Chrissie wiped her forehead. 'It was just an idea. But think about it.'

'Why? We're doing fine here.'

'Jimmy's there, and Peter's clever. He needs better schooling. And you could go into service and be home one day a week.'

'I don't want to go into service.'

'Well, maybe you could get a job in a shop or a laundry. There's more opportunities.' She hoped this would satisfy the girl. Peter believed what she told him without question, but Bel watched her with large soulful eyes that looked inward, as if she read the secrets of her heart.

'I don't want to go.' Without another word, Bel began to clip the washing onto the line with a vengeance.

Chrissie said no more. She would bring it up again, at the right time.

During the day, her eyes often turned towards the mainland. The sun, high and bright, danced on the water and a light mist muted the colours of the coastline into soft browns and greens. There was always the fear there would be a sheet on a peat stack or a bonfire on the beach, the sign that someone wanted to come to Raumsey. And the greater fear of whom that someone might be. Today the coastline remained empty. Relieved for now, she turned back to her washing.

Like the lifting of a shadow, her anger towards Charlie softened. He was right, the boy she had known had gone and it was suffering and pain that had twisted his soul and shaped him into someone else. Once she had fallen in love, she failed to acknowledge his immaturity. Since she'd refused to listen when he'd tried to talk about that night, how could she now set the blame at his feet?

The cow's mournful bellow reminded her that it was past milking time. Not having slept until the early hours, her daily chores were piling up before her. How she wished she could talk to the Reverend Charleston and lean on his wisdom and understanding, but he too, had not returned from the war. Word was he had survived and had taken a post in his native Glasgow. The new island minister was older and stricter and far less approachable.

Images of the past drifted like smoke across her mind. Realising she was shaking, she set the milk pail at her feet and the handle clanked against the rim. The air was cooler this evening, though only one pink cloud stretched and feathered its way across the sky.

'We've not seen Angus today. What's wrong?' Bel's accusing voice cut into her thoughts.

Chrissie turned around to find the girl standing in the doorway.

'He's gone to the mainland to look for a place for us.' She pushed a stray wisp of hair away from her face and tucked it behind her ear.

'You've already decided? I can't believe this. Have you told Peter?' Bel's eyes grew so wide that Chrissie could see the darker rim all the way round her pupils.

'No. Please, Bel, trust me. I'll tell him later.'

'What if we don't like the place?'

'Then we won't go.'

'Promise?'

'I promise.' Her fingers tightened. Another lie.

Suddenly Chrissie longed to see Charlie again – she could no longer think of him as Angus. She did not know if they could ever breach the gulf his revelations had put between them, but she did know that there was still a tender place in her heart for the boy she had loved. She could not leave him. If she were to move to the mainland, he had to come too.

***

Charlie didn't hear her come in. He was staring into the fire, but not too near – he never went too near a fire. The memories he had tried to lock in the dark recesses of his mind rose now and then, cramping his stomach and shaking his body. When he returned from the war, Chrissie had tried to persuade him to stay in Scartongarth, but how could he? How could he subject his family to the nights he woke screaming and vomiting as memories of that final battle re-surfaced?

He had fallen asleep in his chair and now sat staring silently into the glowing ash, his arms wrapped round himself, rocking slowly, tears running freely down his cheeks, visions still crowding his mind. He allowed the memories to come, reexamining them, wishing he could relive the past, make things turn out differently. He had let Chrissie down with his weak cowardliness, but worse than that, the same cowardliness had caused his own brother's death.

'Charlie.'

Her voice startled him, and for a moment his mind whirled, disoriented. Embarrassed by his tears, he dashed his hand across his cheeks. He had always been able to hide these moments of raw anguish from her before.

'Chrissie.' He stood up, and saw her through a film of moisture. The dislocated images from a moment before fragmented and dissipated like mist in the sunlight. He wiped the sweat from his brow and rose.

She counted each breath as he stood before her. In such a short space of time he seemed diminished, shrunk beneath his clothes. He held his head at an angle so that his undamaged cheek was presented to her. His eyes held hers, almost shyly. For a heartbeat they stood like that, the air between them thick with unspoken words which should have been said long ago.

'Are you all right?' she asked finally.

His gaze slipped to the floor. 'I haven't slept. I'm so sorry, Chrissie.'

Taking a step towards him, she held out her hand. 'I don't blame you – not in my heart. I know what you did was for me. You're not the way you were, but then neither am I.'

In his vulnerable state, her kind words unleashed all the trapped emotion inside him. In one swift movement, he grabbed her and buried his face into her shoulder. Unable to stop himself, his whole body shook as he fought the urge to cry out loud.

She held him and rocked with him, until she too was weeping. 'It's fine. We can go to the mainland, all of us. I love Scartongarth, but it's better we're well away from Jack.'

'Thank God you came. And thank you for the offer, but I can never live in the same house as anyone else – I would keep them awake – night after night.'

Her mouth was dry. 'We've both made mistakes,' she said. 'But I don't want to lose you as a friend. We've been through too much.'

'I'll make us a tea.' He rubbed his hands up and down her arms, then turned to swing the kettle over the flames. She sat on the edge of a chair, fingers clutching at her skirt. 'You've not been eating properly.'

He took a seat opposite her. He reached out his hand towards hers, then drew back, colour creeping into his face where there had had only been pallor before. 'Tea'll not take long.' He glanced at the fire. One knee jerked.

Remembering how nervous he was around naked flames, she knelt beside him. 'Charlie,' she said and traced her finger along his damaged jaw. 'Oh Charlie.' And then she was in his arms, and the years fell away and for one brief moment in time, she was young again.

'Tell me,' she whispered. 'Tell me about Angus.'

He shook his head.

'I know you were with him – when it happened.'

Charlie pulled away from her and wiped his face. 'I saw bodies mutilated, torn apart – I still see them every time I close my eyes. How can I talk about it?'

'Maybe it would help.'

'I'm sorry,' he said. 'Sorry you had to see me like this. Sorry I lied.' His body began to shake. 'Please go, I've lived through this before.' The shake grew worse. 'I... don't... want... you... to see... me . ., . like this.'

Chrissie wrapped her arms around him. 'No, I'll stay. You don't have to tell me anything. I'll make the tea.'

Later, when Charlie's tremble had stopped and his breath no longer rattled itself from his chest, when night had squeezed out the last of the daylight and they pressed together on the battered couch, he felt able to speak again. He would tell her what she wanted to know. He owed her that much.

'Angus was running in front of me when the second torpedo struck the ship. I was hurt, badly. If only I'd stayed quiet. I knew he should run – get out of danger, but I was so afraid. I called out to him. He could have saved himself, but he didn't. He stopped. He turned. I saw his face, twisted with the same fear I felt, but he came back – back to save me. He pulled me to my feet. He dragged me over his shoulder and then he tripped. We fell onto the deck. The ship was listing badly. I rolled away – I couldn't stop myself. And then the mast came down and....' His voice faltered. For a moment he couldn't go on. But he had to – had to tell her now – now that he had begun. 'It struck him – and I... I could do nothing. It was... it was hot – so hot and I crawled away. I heard him scream and the flames... the flames were all around him.' Charlie began to shake again as the images drifted across his mind like smoke. 'But I didn't go back.' His voice became strong again. '*You* know I'm Charlie.' He set his hand on his heart, 'But in here I'm both of us. I *want* to be both of us.' He covered his face with his hands.

'What could you do? You were injured yourself.'

'If I... I hadn't called to him... he would still be alive.'

'And you would be dead. He would be the one in torment now.'

He squeezed her hand. 'I wouldn't wish that on him.' For a long time he said nothing more.

Finally, he found his voice. 'I'll get you a place, then I'll come back. I have to face Jack, finish this, so you can return to your old home.' Aye, he would give up his own life gladly, if that's what it took, to compensate for all that was wrong.

'No. Jack must never know you are alive. We can make a new life away from here – as soon as possible.'

'I'll go tomorrow, on the early mail boat.' He wouldn't argue now, but he would return. He had to.

'Thank you.' She kissed his scars. 'I'll have to go now, the bairns will be wondering where I am. I'll see you when you get back.' With that she rose and left.

After she had gone, he stood looking at the firth for a long time. In the distance the restless water shifted and swelled against the shore, a sound that was as much part of him as his heartbeat. Even with his eyes closed, even while lying in bed he could guess the state of the firth, the direction and strength of the wind. And he knew Chrissie felt the same. Once he found a safe haven for her, he would return to Scartongarth, he would face Jack if he had to. He had sworn to protect Chrissie, and he would, with his life. That night, Charlie's nightmares did not return.

Part Three

Chapter 26

On the other side of the Atlantic, inside Brooklyn's City Prison, in a stinking black cell with no light except that offered by an unsteady candle, a man sat alone. The air beyond the door was filled with the clanking of iron chains; rattling bars, screams, sobs, curses and the steady tramp of the warden's heavy boots. More footsteps. Doors opened and slammed shut. Shouts from the guards. Booted feet stopped outside his cell, chains rattled, a click of metal against metal, a key turned and the door opened. The bulk of two wardens blocked the shaft of light which fell across the floor. The man did not raise his eyes – did not object when an iron band was placed around his ankle. His hands clenched into slow fists. His eyelids pressed shut.

'Yo are one lucky bastard,' said the warden. 'Yo to be shipped to Georgia. Hard labour on the railroads. Why the hell they don' have enough damn convicts of their own sure beats me.'

Outside, a guard chained him to a row of pale faced men, dressed like himself in black and white striped uniforms and linked together ankle to ankle. They blinked, rubbed their eyes and squinted at the sky. Prison guards with rifles swore at them and shoved them towards the paddy wagon, a black vehicle without windows. A prisoner, who called himself One Lung, turned to the man. With a thick Irish brogue he said, 'Told you the Gophers got fucking strings to pull, know what I mean?'

'When you said they'd get us out, I didn't think you meant to a bloody chain gang,' the man hissed.

'Sure, and we'll not be going far. I'm an important man to the Gophers, so I am.'

'No talking,' the guard shouted, striding towards them. He prodded One Lung with the barrel of his rifle. The prisoner grinned, baring his rotting teeth to the sun.

Once the last man stumbled inside the van, the door slammed and a bolt clicked into place. The prison guard slapped the flat of his hand against the side of the Paddy Wagon and gave thumbs up to the two men in the cab. They drove south, crossing the Brooklyn Bridge and towards the North River. Suddenly the Paddy Wagon came to an abrupt halt. The men in the dark airless interior fell against each other and swore.

A horse and cart stood sideways across the road. The wheel had broken on the cart and a load of potatoes had rolled into the street. Ragged children loaded them into cans and buckets; women carried them in their aprons, basins, or bare hands. All traffic came to a standstill.

The guard cursed, leaned out of the window and yelled, 'Get the road clear.'

There was shouting and the crack of gunfire; the driver slumped and fell over the steering wheel. The other guard reached for his gun, but before his hand could close around the handle, the cold steel of a pistol pressed against his temple. He immediately raised his hands. Sweat poured down his cheeks. Two men with black scarves around their lower faces and wielding handguns, indicated to him to get out. One of them hit him hard with the butt of his revolver, knocking him unconscious. The van rocked as the other man dragged the body of the driver from the vehicle. The masked men climbed into the cab, turned the van and drove towards Manhattan. Eventually it stopped. The back door burst open and the prisoner who called himself One Lung laughed. 'No fucking jail'll hold a Gopher.'

One of the masked men unlocked One Lung's ankle cuffs. 'Run, Marty has a motor and a change of togs.' He tossed the key to another prisoner. 'You guys are on your own.'

No spectators gathered. Passers-by averted their eyes or made for the safety of alleys.

It was just another day in Hell's Kitchen.

***

Dizzy with a sense of freedom, the man walked past the corner of Forty-Second Street, mid-town Manhattan. Clothes he had stolen from a terrified woman on her way to the washhouse hung loose on his skeletal frame. The wind from the East River was sharp and he closed his eyes, his chest rising. Finally, with a shaking hand, he scratched his stubbled head, reached into his pocket, brought out a slip of paper which he studied, folded and replaced. His eyes narrowed and darted to either side before he started to walk. The streets were a hubbub of noise, a series of odours, a myriad of coloured billboards.

Shrill-voiced mothers shrieked at raucous children playing in the streets, occasional motor cars and horse-drawn carriages trundled on the cobbles, the distant drone of sea-going liners called their departure, and vendors shouted their wares. Shops signs above the doors proclaimed their produce; McGinty's biscuit factory; Kean & sons bakery; Ruckle Brothers, makers of fine chocolate. The scents were sweet and cloying.

The man had tasted chocolate once when he was a child. A sailor in a striped shirt and trousers that barely came below the knee had given it to him. He remembered him as a pretty man who had been rescued from a shipwreck with others who were dressed just the same.

As he walked on, a different smell filled the air. Worse than the cat piss which permeated the lanes; worse than the unwashed bodies surging around him, worse than the human waste as children squatted wherever they chose, worse than all of that – the stench of death. He closed his lids and shuddered. When he opened them, he was confronted with pale eyes in a grime encrusted face; a mass of bones, skin and rags; long matted hair, grey and greasy; clothes that hung loosely and was more hole than cloth.

'Ah, ain't it terrible tho.' The tramp's face was meaner than his own, and he smelt as bad as anything the streets had to offer. 'It's the slaughter houses; we get the whiff of them when the wind from Jersey comes in.

'Whot's yo name, sonny? Yo sure look like yo need a little guidance.'

The man blinked and looked around, confused. 'Where is this place?'

'They call it Hell's Kitchen. Story goes two patrol men came drivin' through, first time for the young un. He says, "This place sure is hell."

"Oh no," says his partner, "This is worse than hell – this is Hell's Kitchen." Name sorta' stuck after that. Spread through the streets faster than rats. Yo come with me, sonny, I see yo fed. What did yo say yo name was?'

The man turned his eyes skyward, searching his brain. 'Jack Reid. Jack Reid from Raumsey. That's who I am. Yes, that is who I am.'

The morning light found Jack huddled in an alleyway sharing a space with the tramp. Around them lay crumpled newspapers proclaiming post-war dramas and the remnants of food taken from trash-cans behind eating-houses the night before. Food for which they had to compete with confident rats.

Jack stood up and flexed his muscles. The rats scattered. He put up the collar of his jacket and hunched his shoulders against a biting wind.

'Where do the Gophers meet up?' he asked.

The tramp opened rheumy eyes; a startled expression crossed his face. 'Yo shore don' wanna' find em Gophers, Sonny. Them's bad news, them is.' He shook his head. 'Yo wanna make some dough, yo go dockside.' With a grimy finger, he indicated a street stirring with sorry life.

Eyes turned upward, Jack sniffed the air like a predator. He started to walk again, walking to where the wind brought the salt of the sea to his nostrils. And when the sun finally managed to cast straggling rays between black tenements, he was still walking.

The following evening, Jack Reid walked along the darkened streets, his footsteps echoing from the tall buildings which rose on either side pointing into the night like accusing fingers. It was cold spring and his worn jacket offered little protection. The gutters were full of trash, and yesterday's newspapers lifted and wrapped themselves round his ankles. From black alleys, eyes hungrier than his own followed his progress. Bunches of youths stood in corners, watching him like marauding wolves.

The sound of someone sobbing periodically drifted on the wind. Somewhere a baby cried and the cries spread into the air. A coarse male voice swore, a woman screamed and the street was silent again. Night-lights that worked were few and windows were blank. Jack walked by the rays of a hazy moon and occasional flares from fires built in corners around which men and women with skeletal faces and threadbare clothes huddled. They did not raise their heads as he passed.

Then he came upon a maze of streets that were full of life and noise. Everywhere there were men with handcarts, and these carts sported a variety of goods – fish, meat, fabric, vegetables, pots and pans. He stopped and stared. His stomach rumbled.

Up a dark alleyway, a queue snaked its way into a dusty building. They stood in ragged clothes, heads hanging, hopelessness in their eyes. Jack stopped at the edge of the queue. 'What is this?' he asked.

The old timer before him turned. 'A mission, son. A place for people who have no home. Agree to be saved and you'll get a bench for the night.'

Inside a preacher was conducting a service. 'Come up you sinners,' he screamed, thumping his fist on the pulpit. 'Come and be saved.' A few stragglers walked forward. Jack joined them. He would do anything to assuage the ache of an empty belly.

'Do you accept the Lord Jesus as your saviour?' asked the preacher.

'I do,' whispered Jack through a hoarse throat.

The preacher put his hand on Jack's head. 'The Lord be praised,' he said.

A woman dressed in a dirty white robe handed him a bowl and indicated he should join another queue. Two women with red faces and coarse hands ladled liquid, spotted with sparse vegetables, into the bowls and gave each man a crust of bread. 'You can sleep on the benches over there,' they repeated from time to time like a monotone.

Jack found a space on a bench and drank the soup that warmed his insides and tasted surprisingly good. A weasel faced man who smelt of raw sewage sat next to him, sucked his pottage with noisy gulps, wiped his mouth on the back of his hand, belched loudly and turned his rat-eyes to Jack. 'Ain't seen you here afore,' he said.

Jack finished his soup by tipping the bowl up until not one drop remained. 'I need work. I need money to get home.'

'The docks,' someone said.

'Been there. They told me come back tomorrow.'

Weasel Face laughed showing rotting stumps where his teeth should have been. 'Sure, yo'll get work tomorrow. Where yo think half these men go every day? Yo think they don' wanna work. And if yo do get on, for every dime yo make, yo pay the gangers half, just for getting yo the job. One man refused to pay and he got beaten plum near to death. Yo's a fine young man, strength in them arms.' He set a dirt-ingrained hand on Jack's bicep and squeezed. Jack tensed and moved slightly away, keeping his eyes on the pock marked face before him.

'Yo'd sure make money fighting. I kin do that fer yo, I kin fix it up.' Weasel Face grinned again.

Jack stared at the thirsty eyes and nodded slowly. 'Oh yes, I can fight.'

He slept on the hard wooden bench in spite of the cold, the moans, the coughs, the sobs and the curses around him. In the morning, an elderly woman with a hard face handed him a small bowl of gruel and a cup of thin coffee. There was nowhere to wash, but a wooden lean-to provided the means for the sorry souls to relieve themselves.

'Come with me brother,' said the weasel faced man from last night. Jack followed him into the thick morning air and along the street past woody storefronts with various goods on display. Alessandro's fruit and vegetables; Claudio's meats, whose window boasted the carcasses of slaughtered chickens and a pig's head; wooden stands filled with second-hand clothing, an organ grinder with a monkey.

'Come, come.' Weasel Face walked quickly now, leading the way with a jerky uneven gate. He turned sharply up an alleyway and paused at an open doorway. Male voices, shouting and cheering, filled the dank air that flowed from the interior.

'Inside, inside.' Weasel Face appeared agitated, bouncing from one foot to the other as he pushed Jack into jostling crowd. Jack struggled to see through the blue haze of smoke and over the heads that bobbed constantly across his line of vision. All eyes trained on two men who struggled with each other in a makeshift rope ring, their bodies glistened with sweat, their faces bloodied. They grunted and snorted as they fought to remain upright. One of the fighters dealt an uppercut to the other's nose. There was a cracking of bone and blood spurted into the air. The crowd cheered as broken-nose lurched forward, collapsed onto the ground, groaned and lay still. Wads of notes exchanged hands. Someone leapt into the ring and held up the victor's arm. 'Anyone else wanna chance?' he shouted, as the defeated fighter was hauled away, still not moving. 'Beat the champion and win the pot!'

Bundles of notes waved above heads. The victor's evil eyes roamed the crowd. Weasel Face grabbed Jack's hand and held it into the air. 'My man will, my man will,' he shouted, and pushed Jack forward.

The crowd laughed as Jack, thin and wiry, half the size of the champion climbed over the ropes. They cheered and placed bets. Jack turned his head, saw the slack lips and greedy eyes, smelt the thick male smell. They were laughing at him. Hate rose from him like steam.

The bell rang. Jack crouched and faced his opponent who simply grinned and flexed his muscles. The fighters circled each other, the champion still grinning. Suddenly he shot out a fist. Jack sidestepped, ducking as he did so and the blow struck air, the dynamism of it carrying the champion forward. The crowd laughed. Jack clasped his hands together and brought them down on the back of the champion's head with all the force of his hate and frustration. The champion staggered and fell face first onto the ground. With a roar like a bull, he was on his feet in an instant, the smile gone from his face. His eyes closed to slits and he drew his lips over his teeth in a snarl. Ducking low, he charged at Jack's torso, but Jack had learned a lot in prison. He was light on his feet, and his reflexes were quick. The champion rushed past him and went headlong into the ropes, pulling the makeshift ring down around him. He rose, shook his head, bellowed loud enough to drown the cheers and attacked again, swinging his arms in every direction.

In his head, Jack was back in the playground, larger boys taunting him, pushing him, until he learned to fight, to avoid the blows, to strike when least expected and where it could do most harm. In prison, his muscles had hardened and his instinct for survival had turned into an instinct to kill. Now before him he saw the epitome of his pain as the cheers and catcalls faded in a red haze of fury. He continued to dance around his opponent, staying just out of reach of the lashing fists. Finally, when the champion paused to take a breath, Jack struck, hitting his adversary in the right eye, and he received a crippling blow to his own gut. He collapsed to the ground gasping for air. The champion laughed and raised both hands clasped together, bringing them down towards the back of Jack's head in a blow, which, had it found its mark, would have broken his neck. Jack twirled sideways grabbing the other's leg as he did so. The champion staggered, and before he could regain his balance, Jack twisted the leg. The champion gave a howl of rage and fell onto the canvas. Quickly, Jack jumped to his knees and punched the other face. The champion's eyes swelled, his nose spurted blood; nevertheless, he struggled to his feet.

Jack rose beneath him, his head scraping against the champion's teeth and striking the underside of the man's nose with enough force to drive the bone into the brain. The man collapsed on the ground. Jack continued to beat him until many hands pulled him away.

Fists shook in the air. Men shouted. Jack fought the red mist, shaking as he gained control. His eyes found Weasel Face. The skinny hands snatched at wads of notes passed his way. Grinning inanely, the little man turned and disappeared through the entrance.

'Christ!' spluttered Jack, spitting blood, and dove through the crowd, elbowing and kicking his way to the door.

The hobbling gate of the weasel-faced man was no match for the speed of Jack's adrenalin fuelled fury. He caught the runt easily and slammed him against a wall.

'That's my money. I won it,' hissed Jack.

'I was gonna give yo yor share, I shore was, I needed to get away from those dogs.' The man trembled and stuck out a shaking hand. 'Here, here,' he said, 'We'll go half, half.'

'No.' With one hand Jack grabbed the miserable excuse for life around the throat and snatched the fistful of notes with the other. 'You were going to give me nothing.' He tightened his grip, squeezing the neck until the eyes bulged, the face turned blue, and the tongue protruded. The man's legs kicked, his scrabbling hands fell limp, and the body slumped. Jack released him, and he dropped to the sidewalk.

Jack walked away, only then feeling the pain of his injuries. Behind him, heavy footsteps echoed his own. He stopped and turned, a fist clenched, ready to defend what he believed was his. A small fat figure with greased back hair and a paunch that hung over his wrinkled trousers held up his hands in surrender.

'You want the same?' asked Jack drawing back his fist.

'No, No,' said the fat man. 'I am Pablo. You come with me. Pablo weel help you make beeg money.' He stuck out a sweaty, pudgy hand. Jack looked at it then back at Pablo.

He had been hurt worse than he thought and needed to lie down. The hand jabbed towards him again and Pablo nodded. Jack shook the hand, but he swayed on his feet.

'If you try to double cross me I'll kill you.'

'No worries, no worries,' said the fat man. 'Come with me, I have a place you can stay.' He took Jack's arm and led him down the street.

Chapter 27

The crowd cheered, their bodies pressing forward, the smell of sweat and blood filling the smoky air. Jack licked his lips and tasted his own blood. His opponent was bigger than he was, and muscular, with a nose which had been broken so often it lay flattened against his cheek. A swelling closed one eye, a bloody gash stretched from his lip to his nostril.

Jack was thin but agile and hate filled him like a furnace. In the last few weeks, he had become skilled at bare knuckle fighting and was now a firm favourite to win. Facing each other, the boxers moved in a slow circle, fists raised, upper torsos bare and glistening with sweat. The opponent's fist shot out and Jack sidestepped, blocked the blow with his forearm and lifted his head so that the top of his skull made contact with what remained of the other's nose. Blood spurted into the air. His other fist caught the opponent in the stomach. He staggered back. The crowd roared. Jack used both fists to rain blows on the other man before he could regain his balance. And he did not stop, even when the challenger lay unconscious on the ground.

The jeering crowd surrounded him. Money changed hands. Cigars flared to life.

Finally, exhausted, Jack stood up and gasped for air. Someone pushed a wad of notes into his hand. A towel blotted his face. He was led outside and handed his jacket and shirt. Leaning against the wall, he regained his breath. He counted the money in his hand – twenty dollars – a fortune.

'I set up a fight Friday night,' said a smiling Pablo. 'We make much money,'

Jack shook his head to clear it. 'No more,' he said. 'I have enough.'

'No, no,' Pablo grabbed his arm. 'This ees your winnings. Find a hotel and a whore for the night. We talk – tomorrow.'

'The whores I want don't come cheap.'

Pablo handed him another note.

Jack held out his hand. 'I need more. Much more. Call it an advance.'

Pablo peeled off another few notes. 'I weel have this money back next fight, no?'

Jack had waited long enough. It was time to go home. 'I need more money. Give me a hundred. A loan. You know I can win it back within a week.'

'No, no, this ees too much. Why you need this much money?'

'If you won't give it to me there are other ways I can get it.' He pushed himself from the wall and made to leave.

Pablo grabbed his arm. 'If I give you this money, you will fight every night for a week?'

'Yes.'

'And you will stay with me – not go near Gophers?'

'I said I would.'

'If you try to be smart arse – I will keel you.'

'I don't doubt it.'

Pablo dug deep in his pocket and counted out some more bills. After Jack had pocketed the money, Pablo made a cutting motion across his own throat with the side of his hand.

'Every night, Pablo – set it up.' He staggered off into the night. He did not doubt for a moment that Pablo would carry out his threat.

***

Next morning at Hoboken Harbor, New York, Jack walked along the quay as he had done every day for a month. The air was thick with the reek of fish. Horns sounded out in the deeper water, their sources yet unseen. In the air, gulls yelped as they did the world over.

Jack stopped, looked towards the Statue of Liberty and breathed deeply. Now that he had money in his pockets and food in his belly, his face was less gaunt. Although the weather was growing warmer, he turned up the collar of the greatcoat he had recently bought. The pockets were deep. He needed deep pockets.

His head turned often towards the vessels anchored in the bay. He began to walk again, now and then stopping and speaking to one of the stevedores who were unloading freight and staring at them darkly when they shook their heads.

He walked up to an unshaven man wearing a peaked cap and a captain's uniform. 'I need a passage to Scotland,' he said. It was a phrase he had repeated often. 'I heard you were looking for willing seamen.'

The unshaven man eyed him. 'Irish?' he asked.

'Scottish,' replied Jack.

The captain shrugged. 'You sound all the same to me. Now why would you want to leave this land of opportunity?' He laughed as if he had said something funny.

'Can you take me or no?' Jack did not laugh.

I'm going to Liverpool, but I have a full crew.' The captain turned away.

Jack cursed and followed him. In his pocket he fingered the handle of a knife. 'I have money, I can pay.'

The captain stopped and eyed him suspiciously. 'I don't take passengers,' he said. 'If you have money, there are passenger ships. But the law is checking all the outlets – for escaped convicts they tell me.'

'Do I look like an escaped convict?' Jack spat on the ground. From Liverpool he would have been able to find his way to Yarmouth and from there it would be easy enough to join a herring fleet from the north. It would mean not getting back to Raumsey until the end of the season, but he could wait. He had already waited fifteen long years.

'I want to work. I'm a seaman – and I'm tired of this land of opportunity as you call it – that's all. Call the law if you want. I've done nothing wrong.' His face was taut, every muscle strained against expression of any kind. His eyes stared straight into the captain's. A muscle twitched along the side of his face.

'What do I want with the law? It's nothing to me what you do. I do not need another crew member.' The captain headed back to his ship.

Jack waited in the shadows until darkness and watched as the crew left the ship and headed into the back streets and down an alley. Ducking into doorways, he followed. The men talked loudly of bordellos and speakeasies and did not glance over their shoulders once. Finally they stopped outside a door and banged on it three times. The door opened and a shaft of pale smoke-infused light fell across the street. Music drifted through the air. The sailors disappeared into the dim interior. When the door shut, all was quiet once more. Jack settled in the shelter of a doorway, folded his arms across his chest and waited. He had become adept at waiting.

It was after midnight when the crew re-emerged somewhat inebriated and made their unsteady way back to the ship. Jack checked the string and cloth he carried in his pocket and followed a short distance behind. A sailor stopped to relieve himself. As he buttoned up his flies, Jack stepped up behind him. In one deft move, he had a hand over the sailor's mouth and the blade of the knife pressed against his throat.

'I'll no' kill a fellow seaman as long as you do as you're told,' he hissed. Dragging the sailor, who was either too drunk or too scared to put up a fight, into an even smaller alleyway, he bound and gagged him. 'If I see you near the docks within the next day, I promise to kill you.' Then he bashed the sailor's head against the wall, hard enough to leave him unconscious but not dead and he hid the body behind a stack of trash cans and piled debris.

Back at the tenement in Thirty-Sixth Street where he lodged, Jack climbed the stairs, his boots falling heavily on the scarred wooden flooring. It was dark and muggy here and the smell of urine was heavy in the air. These six storey buildings, constructed more than twenty years before by unscrupulous builders using rotten lathe, mortar and plaster mixed with sawdust, were already beginning to crumble. A small, dark-skinned kid dressed in rags held out his grubby hand as he did every night. No words had ever passed between them, but in the dark eyes, Jack recognised a pain that reflected his own. He tossed a coin; the boy grabbed it and grinned his thanks.

Five floors up, he lifted his fist and banged twice on a heavy oak door. It opened almost immediately. Mae, the woman with whom Pablo had provided him, stood back to allow him to enter. Her black hair reached past her waist and her slightly slanting eyes, deep and hollow, fixed only on his feet. Her simple shift dress hung loosely as if she had no shape nor substance beneath. A yellowing bruise ran the length of her cheek. Jack pushed past her. She shut the door and bolted it.

'Today you have luck?' she asked, her voice small and slightly wavering.

He did not speak. Thrusting a stack of newspapers out of his way, he dropped onto the iron bed which sat against one corner, and the springs complained under his weight. He stretched out and stared at the cracked plaster on the ceiling. A cockroach wound its way up the wall among the splattered corpses of its mates. Sounds drifted from the street below; shouts from a man selling pies, music from a grinding organ, yells of children and the clatter as they kicked a tin can in the street; the occasional motor car; the clomp of horses hooves and the rattle of iron clad wheels against the paving; the yelp of a dog. He hungered for the sounds of bleating sheep, of sobbing seals and the dash of surf against a familiar shore. Soon, he told himself. Soon.

Barefooted, the woman moved silently to the stove and began to prepare food. Bread with slices of dried beef. Jack rose and ate, washing the food down with warm beer. He wiped his mouth on the back of his hand and pulled the wad of notes from his pocket. Slowly he unfolded them and flicked through. He peeled off a ten-dollar bill and set it on the chest of drawers by the bed. The woman's eyes grew round but she did not move to touch the note. 'All that money,' she whispered.

'Pablo's.'

Her hands shook as she twined them together. 'He will kill you,' she whispered.

'He won't find me. You've been good to me, Mae, but after tonight you won't see me again. I'm going home. Hide the money. When Pablo comes – you know nothing.'

She visibly trembled. 'Then he will kill *me*,' she said.

Jack looked at her. So small and slight, she might have been a child if not for the lines already creasing her forehead and radiating like fine spider webs from the corners of her eyes. He filled his chest with air and let it escape slowly. Peeling off another couple of notes he thrust them at her. 'Take this and get out of New York. And that kid, the one who hangs about on the stairs, take him with you.' He strode out of the door.

Morning found Jack sitting by the dockside against a crate, a cigarette dangling between his lips. He watched as the captain he had spoken to the day before paced the quayside. Finally, he rose and walked over. 'You look like a man troubled,' Jack said.

The captain narrowed his eyes and spoke with reluctance in his voice. 'One of my crew hasn't returned. I can't wait any longer. If you still want a berth the job is yours, but we sail within the hour.'

Jack saluted. 'Yessir,' he said. 'I can come now, for I've nothing except what you see before you.' He threw the cigarette to the ground and twisted the sole of his boot on the glowing ash.

Chapter 28

A week later a bunch of sailors stood around the bar of the Pig's Ear dockside bar in Birkenhead. They had not long disembarked and the smell of the sea still clung to their clothes. Thirsty for a drop of alcohol they downed pint after pint and spoke about their recent voyage.

The latest member of the crew stood apart from the rest. He threw his whisky back. His dark eyes flashed around the bar room.

'You're a good worker,' said one of the crew. 'Like as not the capt'n will sign you up for another trip.'

Jack had no desire to socialise. He shook his head and set the empty glass on the bar. 'How do I get to Yarmouth?' he asked the heavy set barman.

'Ee, lad, yew's at the wrong side of the country. The barman leaned across and looked at him. 'Yew's not from these parts, then?'

'I need to get to Yarmouth,' Jack repeated without a smile.

'Ah, the ferries across the Mersey will be finished for the night. If yew hurries, yew might catch a train to Liverpool. Go west a'ways and stick close to the shore. Yew'll not miss the station.'

Without another word Jack walked from the public house and into the damp air. A low fog rose from the sea and horns like mournful banshees announced the arrival of vessels from foreign shores.

Inside the public house one crew member turned to another. 'I'm glad he's gone. He were a right strange bastard and no mistake.' There was a murmur of agreement from the others.

Outside, Jack walked on beneath the light of a faded moon. The wind blew sharp carrying dampness and the scent of fish and brine. The water lapped against the walls of the walkway and before him, in the distance, he could see the new railway bridge over the river Mersey.

***

Early morning found Jack in Yarmouth harbour watching the crans of herring being unloaded. Gulls circled above, their cries mingling with the sounds of industry. Wheels over cobblestones; warning shouts, barking dogs, the clomp of horses hooves and the ring of the coopers' hammers as they shaped the iron hoops to go round the barrels. He walked past the rows of herring gutters. Sunlight flashed on the steel of blood-speckled knives that sliced into the smooth underbellies of the fish, bandaged fingers ripping out the glistening innards and tossing the empty bodies into a large trough. Silvery scale-dotted hands moved fast and accurate. The unfamiliar sting of tears clouded Jack's eyes, as the sounds stirred almost forgotten memories. He dashed them away, embarrassed by their presence. He was so close to home now, he could taste it in the air.

The lassies sang as they worked, told stories and laughed. Only one girl noticed him. She stopped singing. Her mouth fell open and her knife slipped from her hands, and made an empty, tinny sound as it hit the cobbles beneath her feet.

'My goodness, Ettie,' said her workmate. 'You look as if you've seen a ghost.'

The man barely glanced her way and walked on. For the first time since leaving New York Prison, a smile flitted across his face.

The girl called Ettie bent to retrieve her gutting knife. 'I think I did,' she said.

He walked past the boats with tall sails and the newer boats – the steam drifters. He walked across the cobbles, dodging through the busy crowded pier, looking at the names of each boat. Finally he stopped. Another fisherman walked towards him, stared and scratched his head.

'By all that's holy,' whispered the fisherman, 'Jack Reid.'

Chapter 29

Peter had finished feeding the calf when a figure he did not recognise appeared over the high rigs; tall and lean, a dark silhouette against the low sun. The boy straightened, wiped his hands on his dungarees and screwed up his eyes in order to see better. The day was dying, and the wind was still. Gulls shrieked their defiance from the roof of Scartongarth and the ocean moved slowly up the shore, splashed against the sea-wall and rattled the shingle as it retreated.

It was unusual for a stranger to walk the fields of Raumsey. He was coming through the field of corn stooks towards Scartongarth. As he drew near, he began to take form. Deep furrows scarred his forehead and either side of his mouth. Hair, black as night, was streaked with grey. But his eyes, glitter-brown and edged with pain, intrigued Peter most. The hens scattered before him. The dog growled and ran into the house.

'Jimmy?' The man swung the haversack from his back and set it on the ground.

'No. Jimmy's away to the mainland to learn a trade. I'm Peter.'

'Peter?'

'Aye. Chrissie's my mam.' It seemed this man must know the family.

The man's eyes popped open. 'And who's your Dad?' His voice was suddenly tense. Frighteningly so. 'Would your dad's name be Charlie?'

'No. My dad drowned at sea long ago.'

The man's head bent a little to one side. 'And what was his name – this dad who drowned at sea?'

'Jack Reid.' Peter decided he did not care much for this stranger with the glittery eyes and hard voice. 'Who are you?' The calf butted Peter's legs, looking for more food. He shooed him away.

The man ran his tongue over his lips and sucked in a noisy breath. He cupped Peter's face in his hand and turned the head one way and then the other.

'How old are you, boy?'

Peter jerked away. 'I'm thirteen.' His cheeks hurt where the fingers of steel had grabbed him.

'When's your birthday?'

'Fourteenth of July.' What business was it of his? He didn't want to answer any more questions, but had been brought up to be polite to his elders. He raised his eyes to the distant harvest fields where his mother worked, hoping she would stop, look towards home and see this stranger. But only unrecognisable figures, dark with distance, bent and toiled.

'I, my fine lad, am Jack Reid.'

The shock of the man's words tightened his chest. 'You... you're my dad?' He couldn't be. His dad was lost at sea.

The man who called himself Jack Reid was quiet for a minute. Peter felt the weight of his eyes as they bore into him.

'Did they ever find the body of this man who drowned?

Peter shook his head. Words were beyond him.

The man circled Peter. 'You look nothing like me, but then I look nothing like my dad.' His words did not seem to be directed to Peter, but more of a thought that had escaped from between his lips. Peter shrank against the wall, the solidity of it holding him in its trap. 'You're my dad?' His heart raced; his skin prickled. This man was not the father he had conjured in his imagination. 'I don't believe you,' he said.

Without answering, Jack lifted his eyes and looked around the bay. He took a deep breath. 'I *am* Jack Reid.'

In that moment, Peter's fantasy of his father crumbled into the earth. He had imagined his dad to be fair with an open, honest face. Someone who looked like the rest of the family. He glanced again at the fields, wishing his mam would come home early.

'Does Chrissie have another man now?' Jack asked.

Peter shook his head. His heart thumped against his ribs. He always hoped his dad would come back one day; that he had not drowned after all; that he would be able to meet him. But this stranger scared him. Could it be true? Could this really be his dad? 'Where... have you been?'

'You don't want to hear about where I've been.' Jack rubbed his chin. 'Where is Chrissie?'

'She's at the hay.'

A clink of pans startled through the open door of Scartongarth. Jack's head jerked round.

'That's Bel,' said Peter.

'Bel? Jamsie's girl? How old is she now?'

'Sixteen.'

'Ah yes, she would be. Come on, I could do with a cup o' tea.' Jack gave a sharp laugh. 'They can't make tea in America.' He set his hand on the boy's shoulder and they walked into the house.

Peter's initial shock slowly evaporated and in its place a glow grew with each step. The hand on his shoulder no longer felt threatening but warm and firm. By the time they reached the kitchen door, excitement had begun to dribble into his veins. Was this really his dad come home?

'Bel, Bel, my dad's come home. He wasn't drowned.'

Turning from where she stood over the stove, Bel gasped. Her chin fell. 'Uncle Jack?'

'Yes, my dad,' said Peter. 'He didn't drown.'

The hand on the lad's shoulder tightened reassuringly. 'Charlie – is he still here?'

'He was killed in the war. Angus lives in Mam's house.' Peter had been aware of Chrissie's relationship with Charlie, but he instinctively knew he must keep this quiet. There was something in his dad's voice when he said Charlie's name – something scary.

'Charlie dead. Does Chrissie live with Angus, then?'

'We live here,' said Peter quickly, gazing up at the man, absorbing his features, not quite believing who he was seeing.

'And your granny and granda'?'

'In the graveyard.'

'I should have guessed.' Jack walked round the room and stopped by the fireplace to finger the worn strop where the men sharpened their razors. 'It's still here. Many a time I had this across my backside.' He gave a bitter laugh, his shoulders shook and he covered his face with his hands.

Peter glanced at Bel. She stood as if in shock, a pan still held in one hand. He felt the embarrassing sting of tears, yet his eyes were drawn back to Jack. He studied the shaking shoulders, the hands. Scarred knuckles; fat wormy veins beneath skin; fingers sprouting hairs black as spider legs; black as the ridges beneath the nails. This man was the dad he believed dead. The dad he dreamed about, imagined, longed for, made flesh. A rush of sympathy filled him up. He reached out and touched Jack's arm. 'Dad,' he said.

Jack grasped the boy's hand. Peter realised he had not been crying as he first thought. He was laughing – a joyless, soundless laugh. 'A son,' he said. 'I've got a son.' His Adam's apple bobbed in his throat. He picked up the stocky thirteen year old as if he weighed nothing at all and swung him round and finished the swing with a coarse hug.

Stubble scoured Peter's face and he breathed in the scent of tobacco and sweat. It was really happening. He was being held in his father's arms and it felt good. Finally Jack released him, dashed his hand across his own eyes and turned to Bel. 'What did Chrissie tell you about me?'

'Nothing. She never spoke about you.' Bel set the pan on the stove and grabbed a tea-towel. A shadow passed across Jack's face. A frisson of unease clouded Peter's joy.

Jack sat down and leaned back, balancing his chair on two legs. 'She'll be in for a grand surprise when she returns, then, won't she?' The bite in his voice deepened Peter's unease.

Bel stirred the tea in the pot, filled his cup and added milk. She set the cup on the table and headed for the door. 'I'll... run and tell Chrissie you're here.'

Jack grabbed her arm as she passed. 'No don't.'

The strength and suddenness of his grip spun her round. Her eyes widened, her face tensed. Peter wanted to tell her not to worry, his dad had come home, and everything was going to be alright, although he wasn't sure this was true. Nevertheless, he wished his mam would hurry up.

Jack lowered his voice. 'We'll sit and wait.'

'You're hurting me,' Bel said. He let go and lifted his palms upward. 'I don't want to hurt you. I don't want to hurt anybody.' He rested his brow on his closed fist. Bel rubbed her arm. Silence, save for the ticking clock and the settling fire, filled the room.

'Yes,' said Peter, with a forced little laugh that somehow sounded all wrong. 'Let's give Mam a surprise.'

Peter's eyes met Bel's. She looked scared.

Memories of Jimmy tormenting him with tales of how Jack Reid was the bogeyman and he would come back and kill them all in their beds returned to Peter now. As a young child, those stories made him cry and Bel would put her arms around him and tell him not to worry; Jack Reid had not been like that at all. Peter chose to believe Bel. What did Jimmy know anyway? He had been only two when Jack left.

Swallowing a knot of concern, he imagined Chrissie's reaction when she returned. It had been lonely for her with Charlie gone. He heard her sob in the night when she thought he was asleep. Hopefully, that awful Geordie MacIntyre who was always sniffing around would stay away now that his dad was home. He hoped she would be pleased.

When his friend Alex's dad had piloted a ship to Hull, he had been caught in a storm and ended up sailing with the fleet to the West Indies. He had not come home for two years. What a celebration there had been on his return. Now there would be another celebration. A seed of hope within him blossomed until it filled him up. The work load would be shared. His mam wouldn't cry any more in the night. Everything would be much better now. Of course, he tried to convince himself, she *would* be pleased. She had to be.

***

Bel was not so sure. As a quiet child, adults often forgot she was in the room and subsequently spoke about things they would never have mentioned in front of the more boisterous boys. Jack's name had only been mentioned a few times over the years, and then it had not been with any degree of affection. If only she could warn Chrissie. She studied the tall stranger, the bowed head, the hand still holding Peter's, noticed the boy's flushed cheeks and anxious eyes, and her heart pounded. 'Are you all right, Peter?' She reached out to touch him.

'Sit down,' said Jack, his voice slicing the air.

Her hand hovered and then dropped to her side. Wanting to defy him, to tell him she would sit when she was good and ready, she returned his glare, but the malevolence she saw in his eyes forced her back into the chair without a word.

'He's tired,' said Peter. 'It's a long way from America.'

'You're right, lad. I am very, very tired.' He leaned back and closed his eyes, one hand still holding Peter's.

Bel stared at the far wall and hoped Chrissie would not be long. The ticking of the clock was very loud.

Chapter 30

Chrissie trailed behind the hay-cart, the soft wind lifting the hair from her face. She sang along with the women, some of them with bairns in tow, who walked beside her. The dust rose as feet stirred the dried earth. The day had been long, gathering in the harvest for the Mains, the only place in the island to own a water-powered mill. They in turn would help the smaller crofters by grinding their bere and oats.

'Give us another song, Chrissie,' said Alexina. Behind her glasses, her eyes appeared enormous. Her body had filled out over the years and she now boasted a family of five.

'Are you not coming with us to the Mains?' said someone else. 'The men'll be there already.'

'Na, I've Peter to see to,' Chrissie indicated a track scarred in the land by generations of tramping feet, a shortcut running from the main road to Scartongarth. 'Bel'll have the tea on.' She waved goodbye to the others and followed the path. To either side grew crops; corn and bere, potatoes, turnips and kale, some still waiting to be gathered in. The warm smell of cut hay, clover and the ozone of the sea filled the dying day. In the distance the sea was a flat blue plateau, and the line where the sea and sky merged was barely distinguishable. The ocean sucked softly at the shoreline and sea-maws wheeled and cried above her head. Over the firth to the north lay other islands of Orkney, lazy humpbacked creatures, blued with distance. Few cobweb-like clouds stretched across the faded blue of the sky. She did not hurry. This was her time to be alone – to gather her thoughts – to revel in the peace. The fear of Jack still lurked in shadows fraught with unanswered questions, but since she'd heard nothing more of him, she'd forced him to the recesses of her mind like a bad dream. Nevertheless, she wished Charlie would return. He was trying to find the best place for them, she knew, but now that the decision had been made, she was eager to leave.

The cottage sat before her, a solid structure beyond the swaying corn fields. Smoke trickled from the chimney in thin spirals and dissipated in the still air. She walked past the crops and across the grazing pastures. Sheep, their excrement covered tails slapping against their hindquarters, scattered out of her way.

As she neared the but and ben, chickens ran towards her, cackled and retreated. Poppy, Bel's collie, greeted her; her tail wagging, her tongue lolling out. Gazing at her indulgently, she ruffled the rough fur.

Straightening up, Chrissie looked at the house. Despite the fine evening, the door was closed. Something was wrong. Something she could sense. Chrissie's skin prickled and a sudden dread clawed her stomach. *I'm imagining things*, she told herself. *I have to stop this.*

With her heart already racing, she walked the last few yards to the house. 'Bel,' she shouted, 'Peter.'

She stepped into the kitchen and froze; became stone. The epitome of her nightmares stood before her, and he was holding her son's hand.

Jack.

Thinner, gaunter, his face lined, his nose bent where it had been broken. Her heart thundered. Ice water ran in her blood and pricked her skin. Only her head grew hot. The room retreated, and she staggered back until the wall stopped her retreat.

'Mam, Dad's come home. He's been in America.' Peter's excited voice punctuated the silent spaces.

She couldn't move.

'Aren't you going to give your husband a kiss?' Jack let the boy go and came at her, opening his arms. The heat in her head slipped downwards and overlaid the ice in her body. Her armpits prickled. Standing statue like, she endured his embrace. She must not pass out – not now.

Bel began to rise, glanced at Jack and sat down again.

217

Speechless, Chrissie gathered her strength and glared at the man before her.

'It's my dad. He came back.' Peter's voice quavered slightly. Bewildered eyes shifted between Jack and Chrissie.

'The prodigal has returned. Aren't you going to kill the fatted calf?' Jack asked.

'What... where...' Chrissie stammered, unable to say more. 'Come... come here, Peter.'

'Stay where you are, son,' said Jack.

Peter didn't move. Chrissie sensed his confusion.

She kept her voice steady. 'It's all right, Peter.' She swallowed with difficulty, her mouth parched. 'I'm... surprised... that's all.' *Breathe in. Breathe out. Stay calm. For the children's sake, give yourself time to think.* She had not allowed herself to imagine this moment, plan what she would say and do, and now her mind was a wasteland.

'I bet you are.' Jack stepped forward and lifted a strand of her hair allowing it to flow through his fingers. 'Still a good looking woman, Chrissie.'

'You can't live here.' She had to stay strong.

'But... but Mam...' Peter bit his lip and Bel rose to put an arm around his shoulders.

'Scartongarth is mine by rights. Jamsie's dead, and I'm the second son.' Jack turned to Peter. 'It will be yours after me. He is my son, isn't he, Chrissie?' His voice was still gentle, but she saw past it to the sharp edges underneath.

'Of course he is.' Chrissie shivered as her mouth formed words she did not believe.

Jack's face relaxed. He stroked the boy's head.

Chrissie winced. 'The croft should be Jimmy's.' she said.

Jack grinned. His teeth, still straight and without decay, were yellowed like a horse. 'Would you deny your own son his birth right? I've been to hell, but I've been guided back. Now isn't that a sign, Chrissie?' He spread his hands. 'I'm not the man I was.'

'And I'm not the woman I was. You'll not find me so easy.' Afraid of losing the power of her legs, she sat down.

'Chrissie, Chrissie, what are you talking about?' He twisted his face as if her words stabbed him.

'Where have you been?'

'In prison for a crime I did not commit.'

She stared at the hard chiselled lines of his face, avoided eyes that spoke of a dangerous undercurrent lying just below the surface and doubted whether he had been innocent. She glanced at Peter, at the worried crease on his forehead. 'I can't go back to how things were.' She kept her voice as smooth as his, willing away the tension. She did not want to risk upsetting Bel and Peter unnecessarily. 'You can sleep in the old salt store.' Her heart filled with a silent prayer that he wouldn't create a scene.

His jaw moved, the muscles tensed and then he spoke. 'I will – for now. Take your wee cousin outside,' he said to Bel, 'I need to talk to Chrissie.'

Bel looked at her aunt and Chrissie nodded. 'Come on, Peter.' Bel placed her hand on the centre of his back. With another worried glance behind him Peter moved before her.

Once the door closed behind the youngsters, Jack turned to Chrissie. His voice lowered. 'Swear on the boy's life that he is mine.'

Steeling herself, she stared into the black pools of his eyes surprised to see a desperate longing there. At that moment she realised he would believe her – because he needed to.

'I never swear on anyone's life. I never have and I never shall.'

'If he is Charlie Rosie's, I'll snap his neck, and then I will snap yours.' He spoke quietly. His voice trembled slightly.

The years rolled away and Chrissie was back in her house the night she had tried to poison this man. That same fear swirled through her body and trapped the breath in her throat. That same fear which prompted her to do anything, say anything to make the violence go away. 'I swear on his life,' she whispered, the hand of dread closing round her heart as the words escaped her mouth. If Jack ever suspected Peter might not be his son... she shuddered at the possible consequences.

Jack smiled and slowly circled her. 'For years I dreamed of this day. In the beginning I wanted to kill you, kill both you and Charlie, for what you did to me. But I can forgive you, now he's gone. God, it's so good to be home.'

He reached for her, and she stepped away. 'Please Jack, no more.'

His face darkened, as if he couldn't believe her words. 'No more what? I'm home.'

Chrissie couldn't speak. She continued to back away.

His expression changed and crumpled. The glitter bled from his eyes. 'No, no, don't be scared.' He reached out to her, 'I just want to come home. I'm so tired.'

'I can't be your wife, again,' she said when she could.

His head snapped upright. 'Who is it? What man have you got now?' The softness in his voice had slipped and she heard beyond it to the raw edges.

What was she thinking? He wasn't well. In the head. Had he ever been? She remembered Tyna's words, and a flash of an unloved child flew across her mind. With that flash came a dribble of pity. Somehow, she had to find a way to deal with this horror.

'There is no man – I swear.'

His expression lightened. 'Then it's just the shock.' He grabbed her hand and squeezed it gently.

'Aye, shock.' With difficulty, she allowed his touch.

Relaxed for now, he went to the door and called to Peter. 'Will you come with me to the salt store, son?'

'Aye.' Peter came in and turned puzzled eyes to his mother. Why can't he sleep in the house?'

'We need to get used to each other again. I've sprung this on her, son. I should've written.' Jack's eyes met Chrissie's over Peter's head and those eyes held the promise of a future – a future she would never give him. She shivered.

'What's for dinner? I've dreamed about your fine rabbit stew,' he continued.

For a minute, confusion clouded her thoughts. Dinner? The evening meal had always been known as tea.

'I've... we've oatmeal and tatties, and a skarf.'

'A skarf? God, that fishy birds? You can't welcome me home with a skarf. Can she, son?' He laughed, his movements quick and nervous, and Peter laughed with him.

'It's been wrapped in peat for the last three weeks. Takes the bitter taste away.' Caution was needed now. She held herself together so tightly she feared that if she were to snap, she would start screaming and never stop. Peter expected her to be pleased. Once she got him alone she would explain the nature of Jack's sickness. Why oh why had she not found the courage to tell him before? But she knew why. Hoping this day would never come, she had kept her silence.

'I'll be out with the blankets in a minute.' She closed her eyes as Peter and Jack went into the old salt store. What was she going to do? What in the name of hell was she going to do?

'You're not happy he's back.' said Bel softly from behind her.

'No, not at all.' She should have known that Bel, with her uncanny ability to see what lay below the surface, would realise what Peter failed to – how much the return of Jack had disturbed her. Bel, for all her youth, could read her like no one else – no one that was, except for Charlie.

'He was bitter bad to me, Bel.'

'Maybe he's changed.' Bel did not sound convinced.

'He's sick, Bel. I'm frightened for us all. He's fine now, but he can change in an instant. But Peter – he seems so taken with him. I should have left the island years ago.' And she would have, if only she'd known he was still alive. The old fear was gripping her by the throat and she fought to hold on to the strength she had gained in his absence. From the linen cupboard, she pulled out the blanket and pillow she had used when she slept in the salt store. 'Take these to him, Bel. I'm going to the shop.'

After Bel had gone, Chrissie stood at the door and looked at her old cottage on the rise. How she wished Charlie was there now. She needed him. She needed him desperately.

Chapter 31

A huddle of elderly women looked up as Chrissie entered the shop and just as quickly their tongues stilled. A few men at the usual corner table glanced up and nodded through a haze of smoke, then returned to their game of dominoes.

'My, lassie, you look fair in a fluster.' Lottie, leaning over the counter towards her, spoke into the hush. 'Is it true Jack's back?'

'As large as life.'

'Yer life was easier with him gone,' said Dol Banks, a woman who appeared to have taken up permanent residence against Lottie's counter, one large breast resting on an equally large arm, which spread out across the surface. 'They say he's a changed man.'

'Who says?'

'He came over in the boat with my Frank. Was asking a lot of questions and all. He said nothing about wee Peter, did my Frank.'

Chrissie caught the sly glance between the women and it pierced her heart like an accusing fingers.

'He'll be surprised to find he has a son,' said one, her voice heavy with innuendo.

Chrissie said nothing. How long would it take in this community of whispers before Jack found out she and Charlie had been together for a time? God, she wished he would hurry back.

'Where did Jack say he was?' asked someone else.

'In America. I don't know.' She could not halt the uncharacteristic sharpness that leaked into her voice.

'But it will be grand for you to have another man around the croft. Angus is no' up to much,' said Lottie.

'Aye'. Chrissie ordered what she needed and retreated outside, away from the sympathetic glances and equally sly smirks.

Geordie MacIntyre rose from his seat in the corner and followed her. 'You're not happy to see him back, are you?'

Chrissie shook her head.

'You can still come and live wi' me,' he said. 'I may be older, but I'm a dab hand with the shotgun. Jack'll no bother you when I'm around.'

'Thank you kindly but no.' Chrissie clutched her basket to her. 'I'll cope with Jack myself.' But would she? She was not at all sure. There was only one person she could talk to. One person who would understand. She glanced at the firth, hoping to see a sheet on the peat stack at Huna, hoping Charlie was on his way home, glad that she had kept his true identity to herself. Jack must never find out. If he knew Charlie was still alive... she could not contemplate the outcome.

Charlie had threatened to kill Jack if he ever came back. She knew those were empty words. *You're a good man, Charlie. You don't have it in you to kill.* She spoke to him in her mind. *But I have,* she thought suddenly, remembering the laburnum tree behind the barn; remembering her intentions all those years ago. Her stomach contracted, threatening to force its contents up through her gullet. She gagged and swallowed bile. 'I wish he did die,' she said to no one. 'God forgive me, but I wish I had killed him.'

But could she do it again? No, for desperation had driven her immature self that night, and what had been self-defence, would now be murder. Now she had a choice. Leaving Raumsey, giving up all she loved to live among strangers, would be hard. The cottage had become her home, the heritage which belonged in her family was rooted in her soul, but for her safety and her sanity, she could not continue to breathe the same air as Jack Reid.

If Charlie had obtained a place for them, they would escape in the night. Convincing Peter to leave his new-found father would not be easy, but she would have to find a way.

As she neared the croft she saw him. Still as a statue among the chickens. With a sudden movement, he reached down, and the fingers of one hand closed around the neck of a hen, lifting it high as it squawked and shrieked in its panic. 'You were sick o' fish, weren't you?' He grinned at Peter and Bel who watched him from where they sat on the wall. With a twisting pull, he cracked the chicken's neck. 'Oatmeal and cabbage and an oily bird that tastes like fish, huh?' Jack handed the still jerking body to Chrissie as she approached. 'Roast this for the tea, tonight.'

'We've little enough eggs as it is.' Chrissie closed her fingers around the legs. 'And it's not been hung. It'll be tough.'

'Do the best you can. You kids, stay outside for a wee while. I want to talk to Chrissie.' He followed her into the house and shut the door. 'Did I kick like that? Did I, Chrissie, when you thought you had killed me?'

The body of the hen convulsed against her. Her fingers tightened around the legs until the bird finally stilled, the wings spreading open, and the head dangling loose. 'I did not try to kill you.' The more firmly she stuck to her denial, the more chance she would have of sounding believable. 'I wouldn't know how to. The only herbs I know about heal.'

'You would know, right enough.'

'I only wanted to make you stop.' Try as she might she couldn't keep the panic from her voice. Turning her back to him, she fetched a pail from the back porch. After settling herself before the fire, she began to pluck the chicken.

'Remember how we were, Chrissie,' he said, his voice soft - the deep velvet voice which had once suggested a more sensitive soul might lie beneath the hard exterior.

She stared at the chicken and continued to dash the feathers into the pail as if they were the object of her frustration.

His fingers ran across her shoulders startling her. She flinched, cringing.

'Yes,' she whispered, not trusting her voice to grow loud. 'I remember exactly how we were.' She lit a taper from the fire and singed off what was left on the white pimpled skin. A strong odour of burning feathers thickened in her nostrils. That done, she carried the chicken into the porch and laid the body on the wooden slab. From the drawer she brought her sharpest knife. She held it for a heartbeat, testing the weight, before pressing the point into the soft white flesh and dragging the blade from belly to tail.

She pushed her hand into the carcass and pulled out the still warm innards. With the liver set to one side to use later, she threw the rest into a basin.

The door opened. She heard him move up behind her, each breath distinct in the stillness.

'We could have been happy, if it hadn't been for Davie and then Charlie. If only you stayed true,' he said.

Chrissie's fingers curled around the handle of the knife. She turned to face him, her voice shaking when she spoke. 'I was once willing to give you all my love – but you destroyed us, not me.' The knife handle burned in her hand. The image of the blade slicing though his chest, glancing off his rib to slide into his heart and the shock in his eyes, flashed through her mind. A shudder shook its way through her body. What evil way of thinking had this man driven her to?

'Are you going to use that?' He held up his hands. 'Go on, Chrissie, show me how much you hate me.'

'Don't try to touch me.'

'I'm not going to touch you. I just want to talk.'

'Talk then.' The hand holding the knife shook. Her other hand found the solid wood of the work top behind her.

His voice, warm as acid, carried on. 'Has any other man ever excited you the way I did?'

'No other man terrified me the way you did!'

'I've changed, Chrissie.'

Afraid to see the icy emptiness of his eyes, Chrissie turned away. The knife slipped from her fingers and clattered on the work top. She lifted the chicken, hung it by the feet onto a hook on the wall and, after wiping her hands on a threadbare towel, she pushed past Jack and into the kitchen. 'This is the last meal I'll cook for you. If you don't leave, then I will.' She forced confidence into her voice. She would not give in. She would not. Yet her stomach clenched with every word.

'Do what you like; you were always a free woman. But my son stays with me.'

She said nothing.

'Get on with the dinner, Chrissie. I'm off to speak to my son.'
How much longer could she bear this?

The family gathered for the evening meal and Chrissie cringed at the expression of adoration on Peter's face every time he looked at Jack. Convincing him to slip away with her in the night was going to be harder than she imagined. She set the tureen of potatoes in the centre of the table and then served up the plates of fried oatmeal with roast chicken. Once everyone was seated, Jack lifted Bel's plate and replaced it with his own. 'I'm taking no chances, Chrissie. Every night I'll change my plate for someone else's.'

Bel and Peter exchanged a confused glance. Chrissie studied the food before her. 'For God's sake,' she said.

'A private joke, son.' With one arm, Jack hugged the boy. 'Well, who's going to say grace?' Jack's eyes travelled over the blank faces before him. 'Guess I'd better then.' He closed his eyes and pressed his hands together.

Our father in heaven
Thank you for what we are about to receive.
Thank you for bringing me safely home into the bosom of my family.
Thank you for my son.
God bless the poor souls left behind in Hell's Kitchen
And punish those who would try to destroy our family
Amen

Much as she enjoyed roast chicken, that night, Chrissie could not eat a bite.

Chapter 32

Chrissie slept little and rose early. Her hand shook as she stirred the oatmeal left steeping from the night before.

His step sounded in the passageway and she counted each footfall. The door opened and he entered, dressed only in a nightshirt; his hair standing on end. 'Best night's sleep I've had in a long time.' He stretched and yawned.

Wordlessly, Chrissie turned back to the stove.

'It's been a long journey – an even longer fifteen years.' Jack lowered his voice. 'Every day and every night I've thought of this place. Of this moment, of you.'

'I'll never live with you as your wife again.' Chrissie increased the speed with which she stirred the porridge. She heard her heartbeat in her ears; felt it in her throat.

'I've been in prison. A stinking hell-hole. You don't know what that does to a man.' His voice was confusingly soft and sad.

Chrissie tried to moisten her lips. 'I don't love you, Jack.' This weary voiced stranger was not the Jack of her nightmares, not even the Jack of the night before.

'I understand why you tried to kill me.'

'I didn't try to kill you. I wanted to make you sleep.' Her inner senses directed her words.

'I wish you did kill me. I'd be better off.' He eased onto a chair.

'Don't make things harder than they need to be.'

Her thoughts blurred. The cockerel crowed outside. 'I need to do the milking.' Filled with a desire to be away from him, she went into the back porch and collected the pail. The handle rattled beneath her fingers. Anyone else might believe his sincerity. But she knew that the softness of his voice hid the malice lying just below the surface.

When she returned to the kitchen, Jack took the bucket from her hands. His fingers brushed hers, and she drew back as if stung.

'I'll get on my clothes and then I'll do the milking.' The eyes that met hers were unfathomable.

She started to protest, but stopped. All she had to do was remain calm. Appear agreeable and wait for Charlie to return, she thought.

'Then I'll take the *Christina* out,' he said. 'Get some fish. It *is* my boat.'

Anger suddenly rose in her like a fire. He couldn't do this to her. He just couldn't.

'Why couldn't you stay where you were?'

'This is my home.' He spread his hands, but a hard glint flashed across his eyes.

'Then I'll go back to my old house. I'll go to the mainland and find a lawyer. We'll see who legally owns Scartongarth.'

The pad of bare feet against wood behind her, and Peter came downstairs, his hair tousled, the marks of the pillow still on his cheek. Chrissie bit back any further remarks. When Peter saw Jack, his face lit up.

'Howdy do, son,' said Jack, returning the smile. 'Will you come and work with me the day?'

'Oh, aye.' Peter's grin widened.

'He's got school,' said Chrissie.

Jack glanced at the clock. 'He's got a wee while yet. Come on, son.' He rose to his feet.

After the milking, Jack collected water from the well. He brought in firewood and peat. All the while, Peter followed him like an obedient puppy desperate for his master's love.

'You'd better get ready,' Chrissie shouted to her son as the hands of the clock moved to eight thirty.

Peter turned his eyes to Jack. 'Dad says I can go with him to the sea the day.'

'You've got school.'

'One day won't hurt him. I've missed most of his childhood. What good is book learning going to do him anyway?' said Jack, his words still quiet, but there was an underlying current. She saw it when his eyes met hers and it chilled her core. She would not have this. She couldn't.

'He's already had time off for the tattie picking. He's clever. He should go to the mainland, learn something better than being a crofter – fisherman. He needs his schooling.'

'Is that what you want, son?' Jack asked.

Peter shook his head. His lips pressed together in that stubborn way he had and Chrissie knew she'd lost.

'Well, he's going tomorrow,' she said.

'Do I have to?' He looked at Jack.

There was a second's silence before Jack spoke. 'Better do as your mam tells you, son. I've always had to.'

'I don't want to.' Peter glowered at Chrissie and a panic rose in her breast, as if he'd already gone from her. Jack had succeeded in making her the unreasonable one.

All that day, Chrissie did her work; mucked the byre, cleaned the house, cooked the meals and tried to avoid Jack as best as she was able. His hours at sea gave her some respite, but he was always there, a scar on her mind. Today she did not sing. Her eyes were constantly drawn to the mainland. What was taking Charlie so long?

Once Jack returned, he moved around the house, his eyes on her whenever he was near. Polite and overly helpful, he stretched her nerves until she became jumpy and unfocused. And she hated him all the more for it.

'I traded some fish for a fine bottle of whisky. I'm away to Lottie's to give the lads a drink. Don't wait up,' he told her, after tea.

His words ran through her like cold water. What was he doing? Trying to ingratiate himself with men who never liked him before? Would the lure of fine whisky be all it took to make them forget? But forget what? No one besides the family knew the extent of his violence towards her. He had the ability to turn on a degree of charm when he needed to, and, she suspected, he needed the islanders on his side now.

'Peter,' she called up the stairs, 'I want to talk to you.'

The lad came into the kitchen. He pushed the hair that fell in untidy curls from his brow with the heel of his hand.

'I think we should go to the mainland, get you some proper schooling.'

His brows dropped and his face darkened. 'Dad too?'

'No.' She took his hand and it lay motionless in hers. Fingers calloused, nails bitten enough to look painful. 'There's things you don't know.'

'Dad says you don't like him. That you wish he'd never come back. Why, Mam? Why don't you like him?'

'There were things, long ago – grown up things.'

'He said you had another man.' His hand tensed in hers.

'I did not. He was bad to me Peter, and I'm scared he hasn't changed.'

'I don't believe you. He's... he's been nice. Look at the fish he's brought home.'

'I think he's ill. Nice one minute, bad the next. If Angus finds a house...'

'Angus? Has he gone to find a place? Well I'm staying here. Maybe things happened long ago, but Dad's different now. Give him a chance, please Mam.'

'I'm sorry, Peter, I can't.'

Peter jerked his hand from hers. His lips pressed down at the edges. 'I'm not going, and you can't make me.'

Tears pushed behind her eyes. How could she leave her son?

She saw little of Jack the following morning, which gave her time to collect her thoughts. Somehow she would have to convince Peter to come with her. But he stayed out of her sight, his face sullen, blaming her because Jack had left without him that morning.

She did not hear Jack return. She was peeling potatoes in the basin in the back porch when he came up behind her. Strong hands caught her round the waist and an unshaven chin scoured her cheek. A scream escaped her throat as she tried to struggle free.

'I've been patient long enough, Chrissie,' Jack said with a low hiss. 'Give me a kiss.' His arms tightened, forcing the air from her lungs, his hardness pressed into her back. 'Now, before the bairns come back.' One hand moved upward, clasping her breast. His breath, hot and urgent brushed her cheek.

'Let me go.' She pushed back with her elbows.

A hand clamped over her mouth. His body trembled against her.

'What's wrong?' Bel's alarmed voice came from behind them. Jack cursed under his breath. 'Just giving my wife a cuddle. Go and finish your chores.'

'Leave her alone,' said Bel, her voice wavering slightly.

Jack's hands shifted and clamped like vices on Chrissie's arms. 'I wouldn't hurt her. Tell her it's all right, Chrissie.'

'No Bel, don't go.'

The hands tightened, painfully.

Bel stared at him, her eyes defiant.

Jack released his hold. The instant he moved away from her, Chrissie bolted past him and into the kitchen. Sweat beaded her forehead and cheeks. 'I can't stay here,' she said. 'Not one more night.'

Bel followed her, slammed the dividing door shut and pulled a strand of her hair forward. 'We'll. . we'll go to Angus' tonight.' She chewed on her lip.

'Peter won't come with us,' whispered Chrissie.

Bel stared at her, the seriousness of the situation mirrored in her eyes. 'He'll come in the end,' she said at last.

'But I can't leave him.'

'Jack won't hurt him. He won't hurt me.'

Chrissie considered this. It was true he seemed to be trying to get both Peter and Bel on his side.

The door swung open, and he stood in the doorway, a solid block of black jersey and dungarees. 'I've had enough of this, Chrissie. You're my wife and you'll do as I say.' He turned to Bel. 'Get the blankets from the salt store. I'm moving into the house.'

'There's no room.' Bel's eyes darted from him to Chrissie and back again.

'I'll share my wife's bed.'

'You'll stay away from me, or...'

'Or you'll do what, Chrissie? Kill me? Is that what you were going to say? You'll need to do a better job than you did before.'

A strangled sound came from behind her. She spun around. Peter had entered silently. She had no idea how long he had been standing there.

Jack saw him the same moment she did. 'Does that surprise you?' he asked. 'That your mother tried to kill me?'

Peter's eyes were wide, his mouth open. 'No, no, she wouldn't.' He shook his head.

'I don't believe you.' Bel twisted her hands together.

Jack twisted to face her. 'Tell them, Chrissie. Go on, tell them the truth.'

'I did not try to end your life.' No, she would not let him do this to the children.

'Believe me, Peter. He was ill. I gave him something to help him sleep.' She shook inside as she told the lie. Please God, she prayed silently, make him stop.

Jack's eyes narrowed. 'Get the blankets, Bel.'

'If you come back in here, I'll take the bairns and move back to my old house,' said Chrissie.

'You will not take my son away from me.' His voice was low and shockingly calm.

'You can have Scartongarth. Let us go.' He was close to her now. She felt the heat of his body, the force of his anger. She heard his intake of breath. Straightening her shoulders and tightened her jaw, she waited for the blow, part of her hoping for it. If he lifted his hand in violence, he would reveal his true self. But he would not. He would not risk alienating his son.

'I can't make you stay, but everything in this house and on this croft is mine.' Jack went into the back porch and returned with the whisky kept for dosing sick animals. After pouring himself a cupful, he sat in the fireside chair and lit a cigarette. He looked at her over the rim of the mug. 'You leave with nothing.'

'I brought a cow and twenty sheep.'

'I told you, you leave with nothing.'

She pulled in her breath slowly. Further argument at this point would be pointless. Fear still trembled on the edge of her anger.

'Mam, don't leave,' said Peter.

'You have to go,' whispered Bel. 'Go on.'

'Come with me, Peter. You can see your dad whenever you want.' She held out her hand to her son. He shook his head.

'*You* go,' said Bel. 'I'll stay with Peter. Jack won't hurt *us*.'

Jack did not look up as Chrissie left the house. He stared into the flames, his silence all the more ominous.

'Glad you decided to stay,' said Jack, rising and putting his arm around Bel's shoulder. She shrank at his touch. 'This is your home, lasgie, is it not – eh?'

Bel nodded and stared at the floor. She had wanted to leave as well, knew Chrissie would never leave Peter on his own with Jack.

'You and me, we'll get on fine. You can cook can you not – clean a house?'

Bel nodded again. *Not for long,* she thought. If only things were back the way they were. 'How's Chrissie going to live?' she asked finally.

Jack shrugged. 'That's up to her. The door's always open.'

'You shouldn't keep her sheep and her cow.'

Placing his hands on her shoulders, Jack bent down and stared into her eyes. 'Chrissie can come back anytime. Scartongarth is mine. All the livestock is mine. She'll come back once her belly's empty, you'll see.'

'Why would you want to live with her anyway?' asked Bel in a rush of bravado. 'If it's true she tried to kill you?'

'Charlie made her – she wouldn't have the nerve.' A shadow crossed his face and he seemed to drift into a dark place. 'Life was bitter bad to me, Bel. I did my best, but nothing was good enough for Chrissie. My brother Jamsie, your dad, he cared for me. Do you know what it's like?' his voice was soft again. 'To lose the only one who cares?' A muscle below his jaw bulged and jumped. 'I'd never hurt you, lasgie. Not Jamsie's bairn.'

'You scared me. Grabbing Chrissie like that,' said Bel.

He let her go and straightened up. 'I want her back. Is that so wrong?'

'You can't force her.'

He studied the floor for a second before meeting her eyes. 'I've got a temper, I'll not deny that. But my life's been hell. Do you hate me?' His penetrating stare captured hers. It was almost as if he could see into her mind, as if he knew the answers before she spoke.

'No. I...' In spite of the warmth of the stove, she shivered.

Peter sat, in silence, his hands dangling between his knees. Jack spun to face him. 'And you, do you hate me?'

'No... no. Did Mam really try to kill you?'

'Aye, I'm sure she did, for she had another man. They planned to bury me in the byre up yonder.' He pointed to the house where Angus now lived. He looked ... weary.

'But... how... I mean. .' Bel stammered.

'Aye, there's things you don't know about your aunt. Things that drove a decent man like me to the edge of madness.'

Fear seemed to sit in his eyes. A flush had climbed up his face where there had been none before. Bel could see he was fighting the urge to cry. 'Who was the other man?' Peter asked, his voice small.

'Charlie Rosie. It's good for him he is dead.'

Peter bit his lip. Realising how hard this must be for him, Bel put her arm round his shoulders. Peter loved Charlie and Charlie had been good to all of them. But Bel did understand how things had been between him and Chrissie. Could it be true? Could her aunt who had cared for them, sometimes with enough love to suffocate, have tried to take another life? If she had, she must have had good reason.

'I don't believe you,' she said.

Jack's fingers found her shoulder. Amazed at his strength, she cried out. 'You're hurting me.'

He stared down at her.

She tried to squirm from Jack's grasp but he held her tight. And he was grinning. A strange light filled his eyes that made her remember stories of possession the older children told when she was wee.

'Let her go,' said Peter.

Jack immediately released her and lifted his hands in the air. 'I wouldn't hurt Jamsie's lass,' he said. His voice was soft again. This constant change in his demeanour terrified Bel.

'Chrissie will come back. And when she does – she'll not find me so ready to forgive.' Jack grinned. 'I've got you now.'

The eyes that bore into Bel disturbed her in a way she had not felt before. And suddenly she knew she should have left. 'Please, give Chrissie what's hers and let me and Peter go and live with her. I'll come back and cook and clean every day.' She sniffed and rubbed at her nose.

'No!' Jack paced to the window. 'And that's final.'

'You can't make us stay.' She pulled the sleeves of her cardigan over her hands. It was hard not to cry. She glanced at Peter whose eyes were fixed on Jack. His face was white, and she knew she couldn't leave him here alone with this man.

Jack spun round to face the boy. 'You don't want to go, do you son?'

Peter shook his head, but Bel believed differently. She tried to put herself in his position. What if her dad had come back from the dead? The dad she had conjured up as a fine, upstanding, loveable man. What if he turned out to be like Jack? She wanted to put her arms around Peter and tell him she understood.

'All right, now.' Jack punched the flat of one hand with the other. 'Let's get to work. You, lad, will come to sea with me tomorrow morning. You, Bel, stay here and do women's work. But if you are not here when I get back…' He gave a deep laugh which made Bel's blood turn to ice. 'Peter, go to the salt store and get my clothes.'

Once Peter had gone, Jack leaned close to Bel so that she could smell the smoke on his breath. 'Do you know why I stayed away so long?' She shook her head and fought to control her bladder. 'I was in prison – for murder. I killed a man on the ship that took me across the sea. Slit his throat as easily as if it was the belly of a fish.

You had better stay, girl, because what I did once I can do again.' He trailed his finger down her arm. 'Not to you. Not to Jamsie's girl. But Chrissie, well, me and her, we have business to finish.'

At that moment the door opened, and Chrissie with Geordie MacIntyre and another islander came into the kitchen. Bel dashed her tears away.

'What's this then?' asked Jack, his voice changing immediately, becoming smooth, friendly.

'Chrissie says you won't let the bairns go with her,' said Geordie. 'That's wrong, man.'

Jack spread his hands. 'You walked out, Chrissie. They chose to stay.' He turned to Bel. 'What do you want to do?'

Peter came in. 'Mam,' he said, his face lighting up. 'Have you come back?'

Chrissie reached out and pulled him to her.

'Well,' Jack looked at Bel.

She shivered, the image of a knife slicing through Chrissie's throat uppermost in her mind. 'I want to stay,' she said, but her voice wavered.

'Peter?' asked Jack.

Peter looked at Bel and she nodded. Please, she said with her eyes. 'I'll stay too,' he said. 'Please, Mam, come home.'

'No, no come with me now, both of you.' She tried to reach them, but Jack barred her way.

'Are you sure you want to stay here?' asked one of the other men.

Bel nodded. 'We'll be fine, Chrissie.' She had to convince her, to keep her safe.

Geordie turned. 'I'm sorry, Chrissie,' he said. 'Seems like you were wrong. But come wi' me now. I'll make a home for you.'

'No, not without Bel and Peter.'

'They'll no come. What can I do?'

'Aye,' said the other man, 'This is not our business.' And he turned and left.

Bel wanted to cry at the defeat and confusion in Chrissie's eyes. 'We'll be fine,' she said, hoping she sounded convincing.

Chrissie straightened her shoulders and glowered at Jack. 'I'll go for now,' she said, 'but I will be back.'

Geordie MacIntyre put his hand on her shoulder and guided her out. 'They'll come in time,' he said.

Bel could no longer control the tears which rolled unbidden down her cheeks. She would have to stay for now. It was the least she could do. The risk to Chrissie's life was too great. Chrissie had even been prepared to give herself to that lecherous old man to get her and Peter to safety.

The next morning, as they walked out the door, Peter turned to Bel with a sad, confused look that tore her heart. She watched man and boy walk down the path and onto the beach. She watched as the *Christina* sailed into the bay, then she lifted the pail beside the fireplace and went outside to fill it with peat.

As she straightened up, Chrissie climbed over the wall and came towards her. 'I saw them leave,' she said, grabbing Bel's hands. 'How was he – last night?'

Bel shuddered and fought the urge to cry.

'What is it – what's he done? Has he hurt you?'' Chrissie grabbed the girl's arm.

Bel set down the bucket and blinked away her tears. 'It was fine. He won't let us come, but he won't hurt us. Really.' She grabbed a handful of hair and brought it to her lips. 'I won't leave Peter. But don't come back. You mustn't come back.'

'Angus has gone to the mainland to get us a place to live,' said Chrissie. 'Then we'll go. We'll all go, even if we have to kidnap Peter.'

Bel forced a smile. 'I think Peter will come,' she said.

'But I've no food in my own house. Lottie offered to give me a little for now, but she's barely scraping a living herself and Jack's being so plausible that people believe he's changed. I need some oatmeal and milk – just enough for today. '

Chrissie went into the porch and lifted the lid of the meal kist. She scooped up some oats and wrapped them in a dishcloth. Suddenly, she heard Bel's stifled scream and ran into the kitchen.

'Didn't I warn you not to steal from me?' Jack stood before her, his eyes narrowed to slits; his body tense, the muscles in his arms standing out and quivering. His hand shot out and grabbed the front of Chrissie's blouse. Oats fell onto the floor, scattering across the flagstone. Poppy began to bark and Jack aimed his booted foot at her flank. The dog's yelps brought Peter running indoors. He stopped behind Jack, eyes round. Pulling his lips back in a sneer; his teeth clenched together, Jack's whole being seemed to shake and Chrissie realised, in the fervour of his temper, he was unaware of Peter. The sight of her son gave her courage. Now was the time to win him back. 'Let me go,' she demanded.

Jack laughed and tightened his hand, twisting the material of her blouse around her neck until she could hardly breathe.

'Leave her alone,' shouted Peter, his face white. Shock registered on Jack's face, he glanced over his shoulder, and then flung Chrissie from him with enough force that she fell against the range, the pain of it jarring her very soul. Wanting Peter to realise the full extent of Jack's nature, she did nothing to stifle the scream and allowed her legs to buckle beneath her.

'She stole from me, the thieving bitch,' Jack hissed through his teeth. The devil was in him now. He turned to Bel. His whole body shook. 'What are you looking at?'

With terrified eyes on Jack, Bel edged to where the still whimpering collie stood three legged. She felt along the limp paw. The dog yelped. 'You've broken her leg,' she shouted.

Chrissie righted herself and fixed her gaze on Peter. 'Do you still think he's all good?'

'Shut up,' screamed Jack. The temper rose from him like steam. His shoulders hunched; teeth clenched, spittle escaped from his lips and lay on his beard. His eyes were wide open now and lit with a manic gleam.

Peter said nothing, but colour drained from his face. He crept to Bel and sat on the floor beside her. Jack pointed his finger at Chrissie. 'Steal from me again, and it will be the last thing you ever do. Get out of my house now!'

'Not without the bairns.' She turned to Bel. 'Run, now.'

Bel rose and took a hesitant step towards the door.

'Where do you think you're going?'

'Nowhere. I... please don't hurt Chrissie. I'll stay.'

Chrissie grabbed the brass lamp from the table, knocking the globe off in her haste. Launching herself at Jack, she raised it and aimed for his head.

Both his hands rose, grabbing her wrists. The lamp fell to the ground.

'Run,' Chrissie shouted, not understanding why Bel did not move.

'But the dog,' Peter's voice was high.

'Damn the dog. I'll drown the bitch later — put her out of her misery, hah.' Jack laughed. A high-pitched, mad laugh. His fingers like toughened prongs dug into her flesh. He spun her around and held her against his chest with one arm as he opened the door with the other. 'You want to go? Then you're going. But Bel and Peter stay. And don't you even think of bringing help. I'll flay them both alive rather than let you have them.' Gone was any sense of reasoning, and the madman of her nightmares had returned. Revulsion leaked into her soul. With a push he flung her outside and she landed on the ground, the gravel peppering the skin on her palms. 'I don't want you anymore. Go back and live with that freak Angus. I've got Bel now.' The door slammed behind her.

Peter,' she screamed, 'Bel. Can you hear me? I won't go. I'll sleep out here all night if I need to. I'll be listening – and if you harm one hair of their heads...' She beat on the door with her fists. Eventually her voice grew hoarse and deserted her. She slid to the ground, one hand on the knob, her head against the wood. Her mind whirled searching for solutions. He had the bairns. He was mad. If anyone were to come to her aid, she did not doubt it would anger him more and there was no telling what he would do. The best way was to try to placate him.

'Jack,' she said. 'I'm sorry. Let me stay.' Inside was only silence.

A rap from inside the window of the best room alerted Chrissie. Bel was struggling with the window. It cracked up a few inches, and refused to budge. Chrissie's first instinct was to break the glass, get inside and somehow save the bairns. But the panes were small and the wood solid. Furthermore, the noise would warn Jack and bring the full weight of his fury down on them. 'I'll be fine, Chrissie,' came Bel's wavering voice. 'I'll stay in your room the night.'

'Wait 'til he's asleep, then get Peter and sneak out.'

Bel shook her head. 'He's locked me in this room. But he can't stay in the house forever. And... Angus can't be much longer.'

Frustration swelled in her chest. If only she could get them out, they would run, hide, seek sanctuary somewhere, anywhere, even with Geordie MacIntyre if that's what it took.

Chrissie stayed awake most of the night. From the window of her cottage she saw Jack leave Scartongarth early. She watched him feed the hens then go into the byre. In this state she did not know what he might do, but she did know, that to infuriate him further would be dangerous. An hour later, Jack left the house and went towards the beach. He was leading Peter by the hand.

Her heart raced. If Jack had gone to sea, Bel would be alone. Waiting until the *Christina* sailed around the point, she ran down the field to Scartongarth.

Chrissie tried the door, but it was locked. She knocked. 'Bel,' she called. Silence. She went to the ben-end window and peered through the glass. A humped mound huddled on the bed. She banged on the pane. 'Bel,' she shouted, louder this time. The mound stirred, and Bel raised her blotched face and opened red, swollen eyes.

Without thinking, Chrissie picked up the nearest boulder and smashed the window. The noise cracked into the still morning air. Several panes collapsed inward. Chrissie looked around, her eyes falling on a wooden stake for fencing. With that she knocked out the remaining glass.

Bel climbed out of the bed and stood, shaking. 'I'm sorry Chrissie,' she said, 'He took Peter with him'.

'Hush,' whispered Isa. 'Did he touch you?'

Bel shook her head. 'I made him believe I wanted to stay. After a while he was fine, like he was at the beginning. He let me wrap the dog's leg.'

'Get the dog, hurry.'

'But if I leave he'll hurt you.'

'We'll run and hide if we have to. But come out of there now.'

Bel disappeared and returned a moment later, carrying the shivering collie. 'Her nose is hot. She needs help.' She laid her head against the animal's. Poppy whimpered and licked her face. Chrissie took the dog from Bel's arms. 'Now come, hurry up.'

'I forgot something,' said Bel and disappeared back into the house.

'Bel, please hurry,' shouted Chrissie from outside. The girl returned, a slight look of triumph on her face and climbed out of the window.

'What about Peter?'

'I'll think of something.'

***

Later that night, Chrissie met the boat as it beached. 'Changed your mind?' asked Jack as he tied the rope to the iron ring on the pier for that purpose. 'If you plead long enough I might allow you to come home.'

'I came for Peter,' she said.

'Peter stays with me.'

Chrissie had to get her son away from Jack before he discovered Bel's disappearance.

'Please, Jack,' she said. 'Let him spend some time with me. He can return later.'

'I don't trust you.'

'He's near fourteen. I can't stop him going where he wants.'

Jack turned to the boy. 'You want to be with me, don't you?'

Peter nodded, but his face was white and his eyes were scared. Chrissie understood her son well enough to know he was trying to keep the peace.

'Just for a few hours, please come, Peter,' she held out her hand.

'It's all right, Mam. I'll be all right.' His voice shook a little. His smile was forced and brave. She couldn't let Peter go home with Jack – she couldn't. Although she believed he was probably in no danger, she wouldn't take the risk.

'Then you come too, for tea,' Try as she might she could not keep the desperation out of her voice.

Jack laughed. 'What are you up to Chrissie? Going to try and poison me again? No, no. Bel will have tea ready for us. Come on son.' He started to walk up the slope away from the beach, one hand gripping the boy's shoulder.

Peter turned and gave her a sad smile.

'No, Peter, come with me,' Chrissie ran after them, grabbed the boy's arm and tried to drag him away.

Jack rounded on her. 'What are you up to?' He turned away and, pushing Peter in front of him, marched towards Scartongarth.

Chrissie looked wildly around. She had to get help. Another boat sailed into the bay. She ran down the slope as it beached. 'Aye, Chrissie,' the old fisherman greeted her.

'What's ailin' you the day?'

'I have to get Peter away from Jack.'

'But, lassie, if Peter wants to bide wi' his faither there's no' much we can do.'

'He's crazy. You've got to help me.'

'Look lass, my heart goes out to you, but I've seen how he is with the lad. Jack wouldna' hurt him. And Peter seems happy enough.'

What was the point? The islanders perceived her as a desperate woman, wanting her son back at any cost. Much as they cared for her, they would not get involved in another man's affairs.

She ran after Jack and Peter. Watched Jack stop. Knew he had noticed the broken window. 'Run away from him, Peter,' she shouted. 'Now.'

Peter hesitated. He looked from Jack to Chrissie. 'I'll be fine, Mam,' he said. 'If I leave, he'll come after you.'

He'll do that anyway, thought Chrissie, hiding the extent of her distress from the boy.

Chapter 33

Peter noticed the broken window before Jack did. 'Dad, maybe we should go check on the sheep,' he said, desperately tugging at Jack's sleeve. The fabric of the jacket, damp from sea spray, jarred against his cold fingers.

'Wha...' Jack spluttered, ripped his arm free and broke into a run. He pulled the key from his pocket and it chattered like teeth as he fought to insert it into the metal lock. 'Bitch,' he said under his breath. 'This is your mother's doing, Peter. See what I've had to put up with? She still thinks she'll get the better of me. No more.'

Tears pushed up behind Peter's eyes and he dashed them away. 'Maybe if you talk...' he began, but Jack wasn't listening.

'She's taken Bel. If she's stolen anything of mine... Open it.' He thrust the key at Peter. Knowing he had little choice, Peter unlocked the door. Jack tore into the back porch, hoisted up first the lid of the meal kist and then the milk urn. 'She wouldn't have left with nothing.' He ran to the bed, scrabbled under the mattress, pulled out a leather pouch and emptied the contents onto the table.

Peter shrank back. Never had he seen so much money. One by one Jack counted the notes, visible anger mounting with every second. Finally he threw the empty pouch across the room. 'She's taken half my money.' His eyes glittered, spit formed at the edges of his lips. Thumping his fist on the table he bellowed like a bull, spun around and tore the mattress from the bed, flinging it to the floor.

A hand of terror clamped Peter's heart. He now realised the full extent of what his mam had suffered. He was the man here now – the only man. He should be able to protect his mam and Bel. But he wanted his mam now. A warm wetness spread down his legs, a warm wetness that he knew, should his father notice, would anger him more than ever. Scrunching his eyes tight, he willed his legs to move. A narrow, frightened sound slipped from between his lips. Suddenly finding strength, he turned and ran for the open door and continued to run, tripping, falling, stumbling, sobbing until he reached Chrissie's cottage on the high rise. He flung the door open and collapsed in the passage, his breath hot and hard. Chrissie rushed from the back porch, the carving knife she had been using to chop turnips in her hand. She threw the knife onto the window ledge and gathered her son in her arms. 'Peter, thank God, Did he hurt you?'

'No. He... he has... has money. Some is ... miss... missing. He... he's really mad.' He sank against the soft security of his mother's body, embarrassed at his need of her. The sheer paralysis of being helpless to protect her, crushing him.

'Money? What money?' Chrissie loosened her hold and he slipped from her arms.

From behind her, Bel gasped. 'I took some notes. He *owed*, you Chrissie. I... I didn't think he'd notice for a while – 'til after we'd gone to the mainland.'

Chrissie rose to her feet. 'Oh, Bel. Quickly, get your night things, we'll go and stay with Geordie MacIntyre. He's got a shotgun, and he'll help us – I'm sure of that.'

***

In the main street in Wick, Charlie waited for the bus. Finally he had found lodgings that would accept Chrissie and the bairns, at least until he could get them somewhere better. Right next to the police station. Nowhere could be safer. He checked the position of the sun. If the bus was on time, he should make Raumsey before last light.

***

Back on the island, Sanny the Post hitched his empty bag over his shoulder and wheeled his bicycle into the shed. As he secured the door and turned towards his cottage, he saw Jack in the distance with a rifle in one hand and a can in the other. It wasn't unusual to see someone out shooting rabbit or birds, yet Sanny felt uneasy and watched until Jack vanished over the crest of the hill. He was going in the direction of Chrissie's old cottage. It was not his business, nevertheless, maybe he should follow, see what the man was up to. He scratched his head. Yes, that's what he should do. Chrissie was worried, and remembering the Jack of old, maybe she had reason.

'It's about time you came home,' Sanny's wife, leaning heavily on a stick, yelled from the open cottage door. 'Get yerself away and bring in some peat, the fire's nearly out. And bring in my drawers and semmit from the line, afore the rain comes on. They're my only pair.'

'You mean you've no drawers on?' He grinned, showing the gaps where his teeth had been, opened his arms and ran towards her as fast as his bandy legs would allow. Both his hands clamped round her ample waist. 'Aye, you're still a fine looking woman, Nellie.'

'Go on wi' you, you old fool,' she said with a laugh, 'Before I skelp you with my stick.'

He rubbed his beard across her face, she giggled like a schoolgirl, threw down her stick, and Sanny forgot all about Jack.

***

Jack reached the top of the rise and set down the can of paraffin he carried. The hot blast of his anger had turned into a fury as cold and deadly as a winter sea. He eased a cartridge from his pocket and weighed it in his hand, broke open the shotgun and slid the ammunition into the barrel. Clicking the gun shut, he released the safety catch and aimed at a seagull high above, keeping it within the sights. The late sun glinted on the bird's white underbelly. It rose higher as if sensing danger. He considered shooting it, then decided not to waste a shot. 'I've bigger game than this,' he said to no one. Chrissie's cottage stood before him, a slow trickle of peat scented smoke escaping from the chimney, twirling slowly like the ghost of his past. He caressed the solid barrel of the gun and nodded. 'Now my beauties,' he hissed, 'we'll see what happens to those who make a fool of me.'

***

'Hurry up Peter, what are you doing?' Chrissie called through the house.

'I'm coming.' The boy re-appeared wearing a pair of Charlie's trousers rolled up at the legs and tied with string around the waist.

Chrissie had seen the stain on his dungarees and understood Peter's humiliation.

'Come on now,' was all she said.

'We're too late. Jack's here – he has a gun.' Bel spun round from the window.

Needles danced up Chrissie's spine. 'Out the back,' she shouted. The widow would allow the children to escape, but she knew she would have to face Jack once more. She herded Bel and Peter through to the porch, feet stumbling on the hem of her skirt in her haste. She yanked up the sash window just as the front door burst open.

'Stop.' Jack raised the gun. 'Get back in here. All of you.'

A long thin sound escaped her lips. With an arm around both youngsters, Chrissie led them into the kitchen.

'Who's the bitch that stole from me?' Jack was too calm, his words too brittle, his eyes too hollow. Chrissie feared that any semblance of humanity had flown from him, leaving only an avenging shell. Someone was going to die this day.

'We never,' said Bel, her words forced and brave, her breath quick and hot. Bright pink dots swelled on her cheeks. Her body trembled against Chrissie's.

'Let me speak to him.' Fearing for Bel's reckless nature, Chrissie placed herself between them. 'It's me you want Jack. Let the bairns go.'

Jack cursed and spat on the ground. Hate began to gather in the black glittering eyes where there had been only emptiness before.

***

Young Alex Gordon was collecting whelks on the shore. He stopped for a minute and straightened his spine for relief. His pail was almost full, and the light was fading from the sky. Over on the distant mainland he saw a flame grow in strength on the beach. He picked up his pail and strolled up the road where he retrieved his bike and cycled to Geordie MacIntyre's. Geordie was bending over a stack of peat.

'Fire on Huna beach,' said Alex.

Geordie stood up and stared at the distant flames. 'Who would want to come over at this hour? Could they not have caught the mail boat?'

'Aye, well, I'll give you a hand if you like,' said Alex. 'The last time we saw a fire on the beach it was Jack Reid. He had no thought of the time either.'

'I don't like that man – no, I don't like that man at all,' said Geordie, shaking his head.

'But we'd best not be bothering with things that don't concern us. Though if Chrissie wants out, she knows I'd have her in a second.'

'Aye, Geordie, the whole island knows it well,' said Alex. 'I'd watch out for that Jack, though. There's an evil glint in his eye.' In no great hurry, they walked towards the harbour. The sun had set but the gloaming would remain for another hour or so. The two men launched the boat and hoisted the sail.

'What do you make o' Bel?' said Geordie.

'A real bonny lass she's gonna be once she's filled out a bit.'

'Aye, she's a bit of a spark – like her aunt.' The men laughed and lit their pipes.

In spite of the stillness of the water, the tide flowed strong, and carried the boat at a fair speed to the other side. Before long, they beached at Huna. 'Well, will you look who it is,' said Geordie.

'And you've not come back a minute too soon,' said Alex. 'For you'll not believe who's back in Scartongarth.'

'What is it – what's wrong?' Charlie leapt aboard the boat, the hairs rising on the nape of his neck. His fingernails dug into his palms as he sensed Alex's next words. His worst fears were about to be realised.

***

Back in Chrissie's old house, Jack circled the group. He kept the shotgun levelled at her face.

'Don't move,' he said. 'You know the damage this can do – don't you – you and Charlie?' He looked from one to the other and grinned. 'You are all against me, all of you.' His lip curled up. A string of spittle hung from his teeth. 'You Bel, I thought you understood. You disappoint me so much.' He reached out to her and she shrank back. A sheen of sweat varnished her brow.

'Let… let the bairns go, I'll stay here. We'll… talk. Please, Jack,' said Chrissie, her heart beating against her breastbone like the wings of a trapped bird.

'Hah,' his laugh burst into the air. 'You fooled me once with your silver tongue. It'll no' happen a second time. All out to get Jack. Well who's going to get the last laugh, eh?' Saliva gathered in the corners of his mouth. His nostrils flared as his breathing became quicker. His colouring was high, his eyes bulging.

'No, Dad no,' Peter ran forward and grabbed Jack's arm. 'I'll come back. I'm sorry I left – you scared me…'

Jack stared at him, then indicated with his head. 'Then get behind me.'

The boy did as he was bid.

'You'll never get away with this,' said Chrissie.

He sucked in air through his teeth. 'I left this island once and was believed to be a dead man – I can do it again. Are you with me Peter? We'll go together.'

'Yes. Yes. Dad. Let Mam and Bel go. I'll come with you.'

'No,' cried Chrissie. 'It's me he wants. I'll come, Jack. Take me.'

Jack ignored her and put his arm around Peter. 'I'm sorry, son, but we have to get rid of them. That was my mistake last time, you see.'

'You promised, Dad, you said you weren't going to hurt nobody.' Peter grabbed Jack's arm, the arm that held the gun. Jack drew back his free hand and hit him so hard that the boy staggered backwards against the wall. Chrissie heard the sound of his head as it struck the stone and she started forward. Jack stopped her with the barrel of the gun.

'Stay there, until I decide what I'm going to do.'

'You said you wouldn't hurt *me* or Peter. You promised,' shouted Bel.

'Ah, lassie. It grieves me to do this, but you can blame your Aunt Chrissie for it's all her doing. She could have taken me back, but no,' his lip curled. 'But you're right and I never break a promise. You'll come with us, for I'll be in need of a woman's hand.' Her head began to shake in denial, but Chrissie urged her forward. If Bel could escape there might still be a chance. 'Go on, pet,' she whispered.

Bel turned to look at her aunt.

'Go on,' Chrissie mouthed.

Bel walked gingerly until she reached Jack, and then edged behind him to stand beside Peter. He bent down and whispered loud enough for everyone to hear. 'If you make for the door, I'll shoot your aunt. She'll be dead before you reach the outside.'

***

Charlie, Geordie and Alex hurried up the road towards Scartongarth. As soon as the cottage came into view, the broken window screamed at them. Charlie reached the house first, ran into the kitchen and from room to room, adrenaline increasing with every step. No one here. And the shotgun had gone. 'God, where has he taken them,' he shouted. 'Chrissie's cottage, now.'

***

Bel's eyes grew round. Enormous, tragic holes in the chalk white of her face. Her lip trembled and she stood, statue-like.

'Now then. Where were we? Will I shoot you? No, for the noise would draw attention. That would be stupid, wouldn't it? What do you think, Peter? How should we do it, eh?' He glanced behind him.

Peter was holding his head, blood seeping between his fingers.

'Jack, please, let me go to him,' Chrissie pleaded.

'Na,' Jack said, drawing the word out so that it sounded as a naaaaaaaaw. He's maybe not mine anyway. You've lied enough. Fire. That's it. Isn't it, Bel – Peter? 'It took Charlie, and it's only fitting that it should take my wife.' He stole a quick glance at the terrified youngsters. 'And me and you both, we escape. Simple.' He backed to where he had set the can of paraffin, feeling behind him until his fingers found the handle.

'Bel, run. Take Peter,' screamed Chrissie.

'She won't, for she knows what will happen if she does,' said Jack.

Bel's eyes flicked to the carving knife Chrissie had set on the window ledge, then back to meet Chrissie's. She edged slowly towards the wall.

Chrissie tried not to watch lest her eyes gave her away. 'We can talk about this, Jack. You're ill, let me help you.'

Ignoring her, Jack eased the lid from the paraffin can.

Bel's fingers closed around the shaft of the knife. Her hand shook.

'Jack, give me one more chance.' Chrissie had to hold his attention. She doubted whether Bel would have the nerve to use the knife, and even if she did, Jack would surely be able to fire at least one round when he realised what was happening. She walked towards him holding out her hand. 'Please, forgive me. I'll come back to you – whatever you want – I promise. Your mother told me how she treated you. She said she was sorry.'

***

Charlie and the other men reached the high road, and Sanny the Post came riding along on his bike. He stopped and dismounted when he saw them. 'I'm right glad you've come back, lad. That Jack has me a wee bit worried.'

'Well he's not in Scartongarth,' said Charlie. 'No one is. Have you seen any of them?'

'Aye. I did see Jack going over the rigs. Had a gun in his hand and all. I meant to follow him, got a strange feeling – know what I mean? Then the wife needed me and it clean went out of my mind 'til this very second.'

'God,' said Charlie, 'I should never have left. Come on.'

***

Jack's face froze. His eyes widened and gleamed with a stronger hate than she had ever seen before, and she knew she had made a mistake. 'You're a lying bitch. You're all the same, all the same.' He grabbed the can of paraffin and swung it at Chrissie's head. It missed and crashed against the wall, the liquid splashing over the brickwork, some of it landing on Chrissie. He cursed. He laughed. 'You will burn. A fitting end for a witch.'

Behind him Bel could no longer contain her tears, and began to sob out loud, but he did not turn. Instead he splashed what was left of the paraffin around the floor and across the table – anywhere he could reach. Bel raised the knife, but her shaking fingers betrayed her and the knife fell from her grasp and rattled on the floor.

Jack spun around. With one hand he grabbed Bel's wrist. Her eyes popped open, and she started to scream for help. 'Shut up.' he yelled into her face. 'I gave you a chance.' He threw her back into the room with enough force that she fell on her knees. She crawled over to Chrissie. They clung onto each other.

Jack pulled the matchbox from his pocket. With one hand still holding the gun, he edged open the box, cursing when the contents fell and scattered. He wedged the matchbox into the waistline of his trousers and, without taking his eyes off the

251

women, knelt down and picked up a match. 'Get away from Chrissie, Bel, or you'll burn with her.'

'Go Bel,' said Chrissie. 'Get away.'

But Jack had blocked any means of escape. The match flared. At the same moment, his eyes opened wide and bulged, a look of surprise on his face. He pitched forward, crumpling to the ground.

Peter stood behind him holding the knife in his hand. The blade was covered in blood. He looked up and Chrissie saw the cold, black flash of hatred in his eye, a fraction of a second before the match hit the floor and the room was engulfed in flames. She heard Bel's sobs, saw her son through the raw, red wall of fire. 'Get out,' she yelled, scrambling as far away from Bel as possible. The girl could dive through the young flames. With paraffin on her clothes, Chrissie had no such option. 'Both of you – quickly – out.'

A sob tore from Bel, and she ran, leaping over the trail of flame that erupted behind her and reached for the ceiling, cutting Chrissie off from her only means of escape. She backed against the furthest wall. Knowing that if the flames touched her she would become a human torch, Chrissie struggled out of her cardigan and blouse and threw them as far from her as she could, but she could still smell paraffin on her skin.

Jack groaned from where he lay and lifted his head. He coughed and blood sprayed from his lips. 'Ha, Chrissie. So he is my son, after all. A fitting end this, isn't it, me and you, killed by our own spawn.' His voice rose above the roar and spit as flames devoured the splashes of liquid. He dragged himself across the floor towards her, flames igniting his clothes, yet he didn't as much as flinch at the burn. The curtains caught fire and burning cloth detached, wafted upwards and set the dry thatch alight. Pressing herself tighter against the corner, Chrissie choked on black, rolling smoke and waited for her death.

***

Dragging Peter with her, Bel staggered outside, into the arms of islanders who tore off their own coats to smother the smouldering clothes. All eyes turned to the cottage. Women screamed. Peter, realising that his mother was not behind him, tried to rush back inside. Strong arms held him fast. Other islanders had formed a human chain from the well to the house, passing buckets of water along. In spite of their haste, the water that splashed against the flames was too little and too late to be effective.

Charlie was half a field away when the fire began. One look at the stricken faces and the struggling Peter and he knew that Chrissie was still inside. He grabbed a passing bucket. Before anyone realised what he was doing, he doused himself with water and pulled his soaking jacket over his face. Shrieking like a banshee, he flung himself into the raw red maw. The windows burst outward with a shattering crump. Creaking beams gave way, crashing into the interior. Burning pieces of thatch drifted up into the darkening sky. And for a long moment the only sounds that could be heard was the crackling of flames, falling timber, shouting men and sobbing women.

***

Charlie fought the heat on his face, the sting of smoke in his eyes and the sear in his lungs, and suddenly he was back in the battle of Jutland. He had heard the cries of his brother as the burning mast crashed into his body, pinning him beneath it. Charlie had stopped for a heartbeat, and the wall of flame had sprung up before him and the screams had stopped. Filled with the instinct for self-preservation, Charlie ran, and kept running until he collapsed.

This time he wouldn't run away. This time he would succeed or die in the attempt. 'Chrissie, Chrissie,' he gasped. A burning beam crashed at his feet and in the rush of air from the gaping hole that once was a roof, the smoke dissipated enough for him to see her against the far wall. She lay still, her face pressed to the ground. Jack, his clothes black and smoking, was beside her. His hand reaching towards her, but not quite touching.

Charlie leapt over the burning beam. He landed awkwardly and he fell among the flames. The immense heat overtook him.

The smoke sucked the oxygen out of the air. With a brief flash of insight he knew he was going to fail again. Only this time, thankfully, he would not live to face the regrets. The only thing that spurred him onwards was the determination to reach Chrissie and die beside her.

Suddenly a figure appeared before him, holding out his hand. A figure who walked seemingly untouched by the flame. 'You can do it,' said a voice he recognised. He grasped the hand and felt himself lifted upwards and dragged forward. He stumbled and fell on the floor beside Chrissie. He laid his head next to hers, and breathed in air. A draught was coming from somewhere, blowing the smoke towards the front of the house. He gulped in a few mouthfuls, enough to clear his head. Through the murk, he could see the outline of the porch door. There must be a window open. If he could get to the back porch, there could still be a chance. He pulled off his steaming coat and wrapped it around Chrissie's head and shoulders. 'You still have more to do,' said a hollow voice. Charlie glanced up and the figure, standing there untouched among the flames, gave a salute and vanished.

Outside, silence fell over the little group as the blackened smoke poured into the evening sky. The last of the rafters from the cottage collapsed inward. Geordie MacIntyre held Peter until he ceased struggling. 'I'm sorry, son, so sorry,' he whispered. Suddenly Peter tensed in his arms. 'Look,' he shouted. There was a gasp from the onlookers as, from behind the cottage, a hunched shape, black against the red and orange guts of the building, staggered forward and fell onto the green. Charlie, with Chrissie across his shoulders, collapsed coughing onto the ground. Other islanders threw soaking blankets over them and pulled them away from the fierce heat. Sanny the Post was instantly beside them pressing a can of water to the blistered lips.

No one asked about Jack. The others stood silently around, watching, as Chrissie's house went up in brutal flames.

Chapter 34

The first thing he heard was the ticking of the clock, minutes before the pain became real. From then on he became aware of things by degrees. His eyes opened. He saw Chrissie's face. He heard her voice. 'Doctor, he's awake!' He saw hands move her away, became aware she was using two sweeping brushes as crutches, their bristles flattened below her armpits. And then the doctor from the mainland was bending over him, his face large. 'How bad is the pain?' he asked.

'Bad.' Charlie's lips parted and cracked, his voice was hoarse. 'I can't give you any more laudanum,' the doctor said. 'Codeine should suffice now. Your vital signs are good.' He straightened up and snapped his bag shut. 'No more smoking, though. Your lungs have taken a severe beating as it is.'

'How long . . has it been?'

'You've been unconscious for five days. '

'How's Chrissie,' Charlie whispered. It hurt to talk.

'Her legs are bad, but thanks to you, her face and upper body have been untouched. Her cough is still there, but without her herbs and concoctions, I doubt modern medicine would have helped so quickly.'

Bel came in, carrying a plate of chicken broth and a wedge of bread. Between them they raised him high enough to slip another pillow behind his head. He suddenly realised he was hungry.

'Are you all right, Bel?' he asked.

'Still shaky, but Peter and me were out before the flames got us too bad.' She spooned some soup into his mouth.

Chrissie swung over on her make-shift crutches and sat on the bed. Reaching out, she set a gentle hand on the raw blistering of his cheek. 'Finish your soup, then sleep some more. I'll be here when you wake up.'

A few days later his voice was stronger. 'I'm afraid I'll be even uglier than I was before. I'm sorry Chrissie. I shouldn't have stayed away so long – I should have known there was a chance...' He grabbed her hand, glad he could finally use his voice, even though it was still hoarse.

'Hush. You weren't to know he was nearly on our doorstep. And you'll never be ugly to me. You came back, in the nick of time too.'

***

After she had changed his dressings, she pulled her legs up so that she rested on the bed and laid her head in the hollow of his shoulder blade where it was warm and smelt of him. 'Are the burns awful sore?'

'Nothing I can't stand. Your legs are bad though, I'm told.'

'Aye, they're bad, but they'll get better. You were right. You saved me once, and you did again.'

'And I've saved myself.'

'What d'you mean?'

'My fear of fire. I felt so bad – there wasn't anything I could do to save Angus, but it destroyed me that I was too scared to try. It was... like I was back there. The heat, the fear. I couldn't let it happen again. I'd have rather died.' He relaxed and closed his eyes. 'I've got the better of it, Chrissie.'

'Oh, Charlie.' She heard the breath rattle in his chest.

'And for a moment, in there, I thought... no it's too daft,' said Charlie.

'Tell me.'

'I fell, couldn't go on. I...knew it was the end. But then... I thought I saw Angus.' He held out a hand and studied it. The hand was unblemished. 'This hand. He took this hand and helped me up.' He shook his head. 'Probably hallucinating.'

'Maybe not,' she said. 'I often hear my granny's voice. She's always right.'

'What does she say?'

A mischievous smile trembled at the corner of Chrissie's lips. 'She says, "Hold onto that Charlie. He's a good lad," and again, Chrissie traced the untouched line of his upper lip with the tip of a finger, 'she was right.'

Charlie looked at her with his grey-green eyes as if she was the only person in the world, and she relaxed against him.

They lay in silence for a time.

'No more secrets?' Charlie said at last.

'Not from each other.' But as she spoke the words she closed her eyes, the memory of the black anger that flashed in her son's eyes before he stabbed his father, uppermost in her mind. She had only seen that unmistakable black anger in one other person. *Except one secret*, she thought. *Except one.*

She eased herself upright, picked up today's soup bowl and fed Charlie until it was empty.

Two years later

Chrissie and Charlie closed the gate of the cemetery and pushed the bolt home, shutting the past away. Chrissie took a deep breath of fresh sea air. Charlie reached over and clasped her hand. A seagull whirled above their heads, the sun glinting off its white underbelly. It was a fine day, and the air was thick with summer.

Without speaking they walked up the footpath. In the distance they made out the slim form of Bel with a baby in her arms.

Charlie stopped. 'I still can't believe how lucky I am.' His fingers tightened around hers. His voice faltered. Tears rose in his eyes. 'I never thought...'

'Hush,' said Chrissie.

'She's missing her mam and dad,' said Bel and handed the baby to Chrissie.

'Come on little Mary.' Chrissie hoisted the baby against her breast. Her eyes caught Charlie's and she saw the love shining there.

From the night they had shared a bed again, too badly burnt to even touch, they had begun the healing progress together. Eventually, not expecting anything more than affection, they had spent the night in each other's arms. Then there was that magic night when they both realised that his inability to make love had been all in his mind. Since then he had grown in confidence and the birth of Mary had been a miracle.

'I've put on the pork to roast,' said Bel. 'Jimmy should be here soon. Peter's away over for him.'

Charlie slipped his free arm around the girl's shoulders. Mary reached out a chubby hand and touched his scarred cheek. He nuzzled the tiny palm and the baby chuckled.

Chrissie turned her head to watch the *Christina* bob across the sound. This night her family would be all around her at the dinner table, and for the first time, she would meet Jimmy's new girl.

She had never felt happier.